Home Is Where the Body Is

Home Is Where the Body Is

A Wannabe Sleuth Mystery

Jody Holford

TULE
PUBLISHING

Dedication

To my readers, thank you for diving
into a new series with me.

Don't be afraid to start all over again;
you might like your new story better.

~Anonymous

Chapter One

SLEEPY SEEMED LIKE the wrong adjective for a town so dearly dedicated to caffeine, but it was the only word that fit. When Annie Abbott read the brochure her parents sent—via mail, as if she couldn't just Google the place—it boasted ten different coffee establishments. It might not seem like much, especially to someone moving up from the Portland area, but in a town with less than two thousand people, it showed serious dedication to the beverage.

She drove under the massive, arched sign that stretched from one post to another, the words RAINBOW FALLS etched into the weathered wood. It felt as if she'd rolled onto a movie set from the fifties. It was so different from the area she'd lived in where apartment complexes were stacked side by side like blocks.

These streets were lined with colorful picturesque houses, manicured lawns, lush trees, and black lampposts standing like wrought iron sentinels every twenty feet. She'd recently taken on a new client who wanted signage for their real estate business. This was the perfect backdrop. She might need to come back with her camera and get a few shots.

The town was a weird combination of eerie and welcoming. Maybe that was because, for the most part, she was used to a bustling city. On a typical Sunday morning, she would sleep late in the two-bedroom condo she'd shared with her college bestie, stumble into the kitchen for coffee, then laze about on the couch.

Maybe Portland was secretly just like this quiet cove every Sunday morning and Annie had no idea. She'd have to ask her friend, Vivian, who'd moved her boyfriend into the condo three weeks ago, to solve that mystery for her some time.

A man in knee socks and a striped robe sat on one of the porches she passed, a newspaper in his hand. He didn't lift his head as she drove by.

A couple doors down from him, there was an adorable two-story house with gingerbread trim and a mug-shaped sign on the lawn that said, THE PERFECT CUP. It had regular residential homes on either side of it. Annie smiled at the charm of that. *There's one.* Finding the other nine could be like a scavenger hunt. Annie loved anything to do with puzzles, mysteries, and following clues. A coffee-shop crawl might be as close as she got in this town.

The sign on the porch said CLOSED but made her crave coffee anyway.

She stifled a yawn as she drove past. *Mm, coffee and a donut. Or maybe a Danish.* According to Google Maps, her parents' place was close by. She could always make some coffee there. Her mom had promised to leave her all stocked up on non-perishables. They'd only moved in a few months ago. While some people avoided change, her parents embraced it from every angle.

They'd decided to start their retirement by sailing around the world. A few weeks ago, they'd visited her at her condo to say their goodbyes and go through all of the necessary details of taking over their new home.

Annie was surprised when they'd informed her last Christmas of their plans. She knew her parents enjoyed adventure, but this was bigger than anything they'd ever done. Annie wanted to see the world, too, but not via the ocean. It was beautiful and inspiring to look at, but she was content with keeping her feet on land. Maybe dipping her toes in the water.

Turning onto Center Street, the architecture and landscape became more commercial with cobblestone streets and businesses on either side. In the center of the street, there was a large greenspace with trees and benches. She could picture people heading to those benches for their lunch breaks. More charm.

The shops were the old-school kind—squat boxes, many with wide picture windows giving passersby a view of the activity inside. Though she saw a smattering of people through a couple of the windows, the street was quiet. *The town is quiet.*

"Seems a little late for church," she mused, but maybe

that was where people were. Or, like her former self, tucked up in the cozy warmth of their beds.

When her stomach growled loudly, she made a split-second decision and turned into an angled parking spot. Directly in front of her was JUST COFFEE. *That's two.* On one side, there was a bookstore and a pet food store. On the other, there was a bakery and a sandwich shop. All boasted CLOSED signs, and she wondered if it was a Sunday thing. A graphic designer by trade, she couldn't help but notice their signage was outdated.

Her current roster of clients was keeping her busy enough that she couldn't take on a lot of new work. That didn't stop ideas from popping into her head though. There were other shops farther down in both directions, but Annie couldn't read names. Of the ones in front of her, only the coffee shop was open.

Getting out of her truck, she stretched, pulling her thick, brown hair out of its ponytail confinement as her arms moved up. It was one of those stretches that felt good all the way through her body. She stifled another yawn. Between packing up her stuff, transferring her life in Portland to here, and the drive, she was ready to curl up on a couch or a beach chair with a good book. She tried to roll the stiffness out of her shoulders with no luck.

Anticipation hummed in her belly. She'd do two scavenger hunts: one to find each coffee place and the other to try every one. Maybe there was a big difference between them.

There certainly was if she compared this one to the adorable cottage-like one she'd passed. This one lacked aesthetics, but hopefully the coffee would make up for it.

Pulling the door open, the smell of roasted beans tickled her senses. Quiet music that was typically reserved for elevators and driving people on hold batty played through the speakers. A few people sat in the booths that ran along the edges of the shop. It was small, with seating for maybe ten to twelve. A tall—even giant-sized—man with his blond hair wound into a bun on the very top of his head sent a lazy smile her way. His shoulders were linebacker massive, but he moved with grace as he poured coffee, pushed it toward an older woman.

The sound of shuffling along the linoleum came from the narrow hallway at the back of the store. Annie moved to the counter, aware of the people watching. The newcomer always drew attention.

"Welcome to Just Coffee. Small, medium, or large?" Man Bun asked.

She laughed, thinking he was joking. A glance at the menu made her smile slip. *Really? They only serve coffee? That's ridiculous.* The sign over the counter listed three sizes and two options: decaf or regular. Her stomach complained. Scrunching her brows, she looked from left to right. Not a baked good in sight.

"Hi. Uh, I'll get a large—two creams, one sugar, please. Is there anything to eat here?"

She knew a bistro in Portland that served the best chicken fingers ever but didn't show it on their menu. Maybe this place was the same. Only the locals knew what could really be ordered. Well, she was about to be local. She wanted in on the secrets.

"No, ma'am," the barista said. Was that title too fancy for what he did? Didn't he have to steam milk or add syrups, maybe little foam letters to the drink?

She smiled, leaned in. "Oh, come on. You must have a stray muffin or something." She'd been too wound up this morning, worried about forgetting something or having to go back. She'd missed breakfast and hadn't even packed a snack. *Definitely regretting that.*

"Either you can't read or you don't understand the very simple words this man said. Get your coffee, and move on. Some of us have things to do."

Shock widened Annie's gaze as she turned to face the gruff-sounding voice that spoke behind her. A hunch-shouldered man with salt-and-pepper hair glared at her through unhappy eyes. His lips were tipped downward. Even his wrinkles were frowning. He wore a flannel shirt and a pair of baggy jeans. A couple of his buttons were askew.

He shook a travel mug in front of her. "I'm empty. I don't have all day."

Annie narrowed her gaze. "I was asking a simple question."

"An unnecessary one. Waste of time. 'Just coffee' says it

all. You want all those fancy add-ins or a buffet, head to one of the other places." He shuffled around her, moving like he had a bad back. Holding his cup out, he shook it at the man behind the counter. "Come on. Top me up."

Annie frowned. What a jerk. At least the barista gave her a nod and mouthed "Sorry."

"That's not a very nice way to welcome new people," Annie muttered under her breath as she waited. Plus, he'd barged in front.

The man turned. If she had to guess, she'd say he meant to intimidate her with his glare. All it did was raise her hackles further.

"It's not very nice to ask stupid questions when the answer is right in front of you."

"That's enough," Man Bun said.

The few other patrons stared. Annie suddenly felt foolish for causing a commotion. She'd be known as the newcomer who caused a ruckus. Over coffee. Rooting in her purse, she pulled out a five-dollar bill, handing it to the guy.

He waved her money away. "It's on the house."

Before she could say thank you, the grumpy man turned back to the barista—she'd just go with that title. "Why does she get free coffee? I paid full price for mine. Want me to show a little leg?"

Annie's mouth dropped open. What an annoying, ignorant—

"One more word, Gill, and you're out."

Annie picked up her coffee, gave *Gill* a satisfied smirk. Looking back at the barista, she smiled politely. "Thank you. I appreciate it."

"Least we can do for the greeting you got."

Gill set the lid on his travel cup, looked back at the other man. "I heard that, Simon."

Man Bun had a name. Simon rolled his eyes, sharing a smile with Annie. "I said it loud enough so unless you're going deaf, you should have."

Annie bit back her smile. She mouthed "Thanks" and hurried for the door. Now she was really craving baked goods. In her truck, she took her first sip and sighed. It would have sucked if a place known for only one thing wasn't any good. Fortunately, that wasn't the case, but Annie still wondered how the place stayed in business. Especially if there were nine other options. Maybe *Gill* hung out at this one frequently. That would be reason enough for her to head to any of the others.

Let it go. She set her drink in the cup holder and backed out of the parking spot. As she pulled out onto the road, she caught a glimpse of the miserable old man watching her go. This was a small town, but hopefully not so much that she'd be running into him again any time soon.

Chapter Two

THE GATED COMMUNITY of Rainbow Falls Estates was charming with its eight nearly identical homes, each with a detached garage. The ocean sat just behind the U shape formed by the homes. A common house with land-scaped shrubbery, greenspace, and a couple benches separated the lane that went in one direction only. Annie knew this because it was clearly marked with a handwritten sign that seemed out of place on the wrought iron gate.

Annie made her way past homes with arched peaks and adorable porches. Even her parents' cottage, which sat in the corner of the U, had a dormer window despite having no second floor. It just sat on the roof like a space to watch the world go by.

She parked her truck in the driveway, noting the soft, almost rust color of her parents' home. Each house was a beach-home shade, but she liked the uniqueness of theirs over the yellow, blue, or green.

Getting out of the vehicle, Annie felt a slight pang at the realization that she wouldn't see her parents for a while. They'd keep in touch, but it wasn't the same as getting pulled into one of her father's hard hugs or having her mom run her hand down Annie's oft-unruly brown hair.

Her dad had recently retired from his job as the dean of admissions for a nearby college. Her mom had gone down to part-time years ago, retiring from her job as a lab technician at the same time as her dad. With all of them having busy work schedules, plus the minimum few hours' drive between one place and the other, she'd grown used to seeing them once a month or so. Now it would be at least a year.

She swallowed around the lump in her throat that came from missing them, grabbed her purse, duffel bag, and coffee. Taking the paved path toward the couple steps leading up to the porch, she opened the white screen door, punched the security code into the panel on the door handle.

After kicking the door shut behind her, she dropped her bags. The entryway was part of the large, high-ceilinged living room. Annie set her coffee on the side table by the door, going to the wall of windows that looked out on the front lawn. She pushed two upper ones open, letting in the fresh breeze to combat the stale air. Turning, she smiled, recognizing the familiar couches, the coffee table her father had made a few Christmases ago, and a large television mounted over a stone fireplace. They were all a welcoming way to mix the familiar with the new. Even without her parents here, it felt like home.

When they'd moved in, they'd given her a FaceTime tour, so she knew the archway to the left, off the living room, led to a hallway, two bedrooms, an office, laundry, and a bathroom.

To the right, another rounded arch led to the kitchen. Unlike so many homes today, these houses didn't have an open concept. She headed for the kitchen—what her mother always called *the heart of a home*. Annie wasn't much of a cook, but she loved to eat. Her DVR recordings were an eclectic mix of cooking, crime, and reality shows.

Light poured in from the many kitchen windows—one over the sink, French patio doors, and a picture window over the built-in eating nook—making the room feel large and homey.

Through the nook window, she watched an elderly man shuffle toward the other end of his kitchen. Her parents hadn't said much about their neighbors.

"Small place like this, I'll probably meet them all inside a week."

Turning, she walked the few steps to the double doors, pushing them open. Salty, ocean air slapped her face, filling her with energy and happiness.

She might not have been a great cook, but she'd make use of the grill sitting out there. Beyond the deck rail, the water crested against the rocks soothing her soul. It was impossible to tame her smile. She breathed in as much salty air as her lungs would allow.

The yard was teeny-tiny, postage-stamp sized. It was edged by large—nearly waist high—ocean-smoothed stones, like a nature-made fence. Feeling adventurous already, she took the couple steps down from the porch to the perimeter of the yard. Between her house and the one to the right, there was a trail leading to a set of steps. As soon as she'd eaten and was settled, she'd make her way to the beach.

Waves continued to slap the rocks below her while gulls called out to each other. Her tummy rumbled again, reminding her she really needed some breakfast.

Though there was a perfectly good guest room, Annie took the master because it had the attached bath. One she planned to use tonight to soak and stare up at the stars through the skylight.

She turned in a circle, loving the fact that she was going to wake up to the ocean. A seagull hovered on the rock wall before landing to look around.

Giving a giddy laugh, she fell flat onto the king-sized bed, staring up at the ceiling. "This is my house for the next year." She'd enjoyed her condo with Vivian, but it'd always been her dream to own a house. The condo had its perks. It'd been perfect for that time in her life, but she wanted her own space, a home to call her own. One by the ocean was a whole other step up on the dream ladder.

She clapped her hands together. "Time to move in."

SHE STOPPED LONG enough to make herself a peanut butter

sandwich on toasted bread. Her mom had loaded up the freezer with several of Annie's favorites, including baked goods, bread, bacon, and some individually packaged chicken. Annie took a pack out to thaw, thinking about using the grill later that night. She thought back to the drive through town, trying to remember if she'd seen a grocery store. Seeing as she'd only driven three roads to get through town, she'd probably missed it.

After polishing off her sandwich, she lugged in all of her belongings, which, truthfully, wasn't much. Knowing she was coming to a fully furnished home, she'd brought her clothes, personal items, her laptop, and her favorite books along with a few other odds and ends. She'd sold the living room furniture she owned to Vivian and stored a few of her larger items like bookshelves and her four-poster bed.

By the time she had all the boxes in, she was ready for something cold to drink on the deck. Annie smiled when she opened the pantry to find her childhood favorite iced tea crystals. Rooting around to find a pitcher, she made the tea, added mountains of ice from the fridge's handy ice maker and had just about settled into one of the porch's two Adirondack chairs when the doorbell rang.

Not trusting the seagulls, she brought her tea back in with her, set it on the counter just as her phone rang. *Everything or nothing,* she thought with a smile. Vivian's name popped up on her screen. She swiped to accept as she walked through the house.

"Hey."

"Hi. You there?" Vivian's voice was Sunday slept-until-noon sleepy.

"I am. It's gorgeous. I'll send you pictures. I just have someone at the door though, so can I call you back?"

"For sure. Glad you're there. Miss you."

Annie smiled. "Miss you, too. Talk to Danny about coming up in a few weeks. There's a guest room."

Vivian mumbled agreement and hung up. Annie pocketed her phone just as she reached the door. Looking through the shell-shaped peephole—cute—she didn't see anyone. *Weird.* She pulled the door open.

With the porch being a step down and the tiny wisp of a woman being so short, it was no wonder Annie hadn't seen her through the door. The curly white hair—even fashionably styled—indicated an older age, but this made her shadowed, smoky eyelids that much more dramatic. Annie envied the ease with which the woman pulled off a look Annie never could. Her typical makeup regime consisted of a washcloth, some soap, and a swipe of both mascara and lip gloss. This woman's painted red lips, sparkly gaze, and wrinkles showing a lifetime of smiles and laughter could have made her the poster child for how to age well.

"Hello, dear. You must be Annie. You're just as beautiful as your parents described you to be. Tall thing, aren't you?" This was all said as the woman hustled her way indoors, a large covered basket in hand. "I'm Margie. I live three doors down to the left. I saw you pull in and wanted to welcome you. Gave you a bit of time, but you haven't headed back out to the truck again so I decided you were finished. I'm head of our social committee."

Annie grinned, amused and a little overwhelmed by the speed with which this woman spoke.

"It's nice to meet you, Margie."

"You, too, dear. I've brought you some muffins. They're my personal favorite, double chocolate. I hope you're not one of those city girls who's into all sorts of weird additives like kale and celery root."

Annie followed behind the woman, who clearly knew her way through the house. She scrunched her brows, wondering whether kale could be considered an additive and what the heck celery root was. Why even eat celery? Just have a glass of water, people.

"I love chocolate. That sounds delicious. Thank you."

Margie put the basket on the table in the nook, opened it to reveal the most amazing-looking muffins, large with perfectly domed tops. She'd eaten, but there was no way she wasn't attacking those treats.

Her mouth watered with just a glance. "Wow. Those look incredible."

Margie moved to the cupboard, helped herself to a plate, then pulled a fork from the drawer. Her happy yellow sundress wafted around her tiny figure like the wind trailing after an unstoppable force. She set a muffin on the plate, handed it to Annie with the fork.

She nodded, gestured with her hand. "Go on, take a bite. Not one of those city girls who won't eat, are you?"

Annie laughed, wondering which city girls this woman knew. "I'm not."

She broke a piece off with her fork, slightly unnerved with the bossiness of her neighbor and being watched while she ate. But heck, for chocolate, she could be bossed around. When she took the first bite, Annie sighed in delight, closing her eyes to fully immerse herself in the flavor. When she opened them, Margie gave her a knowing grin.

"Can you bake?"

Annie's brows furrowed. She wasn't Betty Crocker, but she could follow a recipe if she had to. She shrugged, hoping that her full mouth would keep her from having to answer.

"It's not hard. You'll be fine." Margie reached into the basket, pulled out a piece of paper, took it over to the fridge. "Here's a schedule. You make six dozen of your choosing every six weeks. Only six of us take part because the others are sticks in the mud."

The muffin turned dry in her mouth. Schedule? Six dozen what? Muffins? Had she ever made that many of anything? She'd never even bought that many.

Margie went on, pointing to whatever she'd put on Annie's fridge. "We try to make it easy to keep track, so we arrange everything for Mondays. That's when you deliver the muffins and pick up prescriptions. We'll add you to the group text thread, and that way if anyone has library books they need returned or picked up, we know in advance. Now, not to throw it at you but your mom's turn was next Monday. It's easier to keep you on the same schedule. Can you handle that?"

Annie nearly choked on the last bite. She cleared her throat, going to her tea and taking a long swallow. "I'm sorry," she said, her eyes watering as she looked at Margie. "But *what?*"

Margie smiled like she was talking to a young schoolgirl. "It sounds like a lot, but you'll be fine. You'll see how nice it is in the weeks these chores aren't yours. It's important we all work together. We're a community. We watch out for each other."

Annie set the plate down, trying to keep her tone polite. "Prescriptions?"

Margie nodded. "Yes, dear. Most of us are on anywhere from one to a dozen. Well, not all of us. You probably aren't, unless you're on birth control, but you don't likely need to have that picked up more than once every few months."

Annie was positive her cheeks flamed, but Margie acted as if she was just sharing the weather report.

"Raj is on several because of a back injury. Of course, Tate isn't on any though I'd say he needs one now and again that adjusts his teenage attitude. Mostly, he's a good kid though. His grandfather has several, what with the glaucoma and the acid reflux and the lung condition."

Annie's eyes narrowed. Who were these people, and why on earth was she getting a list of their ailments?

"I have no idea who or what you're talking about," she finally said.

Margie walked over, patted her arm and hooked her own through Annie's. "I'm throwing a lot at you, aren't I? That's just because I'm eager to get to the senior's center. Joseph and I have started a games afternoon there, and today is the first one. You look a bit tired today, but maybe you can join us another time."

She pulled Annie along. It never occurred to Annie to dig in her heels.

"Your parents showed me a couple of your fancy designs in that magazine. You're good."

Annie's gaze widened at the quick topic change and the whirlwind that was this woman. Magazine? Right. She'd done a freelance job for a popular home magazine, and it'd received some great praise. She hoped to work with the magazine or possibly other ones again the future. Not just for the way it padded her bank account, either.

"Thank you. I'm really proud of that layout."

Margie opened the door, leading them both to the porch. Annie was feeling like she'd worked out too hard, but apparently, her neighbor was just warming up.

"Let me give you the rundown." She then proceeded to point at each house, telling Annie who lived in it.

There was no way she'd remember all of this. Margie

stopped when a shiny white convertible pulled down the lane, turning into the driveway next door.

"You can skip his house on the muffin drop. Old miser never takes part in anything. I swear, Scrooge was a kinder man in his dark days than Gill on a good one."

Gill? *Nooo.* As if on cue, the unfriendly, hunched man from Just Coffee got out of the vehicle that seemed way too low for him. No wonder he had back trouble.

"He's about as friendly as a starving lion, but pay him no mind."

Gill slammed his door shut, looked their way. Margie waved as if she'd missed him terribly, only to have him send her a growly look. If he scrunched his brows any farther, they'd simply become one.

Great. She was on muffin duty which meant learning to bake, knew more about a bunch of strangers' ailments than anyone should, and to top all that off, she was next-door neighbors with a jerk. Somehow, the chocolate muffin didn't seem worth the trade-off.

Chapter Three

The Sleuth Chronicles
A place to share the love of a good mystery. In any form.

Hey, Sleuthers. I was so surprised by the support of my idea for a book club. When I started this blog a few years ago, I had no idea I'd meet so many awesome people who shared my love of a good whodunnit in whatever format we can find.

I'll put a poll on my website and Facebook account as soon as I come up with some good options. If you have any suggestions, email me. Good job to @arealsherlock for correctly answering my mystery riddle in last month's newsletter. Send me a DM on Facebook or an email through this website with your address. So many of you were close! I'm adding another riddle to the bottom of this post. Answer will be revealed in next month's newsletter.

As many of you know, I've been in the middle of packing up my life in Portland so I can housesit for my parents. Normally, I'm pretty organized and on top of things, but I just realized: IT'S MY TURN TO PLAN AN EVENING OF MURDER! It's going to be hard to top April's event, but ideas are already churning.

That might be thanks to the little town I'm staying

in. It's the perfect setting for one of our favorite cozy mysteries. Honestly, the houses are adorable and serene. So far, it's been full of inspiration.

Our event will take place at the end of the month, as usual. I'm calling it Caffeine and Corpses, a coffeehouse mystery.

As usual, the monthly host (me, this time) will assign roles to the other group administrators and post them on our Facebook page. Throughout the next few weeks, I'll give clues and red herrings. You guys are all invited to take part in the live event on Instagram at the end of the month. Here's what I can tell you so far:

There'll be no shortage of suspects for this murderer. The victim—a squat, hunchbacked, grumpy-faced man with a raspy voice and unwelcome glare—had a number of enemies. With a sharp tongue to match his angry snarl, he had plenty of haters. Including his neighbors, the local coffee shop patrons, and those closest to him. The admin decided to up the ante this month. One of YOU gets a chance to play a suspect. All you have to do to enter for your chance to take part is confirm your attendance on our Facebook page.

ANNIE JUMPED IN her seat when her phone buzzed. Rolling her eyes at herself, she pressed the Minimize button on her document. She picked up her phone to see it was an email from a client. She'd only meant to add a few notes to her blog, but a message from one of her online friends, a fellow Bimonthly Murder Mystery Events administrator, reminded her that she was supposed to be planning this month's event. It hadn't slipped her mind entirely; it just got nudged to the side with everything else she was doing.

A few years back, she'd read a cozy mystery and fallen in love. The need to rave about it led her to creating her own blog. First, she'd just posted a weekly book review and put up links. That blossomed into getting to chat with authors, doing some interviews with them, and expanding her online network.

When a local Portland bookstore asked her to do some design work for them, she was invited to an in-store murder mystery event as a thank-you. Annie had so much fun being part of a live whodunnit. It was like dinner theater with a mystery focus.

She'd even done a few reviews for the bookstore's news-letter. That led to a couple people contacting her to see if she was interested in an online murder club. Which wasn't nearly as ominous as it sounded in the subject line of the email.

It was incredibly fun and satisfying to use her design skills in a non-work-related way. She was able to design character cards and cool graphics for some of the events. She'd met several authors through the club and even done some design work for them.

Vivian and her mother worried it kept her from engaging with the outside world, but Annie didn't see it as being much different from being in a book club that met once a month. More planning, sure, but it was loads of fun.

Stretching her arms up over her head, she lowered them with an intense sigh. Her hobby didn't usually interrupt her work, but she needed a list to make sure she got everything done in the next few weeks.

She'd catch up later tonight. "Another perk to not having set hours."

Maybe she shouldn't have made the victim resemble Gill so much, but he'd gotten under skin. She'd already been turning the idea for the event around in her head, and seeing him today cemented the victim in her mind. Fictionally speaking, of course.

Annie had only planned two other events despite being part of several. It wasn't the first time she'd used real-life inspiration for a made-up victim.

Pushing away from her parents' desk, which she'd organized to make her own, she stood up, hoping the event would be a success. Occasions such as this this relied heavily on buy-in and attendance.

Vivian always suggested adding her "real-life" friends, but Annie knew not everyone wanted to spend the evening playing murder mystery games. In fact, she couldn't think of many people she knew in real life who would be interested, including Vivian.

Her phone buzzed again as she put on her shoes to get a little fresh air. She hadn't tried out those steps yet.

She swiped her phone screen, smiling. Speaking of...

Vivian had texted, *Danny says we're good to come up for the*

4th if that's okay. I'll bring your mail.

Annie typed back a happy-face emoji. It felt weird to know she wouldn't see Vivian for a month after seeing her every day for years. Annie grabbed the mailbox key from her parents' side table. Good idea. Theirs was probably piling up.

A large seagull squawked from somewhere in the distance as Annie's feet hit the front porch. She'd had her coffee on the back deck this morning, watching the water and the boats. She thought of her parents, wondering where they were right this minute.

The sun was high above, shining like a warm spotlight. It was lovely, even with the slight chill from the ocean. She'd head into town today and grab some groceries. The ocean was making her crave fish and chips.

Annie wasn't even to the end of the driveway when she caught sight of Gill. He scowled at her from over the hood of his car. She continued walking, ignoring him and pushing down the guilt of describing him for her blog. *It's his own fault for being the perfect candidate.* Annie turned her head, looking over at the house to the right of hers. She'd heard something. The curtains ruffled closed. Margie had given her a rundown of who lived where, but she couldn't remember everything the woman said about the eight homes in the complex. That one was the older man though. She knew that.

Carrying on down the drive, she stuck to the grass in the

middle of the complex. Seconds later, she heard heavy, shuffling steps. Glancing behind her, she confirmed her suspicions. Gill was heading her way. *Keep walking. Just ignore him like you did the seagull this morning.* Well, she'd mostly ignored it. After she'd tried shoeing it off the railing by waving her arms as if she was trying to fly. Those birds were bigger than they looked from far away. A silver Lexus pulled into the complex, turning into the first house. The tinted windows made it pointless to wave so Annie turned into the little alcove that held the mailboxes. It had a cute little overhang, almost like a summer awning that would keep them dry in bad weather.

Gill sidled up to Annie as she stopped in front of the row of mailboxes.

"Tampering with someone else's mail is a federal offense," he said.

It took effort not to roll her eyes. She glanced at him without turning her head, ignoring the implications of his statement. Instead of snapping at him, she returned his useless fact with a few of her own. "So are bank robbery and identity theft."

He turned to face her, his hands on his hips, surprise at her response registering in the deeper creases of his forehead. "Oh. A smart one, aren't you? Who are you, anyway?"

This close, she could see that his skin was covered in age spots and deep grooves. Taking a deep breath, she told herself that she'd be his neighbor for the next year and there was no reason not to take the high road. She could take the low one on her blog.

She held out her hand. "I'm Annie Abbott. My parents are your neighbors. They're sailing around the world. I'm staying in their house while they do."

A car door closed in the background. Gill harrumphed, ignoring her hand even as he nodded his head like he'd expected this. "Freeloader, huh? That's the problem with today's generation. You want it easy. Won't work for something if someone will give it to you."

Her jaw dropped. She pulled her hand back like he'd spit on it. "I don't know what your problem is, but you have no idea who I am or anything about me."

Bushy, gray brows furrowed, adding more wrinkles to his forehead. "I know your type." He turned to open his small mailbox.

Anger coursed through her veins. Slamming the key into the slot, she opened her parents' box and pulled out flyers, a few magazines, and some envelopes. She slammed the door shut. Gill had already closed his box and was shuffling away.

Locking up hers, Annie stormed after him. "Hey."

He didn't turn around. She quickened her step. "You are a nasty, mean old man," she called after him. Not the best insult, but completely true.

"You tell him," a man on the porch of the second house on the right said. He held a broom in his dark hands, a smirky sort of smile gracing his face. He looked somewhere between Annie's age and Gill's. His black hair was perfectly styled. To the right, the house with the Lexus, a woman stepped onto her porch steps, her hands holding several shopping bags. She stared at them, and Annie briefly wondered if there was an outlet center around somewhere before her attention went back to the men.

Gill stopped in front of him. "Mind your business, Raj."

"You harassing that poor girl is everyone's business." Raj came down the steps, leaving the broom behind. "You hitting my car is also my business, and we're not done with that conversation yet."

"Fool. Get your eyes checked. My car is in pristine condition." Gill pointed toward his house, which couldn't be seen from where they were standing.

From where she stood, Annie didn't see anything wrong with the navy-blue BMW in Raj's driveway.

The man walked toward Annie, shaking his head. "Because you've already had it fixed."

"You can't prove that." Gill smiled meanly at him, his gaze wandering over to the woman who kept watching them. "Good morning, Ginger."

Annie's jaw dropped at the friendliness in Gill's tone. Annie looked over to see the woman attempt to wave. She hurried into the house.

"You're good at scaring off people," Raj commented.

Annie bit back the groan. Gill was no treat, but Raj could have stopped baiting him.

"Says the never-been-married man," Gill said. He leaned closer to Raj. "Quit spreading rumors. Try being a good, quiet neighbor like Ginger there."

Raj's chest puffed up on his sharp inhale. "Is that a threat?"

With a derisive laugh, the older man turned and walked away. Gill kept grumbling and walking until Annie couldn't hear him anymore.

"You must be Annie." Raj held out a hand.

Annie shook it, met his dark gaze. "I am. Nice to meet you, Raj. Good to know it's not just me Gill doesn't like." Though, he'd been almost pleasant to the neighbor woman who was probably close to the older man's age.

Raj stared at Gill's retreating figure. For a minute, it seemed as if he forgot Annie was even there. "One day, he'll get his."

Her gaze widened at the contempt in his tone. When he turned back to her, his features had softened. "I think his biggest problem is he doesn't like what he sees in the mirror so he blames everyone else. Don't let him be your impression of the place. We're nice people. Even if some of us are a little much."

His lips lifted on one side, his eyes drifting toward Margie's place. It was as if she'd imagined the earlier antagonism in his tone. *Or maybe Gill just brings that out in people.*

Giving a rough laugh, Annie nodded. "Yeah. I saw your name on the calendar. Any chance of getting off that schedule?"

Raj's deep chuckle erased any earlier tension. "Good luck. Margie enjoys her muffins." Raj leaned in closer. "Insider's trick? I buy mine at Costco. She raves about them."

Annie laughed. "That's brilliant. Thanks for the tip."

They chatted for a few more seconds about the complex before Annie went on her way. She pushed Gill out of her mind.

Dropping all of the mail in a bin by the door—she'd sort it later in case there was anything she had to take care of for her parents—she slipped off her shoes to head for the bedroom. Her mom said they'd bought a treadmill to get their bodies ship worthy. Annie did not want to know what that meant, but maybe a good, hard run would solidify her ideas on one or both of her stories. She wasn't quite ready to run on the beach yet, though she'd be taking a walk later.

She changed into a pair of shorts and a T-shirt that read: I'M IN A COMMITTED RELATIONSHIP WITH CHOCOLATE. Not only was the sentiment true, it was currently her longest-running relationship. She grabbed her phone and a bottle of water and headed out the front door to the garage.

The lock on the side door of the garage was sticky. She put her water under one arm and shoved her phone in the waistband of her shorts, jiggling the doorknob. She hadn't worked out in a while. Not being able to open the door didn't bode well for her success. She let out a sigh of relief when she heard the click.

Automatic lights illuminated the space as soon as she crossed the threshold.

Putting her hands on her hips, she looked around. The treadmill sat in the center of the space beside a yoga mat— which would *not* be comfortable on a cement floor—and some free weights. Her mom was a long way off from a gym, but it would do.

As she stepped onto the machine, something rustled to the right of her. Her gaze shot to the far wall lined with cardboard boxes, each labeled with black Sharpie. The fine hairs on the back of her neck prickled. She held her breath. Waited. Nothing. Another sound, a quick scurrying, froze her on the spot. Slowly, she put both feet on the floor.

The low, strange growl-type noise set all of her senses on high alert. *What if it's a raccoon? What if it has rabies? Oh my God, or babies?* She didn't know much about animals, having never had one but she'd seen a documentary on those grabby-handed masked bandits that had scared the life out of her. They had no mercy.

A low hiss stopped her in her tracks. The plastic of her water bottle crackled. It must have scared whatever creature she was dealing with because Annie heard scuffling, like something trying to escape. A burst of white caught her gaze, heading straight for her like a shaggy missile.

She screamed, dropped her water bottle, ready to defend herself at all costs when she realized, it was a cat. A very angry, large cat that took one solid swipe when it launched her way. Before Annie could even bend over to check out the scratch on her shin, the cat scurried behind her, heading toward the kayaks at the back of the garage.

"Ouch!" She cursed when she saw the trickle of blood on her leg. Could cats have rabies? Wincing, she picked up her water bottle. *Chill out. It's a cat.* How hard could it be to shoo a cat out of her garage?

"Here, kitty, kitty." She made some weird clucking noises before realizing she sounded more like she was calling a chicken than a cat.

She slapped her hand against the button to lift the automatic garage door, hoping the cat would just run out. Her breath caught as she waited. *Just leave, kitty. There's your escape.* Nothing happened. Tapping some of the boxes, she was rewarded with several harsh hisses.

"Come on. Be nice." She peered behind a box, saw the cat wedged there. Its beady eyes almost glowed in the darkness of the space. Okay. That was a little creepy. "It's okay, kitty cat. Come on out. Go home, or just far, far away."

She had a sudden thought. *They wouldn't.* Her parents wouldn't get a cat if they were leaving, would they? They'd never let her have a pet growing up. They didn't tell her about the muffins. Or the prescriptions.

Annie frowned. "This is silly. Fine. Stay there. I'll just work out anyway." As she moved to the treadmill, she wondered when the last time the cat had had any food. Had it been stuck in the garage? Should she feed it something? What if it was hungry? She'd barely taken a dozen steps when the cat jumped on top of the stack of boxes to hiss and glare at her.

"Are you serious?"

It hissed in response, swiping at the air. Pressing the Stop button, Annie picked up her phone. Cats could be feral? There'd been a horror movie about it. Of course, she'd watched most of the graphic scenes through her fingers and it had about thirty cats in it, not one, but still.

When she searched *animal rescue* on Google, only one hit came up that was in the area: Dr. Benjamin McIntyre, DVM. The cat jumped down, prowling back and forth in front of the treadmill.

"Just go," she said, pointing to the open door.

It let out a strange sound that belonged to a dog or a person in pain. There was no way this cat was willing to share the space. Clearly, one of them had to go. If she couldn't get some help, it was also clear, it would be Annie. She pressed Send, hoping Dr. Benjamin McIntyre was a cat whisperer. Or a trained exorcist.

Chapter Four

WHEN A DARK-GRAY SUV pulled in behind Annie's truck, she was standing in front of the treadmill, locked in a staring contest with a miserable cat. It shocked her that the animal could make such awful noises while not even blinking. The anxiety ramping up in her chest was a tad embarrassing. But it growled like a bear when she moved. A baby bear. *But still!*

She heard the door close but didn't turn her head. When Ben McIntyre spoke, without her looking his way, her first thought was that his voice was sexier in real life than over the phone. That was saying something. It settled some of the nerves racing over her skin.

"Who's winning?" he asked, stopping too far out of her peripheral vision to be seen.

"The cat," Annie said without hesitation. She frowned when the cat mewled in loud agreement. *Rude.* It licked its fur, meowed, walked in a circle, only breaking eye contact with Annie for a second. Her nerves twitched like the cat's tail. That tail was full of more sass than the whole cat.

"Not to interrupt but I'm Ben," he said, walking into her

line of vision.

She started to tell him not to put his back to the wild cat, but the air left Annie's lungs. Unintentionally, her breath changed the tenor of her "Hello" to something much more seductive than she intended. Because *if* she had intentions for seduction at any point in her future, it would not be like this. With her hair in a wild ponytail, a T-shirt revealing her relationship status, and sweat dripping down her back *from facing off with a cat.*

"You're Annie." A smile tugged at his mouth.

Maybe the cat had sucked away all of her conversational powers. She got stuck staring at his mouth and his strong, sharp jaw. Her gaze wandered like a lazy finger over his slightly crooked nose to his dark green gaze that sparkled with amusement. With dark hair cut close but not military close, he made quite a picture. The cat howled. Annie jumped. Ben laughed.

"Sorry. Yes. I'm Annie. You're Ben." She shook her head, muttering, "You are not what I expected. Do you have gloves?"

Ben's full smile struck her right in the chest. That couldn't be good. "Gloves?"

Annie pointed at the cat, who was watching them far too closely. "Yeah. You know, those ones for like raptors and eagles? It's got talons instead of claws."

Now he laughed. Full-on laughed. She would have en-joyed the sound immensely if it wasn't aimed at her. She lifted her leg, held it up for him so he could see the evidence of the cat's malice toward her. "Look!"

Ben did as instructed, but she couldn't read his hooded gaze. When his head tipped back up, he was still smiling. "Got a little scratch there. I might have Band-Aids, but I'm not sure. My patients don't usually need them. I have cones to prevent you from licking it."

Annie lowered her leg with an embarrassed huff. Her cheeks could not get any hotter. *He* hadn't been trapped in this garage with a cat for twenty minutes so it might be funny to him, but it wasn't to her. Not right now, anyway. The cat jumped, meowed, pawed at the box.

"I couldn't get rid of her. She won't go. I didn't want to go in the house and have her hide. Then the next time I come in here, I'll wonder, did she go or is she just biding her time?"

She didn't need to know Ben well to realize he was biting back laughter. He took a gentle step toward the cat. "Do you think she's plotting against you?"

He'd turned so he didn't see that she'd stuck her tongue out at his joke. Nor did he see her checking out how good he looked in jeans and a plain tee.

"You think I'm nuts, but I'm not. That cat has anger issues."

Ben reached out a hand, palm up. The cat nudged it. Annie braced, ready to take Ben's back if the cat attacked. *Wait, what's that sound?*

"You're purring?" Annie didn't mean to yell the last word, but she couldn't believe the running engine sound rumbling out of the animal.

Looking back over his shoulder, Ben shrugged. "I'm good with animals."

Annie rolled her eyes. He was probably good with lots of things. "Okay, well, scoop her up, and I don't know... Where will you take her?" She wanted her gone but not, like, *swim with the fishies* gone. He was a vet, so he probably knew this.

His other hand went to the cat, and she watched as he quietly and quickly checked the animal over in a way that didn't scare or intimidate. She could see he had a soft touch, could hear the murmured encouragement he gave to the cat. *You do not envy a cat.*

When Ben dropped his hand, turned back to Annie, his face was serious. "It's not a good idea to move her."

Her gaze widened. Between the hair, the clothes, and everything else about this moment, she was probably earning herself a spot as the town whackadoodle. Annie crossed her arms over her chest. "You're taking her side?"

Ben's laughter was a distraction. "You are an interesting woman, Annie. I golfed with your dad a couple months ago. He's a nice man, friends with my grandfather. He told me you had a quirky sense of humor and an interesting perspective on life."

Her cheeks warmed even as her pulse accelerated. Was

that a compliment? *Gee, thanks, Dad.*

Sticking to the topic at hand, she said, "Thank you. But, um, why aren't you taking the cat?"

"First, it's not what I do," he said. When he shifted, crossed his arms over his chest, she struggled not to stare at the nice things this did for his biceps. "Second, moving her will only further agitate her since she's just looking for a place to have her babies."

Her mouth fell open. "Wait, what? She's having babies?"

Ben looked back at the cat. "Very soon. She's struggling to make a space. Probably doesn't know the lay of the land, so why don't we take one of these boxes, set her up in a corner where she'll feel safer."

Then, instead of getting rid of her furry squatter, they were working together, emptying the contents of one box into another. Ben found a box cutter before Annie could even look. With a few cuts, he'd made a makeshift bed. Annie found a couple of old blankets her mother used for picnics and set them inside. Ben gently lifted the cat, petting it, nuzzling it. The sight made something delicious and complex swirl in Annie's stomach.

"There you go, sweet girl. You'll be okay," he murmured.

The soft cadence of his voice made Annie feel as if this was true. She knew he was speaking to the cat, but his words made her feel better, too. The cat scratched, turned in circles, starting up with the noises again, making Annie cringe.

Ben, coming up from where he was crouched, walked

over to Annie. He was tall. She was pushing five-foot-nine, but he had several inches on her. Tipping her head back, she saw the hint of a few days' growth on his jaw. Her fingers tingled with the desire to run her hand over his cheek. *Not a good idea.*

"She'll be okay. If there are any complications, you can call me. Can't say how long it'll be for sure, but they can take care of themselves. Though, she'd like the company."

Annie scoffed. "Maybe yours. She does not enjoy mine."

"You just got off on the wrong foot."

What he said registered. "Wait. Call you? As in, you're leaving?"

His lips twitched. "That was my plan."

Of course he had plans. He was a very attractive animal doctor. He probably had all sorts of plans that didn't include babysitting a strange cat for a strange woman.

"I have chicken." She winced even as the words barreled out of her mouth.

When he ran a hand over his mouth, she knew he was hiding a smile but was happy she couldn't read his mind. "Like one? For me to check out? Is it sick? Not that I'll say anything, but I don't think the complex is zoned for livestock."

Shaking her head, trying not to laugh at how foolish she sounded, Annie started again. "Breasts."

His eyebrows shot up, and Annie wondered if she could have a do-over on every moment since she'd walked into the garage.

Taking a deep breath, letting it out, she kept her gaze on his chest as she said, "I took chicken breasts out for *dinner*. Like, to eat. I could grill them. That is, if you could stay." She couldn't imagine a scenario where he'd want to.

Ben sucked in a deep breath. Annie watched his chest rise and fall. She wound her fingers together, waiting.

"Are you telling me you're so nervous to be alone with this cat that you're willing to feed me? A stranger?"

Nodding eagerly, she forced her gaze up. With not one bit of remorse, she said, "Absolutely. You're not a stranger anymore. You know who I am, I know who you are. You're here anyway. I mean, unless you have another patient. Or a date." She frowned when she added that last bit. Not her business, but still, the thought grated over her nerves like the cat's meowing. Why was it so high pitched?

She looked over to see the cat was breathing fast and hard, little huffs of breath. Worry crowded out other thoughts. Without thinking, she hurried over, crouched down. "Hey. Breathe. It's okay. I'll share my chicken with you, too. You're doing all the work. I get that. I'm sorry I said the things I said."

Ben chuckled behind her. "Do I want to know?"

Glancing back over her shoulder, Annie met his warm, amused gaze. "Probably not."

Ben came over, crouched beside her. She didn't think he intentionally let his knee rest against her own, but it felt nice, all the same. Really nice. He looked at her with a sweet smile. How many smiles did this man have?

"What do you have to go with the chicken?"

Her smile stretched. "Double chocolate muffins?"

He shook his head. "Not how I pictured ending my day."

Annie nudged him with her knee. "You and me both."

Chapter Five

ANNIE STIRRED THE iced tea longer than she needed to, giving herself a few minutes to wrap her head around the fact that she had a cat about to give birth in the garage. Not to mention the man in her garage who made her heart do jumping jacks while her mouth spouted silly words. *I have chicken.* She cringed, then remembered to take out an extra chicken breast. *You're just out of practice.*

Taking the two glasses outside, she walked back into the garage. Ben was murmuring to the cat.

"That's it. You're going to be okay." He stroked her fur in a way that made Annie want to arch her own back. Between the voice, the eyes, and everything else he had going on, she figured he was no stranger to attention. Or his impact on women and animals alike.

"I brought some iced tea," Annie said. Ben was sitting, knees bent, beside the cat bed. The cat was stretching out like she couldn't get comfortable.

Ben turned to look over his shoulder with a smile. "Thanks."

He took the glasses from her as she lowered herself to the

garage floor, lifting her knees to mirror his position, then he passed one back.

"You don't know how long?"

Ben took a long swallow of his drink. Annie did her best not to stare at the long column of his throat, the way his Adam's apple moved. When she realized she was staring, she looked toward the cat.

He set his glass down beside them. "Soon, I'd say."

A thought struck her so she set her own glass down. "Should I grab some supplies?"

His hand stroked along the meowing cat's back. A few little white hairs floated up into the space. "What sort of supplies?"

She shrugged. "A clean turkey baster? Boiling water? Some towels?" She looked at the cat, certain it gave her a snarky look. *I didn't get you in this position, missy, so quit giving me the evil eye.* The cat made an awful noise, prompting Ben to lean in close, soothing it.

Annie narrowed her gaze on the cat. *Nice play.*

"I'm going to go out on a limb and say you've never been around an animal giving birth? Or any birth?" When he looked at her, his smile was playful, his eyes dancing.

She crossed her arms over her chest, doing her best not to scowl. "Not exactly. But I've, you know, seen it on television." Sort of.

Ben nodded, snapped his fingers. "Right. Things go just like that."

HOME IS WHERE THE BODY IS

She pointed at him. "Hey. Maybe that isn't accurate, but a lot of television shows check authenticity with experts in the fields." She couldn't believe when she'd read online that some of her favorite shows—*Criminal Minds, Chicago PD,* and *The Rookie*—were based on actual events. It was a creepy world out there. Fascinating. But scary. Even though she loved the adrenaline rush of the shows, she often had to look away from the screen if it was graphic. *CSI* had become too much for her by the end of the series.

His chin tipped down. "Sure, maybe they're loosely derived from real events, but most things are a lot different in real life. I wasn't trying to be mean. I was mostly teasing, but if you ever find yourself in a situation like this again, avoid the turkey baster, okay?"

She laughed. That was fair. "Fine."

"You're here for the year, right? What do you do for work?"

Annie picked up her drink. "My parents expect to be gone for that long. I can't imagine them coming back early. They were pretty invested in the whole adventure. I'm a freelance graphic designer. I do a mixture of things. Signage, magazine spreads, book covers, website design, all sorts of things."

The cat got up, moved out of the box, then back in. Ben tracked the animal's movement before focusing on Annie.

"That sounds interesting. Obviously you won't be commuting, so do you work remotely?"

She nodded. "I used to work for a company in Portland, but I started taking on side jobs to make extra cash and it snowballed. It's nice being able to work from anywhere. My view now beats any others I've had."

He pinned her with his gaze. "There's no shortage of amazing views here, that's for sure."

The breath caught in her lungs. She coughed around it, startling the cat. Reaching out to smooth her hand down grumpy cat's back, she pulled away when she hissed. Annie frowned, but Ben laughed.

"You've clearly gotten on her bad side."

Annie folded her hands together. "I'm cutting her some slack on her attitude given the condition she's in."

"Generous of you," Ben said. She could hear the smirk in his tone.

The cat arched her back, started licking herself. When Annie pointedly looked away, Ben burst out laughing.

"What?" Annie asked. "It seems private."

"Well, she's a cat so I don't think she cares."

She turned her head a little, looking more out of the corner of her eye. "Is it, uh, gross?"

God. She sounded like a little kid who'd never watched YouTube.

Ben's smile was nothing short of magnificent. "It's beautiful. Incredible. I mean, yes, there are pieces that are messy, but the fact that she's about to give birth to probably four or five animals that will fill someone's heart and home…" He shook his head, his gaze filled with wonder. "It's incredible."

She was struck by the passion in his tone. Did she feel that way about her job? She enjoyed it, felt challenged by it and satisfied when she completed her work. But did she feel that intensity? The cat's noises escalated. Ben shuffled back a bit. "Let's give her some space."

Annie followed his lead. "What if she needs help?"

Glancing at her, he shook his head. "They know what they're doing. It's instinct."

It felt weird—and oddly intimate—to be sitting close to this man on the floor of the garage while nature was in full bloom right in front of them.

Ben ran his fingers up and down his glass. "I can't imagine spending a year on a boat. That's quite the trip."

She nodded, hugging her knees close to her chest, resting her cheek on them. "It is. They have every step of it planned. I thought it came out of nowhere, but when they told me about it, they'd clearly been thinking about it for years. Works out well for me."

"I think you'll like it here. What do you like to do? Any hobbies?"

He asked it so casually, she almost said, *I love creating fake crime scenarios so people can try to figure out who the murderer is.* First meetings called for more simplicity.

"I read a lot."

He stared at her like he was waiting. His brows arched. "Favorite genre?"

"Mystery and biography. How about you?"

"Reading is good, but I usually don't find the time until I crawl into bed and then I fall asleep. I like to hike, swim, kayak. I go rock climbing a few times a month."

Wow. Their hobbies were quite different. "You're very active."

"There's so much to do here. I'll have to show you some of the best spots to hike."

She must have looked skeptical because he added, "You can bring a book for when we take a break. Have you met any of your neighbors?"

"I've only met a couple people so far, but they're unique." She thought again of Margie's take-charge bossiness and flawless makeup. She was the anti-Gill, thankfully.

"That's an apt description. Have you met Gill yet?"

Her lips formed a frown of their own accord. "Yes. Let's just say we're not going to be best friends."

"Uh-oh. Not surprising, but sounds as though there's a story there."

She really wanted to see what the cat was doing. It was sure making lots of noise. Watching Ben's expression wasn't enough. He was fixated on the animal.

"Maybe you'll get on his good side with this good deed. There you go, sweetie. That's right. Clean her all up."

Wait. Clean who up? Did she have a kitten? She lifted her head while asking, "What good deed?"

Ben turned toward her just as Annie caught sight of the

cat and her newborn kitten. She only knew it was a kitten because that's what was supposed to come out of a cat. Otherwise, she would not have known. Her head spun. Her hands shook a little as the familiar but infrequent sensation worked through her body. "Oh no," she whispered, trying to block out the image of blood staring back at her as the cat did her thing.

"Annie?" Ben's voice sounded far away.

"What good deed?" Her tongue was heavy.

"Taking care of his cat."

When she turned her head to meet Ben's gaze, she never got a chance to say anything because the sensation consumed her and she passed out, right into his lap.

Chapter Six

ANNIE OPENED ONE eye then the other, then closed them both again. She heard Ben's gust of relief, felt his fingers on her neck, checking her pulse.

"I'm fine," she croaked. Embarrassment never killed anyone. If she wasn't sure of that before, she was now.

"I'm going to help you sit up. Is that okay?" His fingers on her skin were warm, and she sort of wished he'd run them through her hair. She could lie here a while absorbing his touch. Thank goodness her mouth felt too garbled to actually say that out loud.

"I'm fine."

"You just passed out," he reminded her, scooping one arm beneath hers so he could take her weight, shift her body.

"I'm not great with blood." Which was why she didn't have a job involving real crime scenes. Life was ironic. She put a hand to her head, feeling like it was rising from the ground without the rest of her body. She just needed a minute. This day was really not turning out how she'd planned.

"That rules out you being a vampire," Ben said, his face

very close to Annie's.

"Funny guy." She breathed in and out slowly. Closed her eyes another minute, feeling his stare. When she opened them again, she nodded, tried for a smile. "I'm fine."

His mouth tilted down. "I'm disliking that word more every time you say it."

With his arm around her, her head still a bit woozy, she had to resist the urge to nestle into the crook of his shoulder. "Sorry. I'll work on my adjectives. Just give me a minute."

He was smirking when she glanced up. "Can you stand?"

She didn't particularly want to but probably could. He helped her to her feet, then put both hands on her shoulders, staring into her eyes as though he was looking for signs of concussion.

"I didn't hit my head, right?"

Ben's gaze snapped to hers, mouth twisting slightly. "Not on the floor."

Oh God. She'd been sitting right beside him when it came over her. "Okay, then. As long as I didn't hit my head or anything vital on you, we're good."

His amusement made her skin warm. "Nothing vital."

"I'll just go inside, freshen up. If you want to stay with the cat, I'll pretend we never met, I didn't pass out in your lap, and we never had to discuss it. Have a nice life, Ben." She started to pull out of his grasp, but he chuckled, held tight as he looked down at her.

One of his hands tucked a lock of hair behind her ear,

and she nearly purred like the cat. *You're weak, Annie.* Knowing was half the battle. Or something like that.

He continued to watch her closely. "How about I stay with the cat and you don't even look at her until she's done. While I'm out here, I believe you promised me chicken and chocolate. Are you up for that?"

She nodded. "I am. Especially the chocolate. Are you sure?"

This time he nodded. "You're sure you won't pass out again?"

"There's no blood in the kitchen so I'll be all right."

As she moved past him, resisting the urge to look back at the cat, she knew she'd lied just a little. She was okay physically, but her pride was definitely dented.

Better than your head or Ben's... she stopped the train of thought as she walked back into the house. *Focus on dinner.*

She gave herself a minute to down some water, let her head stop buzzing before she dug through a drawer for a BBQ lighter.

The slap of salt air refreshed her when she opened the patio doors. Breathing it in, she felt back to herself. The spells never lasted long. She'd been blood-averse since high school. Finding out had changed her career trajectory. She'd always thought working in forensics would be fascinating. She could watch crime scene shows on TV, read murder in books, plan a murder mystery game down to the trickiest detail, but a hint of blood that didn't belong to her—and she wasn't particularly fond of her own—and out she went. It didn't happen frequently, and she'd never woken up with her head in a hot guy's lap. *First time for everything.*

Annie checked out the BBQ, crouching down to turn on the propane tank. She and Vivian had one similar on the balcony of the condo. Or they had until they realized it was a violation. She missed the taste of grilled meat.

The sound of a door opening and slamming shut jolted her. "That's what you think, Bethany, because you've got the common sense of a pigeon. Just one time in your life, listen to reason." The voice came from one porch over—Gill's. Annie was afraid to stand in case he thought she was listening. She was, but not on purpose. She didn't dare peek around the grill when it was hiding her so well. He'd for sure think she was up to something.

"That's not true and you know it," he said, his volume escalating. "You've poisoned her against me."

The door opened and slammed again. Annie peeked slowly and saw that he wasn't on his porch anymore. Letting out the breath she hadn't realized she was holding, she stood up. Once the grill was warming, she hurried back into the house. Did that man get along with anyone? Who was Bethany? Who had she poisoned against him? If Annie had to guess, she'd say Gill turned people away from him all on his own without any help from others.

Looking in the freezer of the fridge, she found a bag of fries and thought Ben might like them more with the chicken than chocolate muffins. The muffins could be dessert. She froze on her way to the stove. What had Ben said right before she passed out? The seconds before an episode were always a bit hazy.

Annie looked back toward the front door. Something about Gill? "No." She shook her head. "No. That can't be Gill's cat. Though, they have the attitude in common." Gill couldn't blame his on giving birth though. Trying not to panic about what her nasty next-door neighbor would say when he found out she had his cat, she focused on making dinner. Maybe she'd misheard Ben.

It was about twenty minutes after she'd put the chicken on the grill that Ben joined her in the house.

He poked his head into the kitchen. "I hoped it was okay to just come in."

She tilted her head to the side. "After all we've shared? Definitely."

His laughter made her smile. "I closed up the garage. Okay if I just clean up?"

She nodded, walking past him to show him where the bathroom was. She ignored how good he smelled. Mostly. "How'd it go, Doc?"

He looked down at her with a wide, toothy grin. "Four perfect kittens. They're all latched on and doing well. Mama is tired but much better. She said thanks for your support."

Annie scrunched her nose, making a face at him. "Liar."

Ben laughed, closing the door behind him as he went

into the washroom. Annie went back to the kitchen, grabbed some plates and cutlery, set them on the table. Heading out to the porch, she took the chicken off the grill, turned off the propane, grateful Gill didn't return. *It'd be nice to eat outside. Maybe I should get one of those little bistro sets.* It would be lovely as long as her neighbor didn't do the same.

"That's some view," Ben said, walking right up to the railing.

Annie took another deep breath, her smile coming easily as she stared at the ocean. "Isn't it? I think I'm going to love it here."

Ben turned his head, caught her gaze. Something in her chest hitched, like her stomach did when she went too fast over a speed bump. Their mutual staring lasted long enough for her to feel the babble getting ready to erupt.

"Let's eat," she said, stopping herself from further embarrassment.

"I didn't think I'd be getting a home-cooked meal tonight," Ben said, shutting the door behind them.

Annie put the meat on the table, grabbed the bowl of fries from where they were warming in the oven. As she brought them over, she realized it wasn't the most balanced meal.

"I haven't hit a grocery store yet, so I don't have anything for a salad."

Ben waited for her to sit, which was oddly charming. When he sat, he met her gaze again. "One meal without vegetables should be okay."

Annie's eyes widened. How about two out of three most days? Fries were vegetables, right? Sort of.

Ben's grin widened playfully. "I'm joking. I won't judge you for no salad as long as you don't tell my grandmother I hate most things that are green."

She relaxed as they dished up the food. His brows arched at the amount of ketchup she put on her plate. Fine. She liked some fries with her ketchup.

"It's a vegetable," she said, setting the bottle down.

He merely sent her another amused glance as he added a normal amount to his own plate.

"Okay," she said when she'd swallowed down a couple bites. "Tell me the story of Ben."

His lips quirked even as he chewed. When he finished, he cut another bite of chicken while answering. "It's not very exciting. This is good, by the way."

"Thanks. I'm pretty good on the grill. I learned fairly quick in college that cereal gets old fast, but this is the height of my skills."

He speared a piece of chicken. "That's fair. Okay, short version: I'm thirty-two, never married though I came close once, I love animals but don't have any of my own yet. My grandparents are wonderful humans whom I adore. They took over raising me after my parents decided they'd rather live abroad and I didn't want to go. My grandfather ran my vet practice, and though I do now, he's having a hard time letting go. Your turn." He took his bite.

"Nicely done," Annie said, nodding. "Very succinct." She picked up a fry, dragged it through ketchup. She took her time eating it.

He pointed his fork at her. "You're stalling."

Annie grinned. "I'm not exciting, either. Only child, no traumatic stories. Just a girl who enjoys designing, reading, and doing puzzles. I've never been married, never been close, don't like blood, but I do love crime shows and police procedurals. I'm close to my parents. I didn't realize until today that I'm really going to miss them."

His smile was softer. In tandem, they both picked up their drinks to sip. When he set his down, Ben finished cutting his chicken.

"Did you see them much?"

"Portland isn't far, but it's enough of a drive that I wasn't doing weekly dinners. It's just weird knowing they aren't right here waiting for me to visit."

Ben's laughter made her smile. "I get that. When I went away to college, I was beside myself ready to come back, thinking my poor grandparents needed me. I thought I'd be coming back to house and yard chores along with taking care of them. Don't know why I imagined that, but I did. The night I came home, my grandparents couldn't meet me at the airport because they'd booked concert tickets."

She could see her own parents being the same way. "They sound fun. What does your grandmother do?"

"She's an organic gardener. There's a farmers market this weekend. You could stock up on your produce."

Was he asking her to go? Did he work on weekends? "Oh. Where is it?"

Ben focused on his plate. "Over at Blossom Field. I promised my grandmother I'd come help at her stall. She doesn't need it but likes when I'm there. I could pick you up if you're interested in checking it out."

Annie waited until he looked up. "Would I have to work in her stall?"

He chuckled. "No. I think she'd let you have time to browse. There are other things there. Different vendors, coffee huts, sometimes there's entertainment. In a small town like this, a lot of people supplement their income by selling their crafts or hobbies."

Finishing up, Annie set her fork down. "That sounds nice. I have to ask. What is the deal with the love of coffee in this town? Was Rainbow Falls founded by a coffee bean addict?"

Ben's smile was instant, but his words were cut off by yelling that was loud enough to be heard through the closed door. Getting up, Annie went to the glass and peeked out, being careful not to be seen.

"It's Gill. He's pacing his porch. He was out there while I was cooking, arguing with someone named Bethany."

"That's his ex-wife. Gill is always arguing with someone. A day doesn't go by that he isn't railing about a perceived slight."

Annie turned around, unable to hear Gill's words. "That's really his cat? How am I supposed to tell him she's in my garage? With kittens."

Ben had turned in his chair. He paused a beat, like he was thinking, then shrugged. "Maybe leave her on the doorstep in a few weeks with all her kittens?"

She laughed. "Can you imagine?" Maybe it wasn't a bad idea.

Ben stood, cleared both of their plates. "I'm sure you can just knock, tell him what happened, and he'll be reasonable."

Annie grabbed the ketchup to put away. "You've had encounters with him where he's shown he can be reasonable?"

As he loaded the dishwasher, Annie realized she'd never shared a domestic chore with anyone other than Vivian or her parents. Weird. Not altogether unpleasant. She wondered about his *came close once* comment. Was there one who got away?

Ben shut the door on the washer, then pinned her with his emerald eyes. "Nope. But maybe you'll get lucky."

Annie groaned. Based on her experience so far, she didn't think that would be the case.

Chapter Seven

Her day's to-do list was fairly short. It included coffee, breakfast, knocking on Gill's door to share the happy news that he now had grand-kitties, then finishing up a project for a new client. She'd given it a couple days, telling herself that she couldn't let her clients wait, but the truth was, the thought of knocking on her neighbor's door was worse than the memory of watching his cat give birth.

"I hope your dad is happy," she said to Mama Cat who still eyed her suspiciously. "Geesh. Stop looking at me like that. I'm not the bad guy here." The kittens whined, mewled, and crawled over one another like squabbling siblings. It was pretty hard not to smile.

Ben said not to touch the kittens. He'd had some sample products in his truck so he left her with cat food, which she set out for the mom.

"I need coffee to deal with him, but I'm breaking the news today." Annie frowned when the cat looked away. Her tail swished like a dismissal. "Hey. I'm no coward. I just need caffeine. Don't judge."

The cat looked back. Clearly judging. Annie huffed and

left the garage. Ideas tickled her brain for her mystery night. *One of the characters should be allergic to animals. A last minute clue.* She had a victim, some secondary characters, but her mains were still fuzzy. Unsurprisingly, one of them was shaping up to look a lot like a hot vet.

The cat purred softly. Despite having a bit of an attitude, the cat was really pretty and a heck of a lot calmer without kittens trying to work their way out of her body. She wondered what Gill would do with the kittens. And when they'd actually look like kittens. To be honest, they were a little creepy at the moment. Like miniature sci-fi creatures.

Over coffee, she checked her email; messaged with an online friend, Claire, who was helping her organize the details of her event; and demolished not one but two chocolate muffins. She was going to need that treadmill.

Annie texted her parents before putting together a list of items to grab from the store. They hadn't responded yet, but she liked to update them. Annie had agreed to Ben's offer of the farmers market that weekend, but she still needed a few other things. Like caffeine in the form of soda. Chocolate in the form of Kit Kats, and vegetables in the form of Lays chips. She grinned at the list. Sometimes adulting was fun.

When she was dressed, fully caffeinated, and stuffed on chocolate, she knew she couldn't put it off any longer. Locking the house behind her, Annie made sure not to cut across his lawn. The last thing she needed was him coming out of his house accusing her of ruining his precious grass or something. For one brief second, she pictured Mr. Wilson from *Dennis the Menace*. Maybe she and Gill just needed to get to know each other. One day, they'd laugh about how gruff he'd seemed when really, he was an old softy.

A laugh-slash-snort left her mouth as she lifted her hand to knock on his door. Birds sang overhead and, in the distance, she could hear waves crashing. It really was incredible here. That was never going to get old.

When her fist connected with the door, the door squeaked open a tiny hair's width, making her jump back. What the heck? Why was his door open? *Maybe he didn't close it all the way. Maybe he slammed it in anger, and it didn't latch.* She could picture that scenario—no problem.

Listening for a minute, she held her breath, trying to hear footsteps. Inhaling deeply, she debated coming back later or seeing if he was on the back porch. *Chicken.* She knocked again, a little harder, which only moved the door farther open. A strange feeling tickled her ribcage. Like sharp feathers poking her skin.

Annie called through the crack. "Gill?"

She knocked again with more force. The door swung all the way back. Glancing around the complex, she saw no one else up and about. Maybe he'd stepped out, around the side of the house? "Gill!"

His car was in the driveway, his door was open. She *was* his neighbor and the current caretaker of his cat. She took a step in, called him again only to be met with silence. Little hairs stood at attention on the back of her neck. Leaving the door as it was, she glanced around from the entryway. Similar to her home, it opened into the living room, which was empty and starkly quiet.

His furniture was dark. With the drab color on the walls, it felt dreary. Lonely. He needed a splash of color. Even some throw pillows on the brown couch or chairs would help. Deciding she was inside anyway, she headed toward the kitchen, thinking he might be out back. Maybe he was watering the grass?

The floor creaked under her feet. *What if he's sleeping?* She stopped. *If he's not in the kitchen, you'll leave and shut the door behind you.* She'd tell the cat she tried her best. Annie thought about doing that right that second, but the nagging feeling grew stronger, making her chest tighten. *Stop it. Just because you fancy yourself an armchair sleuth doesn't mean darkness is lurking around the corner. Or next door.* Straightening her spine, she pulled in a cleansing breath. Sometimes her imagination was a pain in the butt.

"Gill. Your door was open," she called as she crossed the threshold of the kitchen.

Her gaze went immediately to the left, noting the remnants of breakfast. Pan on the stove, dishes in the sink, the smell of eggs and bacon permeating the air. Eyes scanning the room, landing on the window over the sink showed he wasn't outside. Her head continued its slow-motion turn toward the breakfast nook.

Annie sucked in a hard breath that got caught in her windpipe. Her cough was painful but not as much as the sight before her: Gill slumped over the table, head down, back rounded. He could have been sleeping in his eggs if not for the large knife sticking out of his back. Her gaze moved faster than her brain, taking in the crimson circle spreading outward from the knife like one of those splotch paintings. His arms hung at his sides as if they were pointing to the puddle of blood below.

Bile rose in her throat even as her vision doubled. Reaching out a hand to steady herself on the wall, she missed, falling forward a step. Annie tried to call out, but the bile was blocking her airway. She couldn't breathe. Her head grew impossibly heavy, and the room swished side to side.

She reached for her phone even as she felt herself get pulled fully under. The crash of her phone against the tile echoed as she followed the device down, smacking her face against the cool, hard linoleum. Fortunately, she blacked out before the pain radiated through her entire body.

ICE-COLD WETNESS GRAZED her cheek, making her flinch. Something hurt. *Everything hurts.*

"Come on, girlie. Up you get," a voice said. It sounded like someone was speaking from the far end of a tunnel.

Another brush of icy cold touched her face. Annie forced

open her heavy eyelids. Two Margies greeted her, both out of focus. Unable to tell if it was because the woman had her face so close their noses were touching or if she was still experiencing a spell, Annie reared back. Pain radiated down her neck and from the cheek pressed against the floor.

"There you are. Gave me a scare, you did. Come on. Can you get up? I can't lift you."

Her mouth felt like she'd stuffed it with socks. "Gill." The word came out rough. Her throat was a scratchy kind of dry.

"I know, honey. Let's get you up."

"Blood." Had she lost her ability to form sentences? As Annie did her best to roll to her back, her stomach followed suit, making her worry that she might throw up. A wave of dizziness held her still.

"Go slow. Can you sit up?" For a tiny woman, she had a surprising amount of strength. Maybe Marge couldn't lift her, but she was the reason Annie moved. She pulled Annie up, blocking the view of Gill with her small frame. "There you go. Don't look that way. Look straight ahead. The police are on their way. You're one of those city girls who can't handle blood?"

Her head felt as though it was full of concrete slabs. "Po-lice?"

"Yes. That's some bruise you've got forming on your face. That from your fall or from Gill?"

"Gill?" Why wasn't anything making sense. Gill was

dead. Wasn't he? Had she imagined it? She turned to look, but Margie caught her chin between her bony fingers.

"Nuh-uh. Don't look at him. Let's get you to the living room and settled before the fuzz barge in."

The fuzz? She leaned far too much weight on the slight woman but couldn't bring herself to apologize. Margie practically poured her into the leather recliner, which was closer than the couch. Annie worked on keeping her head up, but her body sank against the cushions.

"Did he hit you? Gill?" Margie held an icy, dripping cloth against Annie's face, making her shiver.

When her brows pushed together in confusion, she realized even that part of her face could hurt. "Why would he hit me?"

"Why else would you stab him?" Margie said the words so casually, they nearly didn't register.

"What? I didn't stab him! What are you talking about? Is he dead?" She tried to stand up.

Margie's chuckle was dark. "There's your big girl sentences. I was just testing you. You were passed out two feet from the body when I came in, and there isn't a drop of blood on you. I think you have a concussion, but you don't strike me as a murderer. But yes, he's dead. If he wasn't, he'd be yelling his head off about the mess in his kitchen."

A murderer. What the actual hell? Murders were for television shows and books. She didn't witness the real thing. Well, to be fair, she didn't witness anything. Other than the blood. *Oh, don't think about the blood.* Her stomach roiled.

"You're a squeamish thing, aren't you? I'm going to grab you a juice. You okay for a second?"

Before Annie could answer, an older man appeared at her side. He had short, curly salt-and-pepper hair and a pair of wireframed glasses perched on the end of his nose. He put his hand on Margie's shoulder, his expression filled with confusion.

"What on earth? Margie, what's going on?"

Margie patted the hand on her shoulder, glancing up at him. "Joseph, this is Annie. Annie, this is my Joseph. He lives in the complex, too."

"Nice to meet you," Annie muttered. That was as much as she could manage.

"You as well, dear. What are you doing in Gill's house? You, too, Margie. Gill's going to yell loud enough to be heard three states away if he catches us here."

Margie's gaze met Annie's. "He won't be yelling at anyone anymore."

Joseph huffed out a deep laugh, clearly not picking up on the tone of the room. "Good one, love."

"Rainbow Falls PD. Put your hands where I can see them," a deep voice boomed.

Annie didn't even try to turn her head. She just lifted her hands as she leaned farther into the chair.

Margie stood, putting her hands on her hips. "Ryan Porter. You can see my hands right where they are. Point that gun somewhere else. I've changed your diapers. How dare you?"

Did anything shake this woman? Annie felt like a wimp in comparison.

"Aw, come on Margie. Don't make this difficult. Stay right there, Joseph. Emily, check the kitchen."

The officer shuffled farther into the room, and Annie got her first look at the cavalry. Tall, with dark hair and thick eyebrows, light brown skin, a curious gaze, the cop's expression was a mixture of exasperation and frustration.

"Body," another voice, this one female—presumably Emily—called.

"For goodness sakes, Ryan. Do you think I have a weapon in my yoga pants?" Margie gestured to herself.

It was only then that Annie took note of the woman's outfit. She wore flower-patterned pants with a lime-green shirt. It was a color Annie wouldn't wear in a thousand lifetimes, but on Margie, it worked.

The officer holstered his weapon, not hiding his irritation. "Sit down, then. Right there on the couch." He pointed, and surprisingly, Margie listened. For the first time, he looked at Annie. "What happened to your face?"

"The floor hit it," Annie mumbled. Her tongue felt thick.

Pressing a button on the radio attached to his shoulder, he said, "How long until the medics arrived? We have an injured female, early thirties, possible concussion."

"Hey," Annie said, her eyes closing. "I'm not thirty yet."

Margie chuckled beside her. "Save your strength, girlie."

He walked closer. "Ma'am. Paramedics will be here quickly. Can you open your eyes again?"

"The rest of the house is clear. I've called in Trenton CSU. They're on their way," the female voice informed them.

With her eyes closed, Annie felt like she was in a live production of a cop show. *CSI: Rainbow Falls.* The theme music played in her head, causing her lips to tilt upward.

"What's going on here?"

Wait. A familiar voice. She liked it.

"Annie? Are you okay? What happened?"

Opening her eyes was worth the effort. Ben was crouched in front of her, his hand grabbing hers, holding on tight.

Her face was sore, but she tried for a smile. "Hey."

He gave a short, humorless laugh. "Hey. Open your eyes, Annie." His fingers probed her skin, making her jump.

She opened her eyes to glare, then swatted her free hand at him. "Ouch. Don't."

"Ben, how do you know Annie?" Margie asked.

"How do *you* know Annie?" another voice asked. Her brain must be functioning because she was pretty certain that voice was Joseph. Margie's guy. This production was getting harder to follow.

"Ben, you need to move away from the suspect," the officer's voice said firmly.

"Suspect? Are you kidding me, Ryan?"

Did everyone know everyone? Annie smiled at Ben's defensive tone. That was nice, right? What was he doing there? What was she doing there?

"Paramedics are here."

Emily. That sounded like Officer Emily. As long as Annie could keep all of this straight, she didn't have to be worried about her cognitive function.

"Cog…cogney…nope. Cog-ni-tive." Annie frowned, opened her eyes again, not realizing they'd slipped shut. Her lips weren't working properly.

"What are you saying, Annie?" Ben leaned close.

She smiled at him. She liked how he said her name.

"Let us through."

Now there were too many voices. Annie shut her eyes again, figuring Ben would wake her when things weren't so crazy.

"We making an arrest?" The words sounded far away.

"The hell if I know," Officer Ryan said.

He didn't sound happy at all. Annie wanted to tell him he should arrest whoever killed Gill but was too tired to say the words out loud.

She'd tell him later. When her eyelids weren't so heavy.

Chapter Eight

B Y THE TIME she finished answering twelve hundred questions—most of which felt like the same query asked in a different way—Annie's head was spinning. Worse than it had been earlier. The police had been very clear that she was not to go anywhere. With her face throbbing, that wouldn't be an issue.

As soon as she broke into the aspirin bottle fighting her, she only planned on going as far as the couch. The paramedics said her concussion was mild, and since it wasn't her first time passing out, she'd convinced them she didn't need to go to the hospital. Maybe if it was worse, the police wouldn't have asked so many questions. How long had she lived here? How long had she known Gill? Did she see anyone else in the area? Did she have a problem with her neighbor? Duh. She'd met him, so yeah. It probably wasn't wise to have answered that way.

"Want some help?"

She jumped, losing her shaky grasp on the bottle. It chose that moment to open, sending pills flying everywhere. Annie groaned even as Ben quickly crouched to gather them up. He'd been checking on the cat; his original purpose in coming over. Once again, he'd gotten more than her bargained for by visiting.

"I'm sorry." She bent to help.

He took her hand, squeezed. "Do me a favor? Go sit on the couch."

She thought of arguing, but she didn't have the energy. When he joined her on the couch, he had a glass of water and two pills. She hadn't realized her eyes filled with tears until she needed to blink them away.

"Are you okay?" His gaze overflowed with concern.

Annie nodded, unable to speak around the lump in her throat. It didn't make swallowing down the medicine easy. Her hand shook when she set the glass on a coaster on the table.

"Annie?"

She turned to face Ben, doing her best to keep her composure. As long as she didn't speak, she should be fine.

"Can I hug you?"

The lump thickened. He was poking holes in her determination not to cry. She inhaled sharply, giving one, quick nod, ignoring the hiss of pain. Ben put his arms around her shoulders, pulling her against him. He smelled like soap, subtle cologne, and cleaner. She supposed the latter was from his vet office, but the rest felt like all Ben. His arms were strong. *Safe.* Annie wasn't one to lean on strangers. She didn't even push that hard to lean on friends. But this was different. She'd never seen a dead body before. The only thanks she could give was that she didn't see his face.

Ben's hold was like a warm blanket on a frosty day. She sank into it, let herself absorb his heat and strength for a few minutes before pulling away. If she didn't, she might want to stay in his arms for good. Or at least until the images stopped jumping into her brain.

"I'm okay. Shaken, I guess. Thanks for checking on the cats."

"No problem. I brought a litter box, set it up, and gave her fresh food and water. She'll be pretty self-sufficient."

"Thank goodness she wasn't with Gill."

Ben's brows tented over his eyes. "Because?"

Annie pursed her lips, started to shake her head but stopped, remembering it hurt. "I don't know why I said that. Just...she doesn't need anymore trauma, right?"

His laugh pushed her back from an unsteady ledge, evening out her pulse. "No. She's been through enough. So have you."

"Who would have killed him?"

Ben blew out a hard breath, ran a hand over his neck. "I don't know, Annie. The cops will figure it out. That stuff about you staying put, it's just routine. You know that, right?"

Her lips lifted. "Been part of a lot of investigations, have you?"

Dropping both hands between his legs, he shook his

head. "No. I just don't want you to worry about that right now. They have no reason to suspect you. They'll figure it out."

She sure as heck hoped so. She'd only just settled into a home by the ocean. She definitely didn't want to trade her view for prison bars. Would she be able to work from prison? Would they let her have a laptop?

Ben glanced at his watch. Annie pasted a smile on her face. "You can go. I'm okay. Honest."

"You've got a mild concussion. You passed out *again*."

"I'm fine. You have things to do other than taking care of me."

He looked as if he might argue, but she steeled her shoulders, refusing to show weakness or keep him from something he'd rather be doing. She was safe. Alive. She wasn't the one on her way to the morgue. Her heart pinched. Gill was an awful man, but no one deserved that ending.

"I wouldn't go, but I need to check on two animals who had surgery today. When you go to bed, you need to set your alarm for every four hours. Text me when you wake up even if it's just *hi* so I know you woke up. If you don't text me through the night, I'm coming over to wake you."

She didn't know him well enough to give him one of the witty, sexy replies that usually came to mind easily. At the moment, her brain was too sluggish to even think of one.

"Yes, sir. Anything else?"

He laughed, reached out to squeeze her hand. He held it

a few seconds longer than necessary, making her wonder if he felt the same sparks she did.

He stood up. "You'll call me if you need anything." It wasn't a question.

Hard no. She'd embarrassed herself enough in front of this man. This wasn't how she wanted to get to know anyone. He stood there in his jeans and sweater, looking like a model from L.L. Bean while she probably looked like she'd made out with a hard kitchen floor. So, no. She wouldn't phone him because she wouldn't need anything. Once the pills kicked in, she was going to curl up with a pillow.

"Absolutely. Thank you for everything."

She walked him to the door. He paused after stepping out onto the stoop. "You still want to go to the farmers market this weekend?"

Oh. Right. She'd see him then. "Of course. Promise my hair will look better than it does right now."

Ben tilted his head, gave her a soft smile that made her wish he would hug her again. "Get some rest. Put some ice on that cheek."

After agreeing to both, she shut the door and leaned against it. Closing her eyes, she focused on the feel of the wood at her back. Deep breath in. Choppy breath out. Deep breath in...and the tears came.

Sinking down to the floor, she didn't try to stop them. If someone cried in private, it didn't count as weakness. Not that she'd ever felt an overwhelming urge to prove her toughness, but people barely knew her here and already, she'd left more than a few less than stellar impressions. *Crying has scientific benefits. It's cathartic and soothing.* Images popped into her brain that she couldn't push away. She let those come, too. The sooner she faced them, the sooner she could put this behind her. Providing she didn't get arrested.

AS LUCK WOULD have it, Annie had cleaned up and was sitting on the deck—the doctor had told her to avoid the computer screen for at least twenty-four hours—trying to pretend it was a normal, sunny evening when she heard the doorbell. Her gaze drifted over the table on her way through the kitchen, and the image of Gill in that spot in his own home flashed in her head with startling clarity. Stomach turning, she hurried toward the door when the bell rang again. Looking out, she saw Margie only because the woman stood far enough back that she was visible.

"Hi," Annie said after opening the door.

Margie stepped forward. "Hi. How are you doing?" She came all the way in, a large bag thrown over her shoulder. She smelled like breath mints.

"I'm doing okay. Thanks for checking. How are you?" This woman, this tiny force, saw the same thing Annie did. She didn't end up facedown on the floor. Not only that, she'd taken charge. Annie had all but curled into a ball.

Margie dropped her bag onto the couch, waved her hand in a dismissive gesture. "I'm fine. At my age, you expect to see a dead body at some point. Not with a knife sticking out of it, mind you. I've got a strong stomach."

Annie winced. It didn't need to be said, even as her own stomach rolled, that she did not.

"Have you eaten? Taken some medication? I've brought lavender oil. Ginger swears by it. Says it's great for headaches and relaxation. I figured it couldn't hurt. Now, I don't mind taking the couch, but if your parents have a spare bedroom, that'd be better. At my age, you want a good mattress under you if you have any hope of getting off it the next day without your bones crackling."

Annie smiled even as she tried to follow the conversation. "How *old* are you?" She covered her mouth with her hand, then removed it. "Sorry."

Margie gave a big belly laugh. "Not as old as I make my-self seem. I'm practicing for when I am. Now, spare room?"

Annie pointed even as she asked, "For what?"

Margie picked up her bag. "For me to sleep over. I'm going to make you something to eat, get you situated, and then I'll wake you every hour to make sure you don't succumb to an eternal sleep."

Shock stopped her from speaking until Margie was across the room. "That's completely unnecessary. Please, Margie. I'm fine." Hmm. She *did* overuse that word.

Margie stopped, turned slowly to face Annie. "We're

neighbors. That's something like being family when you live close as we do. I don't feel right about leaving you alone after what you saw."

"You saw the same thing." They stared at each other from across the room.

Margie nodded. "But I didn't pass out. Didn't get a concussion."

Annie could see from the set of the woman's jaw; she wasn't getting out of this without a compromise. "I'll take dinner since I didn't get to the store, but you really don't need to stay the night. Ben already has me texting him through the night under the threat of showing up if I don't respond."

Margie shook her head, coming back toward the couch. "Girl. Maybe you hit your head harder than I thought. An opening like that, a man like Ben, why on earth didn't you just tell him to stay and check on you personally?"

Laughing made her wince. She sank onto the couch, more tired than she realized. "I've been here less than a week."

Opening the bag, Margie started pulling out items as though it was Mary Poppins's grocery sack. Cheese slices, a tub of butter, a loaf of bread. "Observant girl. In that much time you zeroed in on one of our most eligible bachelors."

"In my defense, I didn't. I had a…cat issue and called the local vet. I had no idea he was…Ben."

Margie smiled, pointed the loaf of bread toward her.

"Bet that was a pleasant surprise. That boy is full of goodness inside and out. Just like his grandparents. You're not one of those lactose intolerant city girls, are you?"

She was pretty sure country girls could be intolerant to lactose as well but just shook her head. "No."

"Good. Close your eyes for fifteen minutes while I throw some grilled cheese together."

She should offer to help but knew the answer she'd get so she closed her eyes.

"Good girl. You rest, I'll cook, then we'll figure out who wanted to shut Gill up for good."

Annie's eyes popped back open.

Chapter Nine

ANNIE WOKE THE next morning with the feeling of forgetting something. There was a hovering in her brain, but whatever it was trying to remind her of was just out of reach. Rolling over in the bed, she stretched her arms wide as she pulled out of her heavy sleep slowly. Cataloging her brain, she scrolled through her multiple to-do lists. *Start the concept art for new client, finish up menu design for Luigi's Pizzeria, visit grocery store, feed the cat…Gill.* She sat straight up in bed, immediately aware of the throb in her cheek.

Grabbing her phone, she winced when she saw the time. Ten o'clock. She never slept that late during the week. Of course, she didn't often have a mild concussion, late-night visits with nutty neighbors who wanted to solve Gill's murder—she'd sent Margie home right after dinner—or middle-of-the-night text exchanges with a certain sexy, charmingly sweet vet.

She really needed to get to the grocery store. That was job one today. *After a shower, caffeine, and some pain meds.* Refusing to look in the mirror, she rushed through her shower before checking out the damage.

Ouch. Her cheek was puffy and bruised, the purple smudges creeping up around her eyes. She was grateful the headache had softened to a dull ache, but there was no amount of makeup she could use to cover the bruise. Instead, she focused on drying her hair and applying some mascara and lip gloss while she played around with ideas in her head. She was sitting in the middle of an actual murder. It wasn't a game on her phone or a setup for the Facebook group. It was real.

If she tried to work around the part where she knew the person and had seen the evidence, she could use the details to make her event even better. She winced. *Way to be sensitive, Annie.* Cutting herself some slack—she *had* witnessed something horrific—she decided this was a good distraction tool. Removing the personal element would let her be objective. Maybe that would stop the images from spinning like a carousel in her head. After texting Vivian, she grabbed her purse, wondering if she should check the cats again. Opening her front door, she nearly tripped on a rock sitting on her stoop. Frowning, she picked it up. Why would an apple-sized rock just randomly appear on her doorstep?

Her stomach clenched hard when she turned it over in her hands. Written in a messy scrawl were the words *I need to talk to you.*

Annie's head snapped up as she looked to her left and right. She ignored the pain brought on by the quick movement. Other than a mower whirring in the distance, the ever-present roll of the waves splashing, and birds singing, the complex was quiet. She set the rock inside the house. If something happened to her, maybe they could use it for fingerprints. Should she take it to the police station? *And say what?*

She huffed out a breath. "Stop it. Nothing is going to happen to you. Why would it? Nothing ever happens to you." Thinking about Gill, suddenly her quiet, uneventful life didn't seem like a bad thing. Casting what she hoped were covert glances each way, Annie walked to her truck. Basically, she channeled her inner Margie. Annie knew she was probably imagining it, but she *felt* as if someone was watching her. Enough so that she locked the doors even before she started her vehicle.

No one could say she didn't have an active imagination. Sometimes, it was a little too active. "You're freaking yourself out. It was probably Margie. She didn't have a piece of paper so she used the first thing she found." *Okay, but why would she have a black marker on her? Why didn't she knock? Heck, it's Margie. She would have just barged in.*

As Annie backed out of the driveway, her gaze drifted to the house on the right of her own. It was one of three homes in the complex that had a second story. The drapes fluttered in an upper window. Was the old guy she'd seen through the kitchen window the first day watching her? Had he left the note?

"You're going to drive yourself crazy." She turned up the

music and forced herself to sing along, making up the words she didn't know. Anything to keep her brain from wondering if whoever wanted Gill dead now had their eye on Annie.

THURSDAY MORNINGS IN Rainbow Falls were far different than Sundays. The town was alive. No other word for it. Shops were busy, cars pulled up alongside her own, restaurants had rolled tables and chairs out onto the sidewalks for customers to enjoy the sunshine. She let the GPS's robotic voice guide her along the main drag of shops. Shop Smart was seven minutes away on the outer edge of the town. She would have found it without the help of her phone. It was in the same parking lot as a tiny Walmart, a 7-Eleven, a giant pharmacy, and a small movie theater showing only two movies. Center Street might have the most touristy shops, but she was willing to bet this was the real downtown core of the tiny city.

The grocery store was bright and cheerful with large rainbow signs announcing what could be found in every aisle. They were cute and on brand but dated. Annie couldn't help but critique signage when she was out. It was where she'd started her career. She grabbed a cart and made her way through the store, orienting herself with what would be her go-to grocery for the next year. It was nice to focus on a mundane chore.

She was choosing between Honeycombs—a childhood favorite cereal—and oatmeal—definitely the more adult choice—when the feeling of being watched hit her hard. Neck hairs up, goose bumps on her skin. A general feeling of unease. It was starting to irritate her how on edge she felt.

Looking up, she tossed the sugary cereal into the cart. No one else was in the aisle. Pop music played over the speakers, and if she listened really hard, she could hear the gentle buzz of freezers and electronics. Hurrying forward, she looked both ways at the end of the aisle. In front of her was the meat section. The entire back wall was devoted to fresh fish and butcher-cut meats. Prices and choices were listed on a huge chalkboard. A couple of people chatted with the butcher. To her right, the aisles became more household products than food. To the left, was the dairy section. People milled about as if she wasn't there. Totally normal. No one watching. *Simmer down, Suspicious Sally.*

She continued, grabbing milk, eggs, and yogurt. The feeling didn't hit her again until she was in the candy aisle. Pretending to crouch down to check out the selection of chocolate bars, she turned her head to the side. A woman in overlarge sunglasses, a cheetah print top, and skyscraper heels was stopped, staring at her. As soon as she noticed, the woman pretended to check a list clutched in her hand and moved forward.

Annie rose from her crouch and decided she'd had enough shopping for the day. She hurried through the checkout, making minimal small talk with the perky teen girl who worked the register. Once her items were stowed in her truck and she was in it, doors locked, she breathed easier.

"This is ridiculous. You've lived in big cities. You're being paranoid." *Cut yourself some slack. You did just experience a traumatic event. It's normal to experience aftereffects of something like that.* According to every show she'd ever watched, anyway.

As she drove home, she thought about what Margie had said. There was no shortage of people who disliked Gill. Margie had given her several names of people who had ongoing issues with the man. Regardless of how Annie had tried to steer the conversation away from murder, Margie kept going back to it, casting her vote for the most likely suspect. Thinking about last night distracted her from her route, sending her down a street she didn't recognize.

The houses in the rest of the town were more varied and distinct in style than the one she lived in. She passed a school—elementary, from the look of the kids on the playground. She found the middle and high schools on her impromptu tour and another business area.

The sight of Gill's large, growly face made her stomp on the brakes, earning a generous amount of honking from the cars behind. Stepping on the gas, Annie glanced back once over her shoulder.

GILL'S CLASSIC CARS. He was a car salesman? Annie couldn't believe it. Weren't salespeople supposed to be friendly? She'd noticed it was open and people were browsing the lot even though there was no way Gill was working the floor today. She wondered who was holding down the fort. Maybe Bethany? The ex-wife. She'd have to ask Margie after she looked up the dealership online.

As she pulled into her driveway, Annie knew she wasn't going to be able to focus on work while an actual mystery was sitting in her lap. It wasn't until she carted the last bag of groceries to the steps that she felt the whisper of unease trail along her arms. Glancing up, this time she saw a huge, dark shadow next door—much too large to be the old man she'd seen—behind the curtains that had definitely just been swept closed.

Chapter Ten

S HE COULD LEAVE it alone. All of it. She'd come to Rainbow Falls to help her parents, save some money, and decide what was next in her life. She'd always been okay with the everyday status quo. Her adrenaline rushes came from the seat of her couch with a bowl of popcorn beside her while she watched the next episode of whatever show was pulling her in. She *always* guessed the killer in those shows.

Television and real life are vastly different. She huffed out a breath. *No kidding. The blood in shows doesn't make me pass out.*

Her perception had shifted even when it came to planning her fictional murder. Until now, it was storytelling. Entertainment.

Taking the steep, wooden stairs from the side of her parents' home down to the ocean, she focused on her feet so she didn't lose her footing. If she fell down these stairs, she'd probably end up washed out to sea. Or, more likely, she'd get found and be labeled as the clumsiest newcomer to the area. Quite a name she was creating. Scared of cats, finder of bodies, paranoid she was being watched.

The stairs were built into the side of the cliff, surrounded by overgrowth that Annie couldn't label. There was a surprising amount. Hopefully it wasn't her job to trim it back. That had to be a city thing, right? She added checking with someone about landscaping to her mental to-do list. Instead of just straight down, there were a couple of twists in the stairs that accommodated the steep hillside. Hill.

"Do not think about how you're living in a house *on* a cliff." The house didn't seem this high up when she was looking down from the porch. The reason was likely that the ocean was straight down whereas the stairs were tucked between the two houses, making a path from what had once just been a rockface.

It was hard to imagine her parents taking these steps down. They were both in great shape, but there were a lot of them. *Just wait until you go back up*. Maybe that was how her parents stayed fit. Who needed a treadmill? They'd aged well, and Annie hoped she could say the same several years from now. She'd have to stop passing out at the sight of blood first. Especially if she wanted to sort through this mystery on her own. Or with the help of an equally nosy neighbor. Margie would be all in for throwing some theories around.

Annie's heart rate settled when she neared the end of the stairs. The overgrowth was still thick, but the beach had to be just on the other side. Hopefully, she'd be able to walk along the sand. After all this, she wanted to walk on the water's edge. Gulls sounded in the distance and Annie heard the hum of the waves. It was immediately soothing.

In less than a dozen steps from the stairs, the beach and the view opened up to exactly what she'd hoped for. She stood a moment, staring out at the sea, just listening, breathing, and existing. The tension from the last day was still locked in her shoulders but some beach time would cure that.

The tide was out. Annie slipped off her shoes and tied the laces together, making it easier to carry them with her as she walked away from her home. From this spot, the houses looked small and far away. Perspective was a funny thing.

Up ahead, a man threw a stick for a huge, shaggy, gray dog. The dog raced into the surf without hesitation. The waves rolled right over him, but he came out with the stick. Annie laughed. The man, who was a lot closer to the water than she was, waved in greeting. Annie waved back, kept walking.

The beach curved with some areas of the shore spreading wider than others. There were several paths that led up and away from the ocean. In the distance, she saw a couple of boat launches. With this much ocean, it made sense that there was more than one.

Tempted to take the little path that had a sign saying, SHOPS THIS WAY, Annie chose instead to sit on a huge rock and just let the waves calm her breathing. Her mind. It didn't work, but it was still nice.

The last few days tumbled through her brain like a cozy mystery novel she'd read. What would her favorite sleuths do? Obviously, they'd get involved but Annie had no real reason to do so, other than being the one to find the body. *But if you use it as your basis for the event, you could actually solve the crime.*

Her phone rang, startling her out of her thoughts.

"Hey," she said after seeing Vivian's name on the screen.

"Hey? That's it? How about, are you okay? I heard there was a murder," Vivian said, her words rushed.

"How?" Annie looked around to make sure she was relatively alone. People were on the beach, but so far apart, she felt as if she had privacy. She hadn't filled her friend in when she'd last texted.

"Uh, there's this thing called the news."

"But it's such a small town." That felt unfair. Death mattered even if the town was small. Guilt pierced her conscience.

"I was looking the place up to show Danny. Seriously, are you okay?"

"I think so. It's been a rough couple of days." She went over the events without being explicit.

"Wait. You saw blood. What happened?" Vivian knew her well.

"What do you think happened? That's how I got a concussion. Another neighbor was there when I came to."

"Holy rollers, Annie. Do you need me to come out

there? I told you small towns were trouble."

Her laugh made her wince. She'd been out in the sun for a bit. It was probably time to head back, check the kittens, and take a break. She had a menu design to finish up for a client.

"You don't need to come up. It has nothing to do with me. It's sad. It was really awful to see, but I'm just going to keep to myself and hope they find the killer soon."

Just saying the word *killer* made her want to glance around, check her surroundings. She didn't let herself. *You're safe. You're safe. Yup. Just keep saying it.*

"Annie." The one word, drawn out by her best friend unlocked so many of the thoughts she'd tried to keep corralled. "What's really going on in your brain?"

Looking around one more time, seeing that there was no one close enough to hear, she spoke quietly into the phone. "Why would someone kill him now? It can't be a coincidence that I just moved in. That I had more than one confrontation with him." She told her friend about the rock, Raj's and Margie's comments about how many people wouldn't be sorry about his death. "I think the timing is a big clue."

Vivian groaned into the phone. "Annie. This isn't one of your mystery nights. It isn't a neatly thought-out murder you can unravel."

Annie pictured her friend's pinched brows and frown. She pushed up off the rock, adrenaline coursing through her.

"They rarely are. Chances are in my favor that the perp left something behind. Some evidence."

"The perp? Do they even use that word on TV?"

She shrugged as she walked. "*Murderer* sounds awful. But you're right. Call it what it is. I should have looked more closely at the scene when I got there. The door was open. Did the killer leave through the front door? Oh, I wonder if the complex has cameras."

"Annie, I swear to Sherlock and all his buddies I'm going to come up there and handcuff you to something inside the house if you get yourself in any trouble."

Her toes dug into the sand. "I didn't look for trouble. It found me. I won't do anything stupid."

"Like go into the house of a man who made it clear he disliked you?"

Annie had no comeback for that one. After promising Vivian she'd call if she needed her, she pocketed her phone. She didn't think she'd wandered that far, but fatigue was setting in.

Looking up at the houses, she noted they all looked really similar from way down here. She took the path to the stairs and made her way up. It wasn't until she was nearly to the top that she realized her error. She stopped on one of the stairs and looked out. Same view, but she was almost positive she'd taken the wrong set of stairs. Sighing at the thought of going back down all of them to find the right one, she kept going. She'd figure it out when she got to the top.

"Well, hey there, neighbor. How are you doing, dear?"

Annie startled at the sound of a man's voice. When she saw Joseph in his yard, she breathed easier. She hated being so jumpy. She took the final few stairs to the narrow green-space between his house and the one next to it.

"I'm okay. Your flowers are beautiful," she said. Inside his fence was edged with roses of all colors.

He looked behind him. "My own version of a rose garden. Margie loves them so I like to have them on hand. Of course, if I can ever convince her to move in with me, they're just a bonus feature."

That was sweet. It reminded her of her parents. They were in that kind of love that people aspired to feel.

"I think I lost my bearings." She looked around, trying to remember what Margie had said about who lived where.

Joseph chuckled, took off his gardening gloves as he approached the fence. "Margie's is right there," he said, pointing to the house beside his. "Then Gill's, then yours."

"Sorry. I thought I took the right one," she said, smiling at him, fighting back a yawn.

"No harm. My trick is I count them as I walk away so I know how many paths I passed. But they all lead to the top so it's never a problem to get home. You just head around the front there."

"Thanks. Can you thank Margie again for me? She made me dinner and checked on me. Is she doing okay?"

Joseph nodded, the concern evident in his kind gaze.

"She is. She's a tough one, my girl. You need anything, you let us know."

"Thank you. I should go. I'm more tired than I thought."

Joseph pointed to the front of the house. "Just go straight and turn left."

She wandered back, more relaxed but also close to exhausted. She'd forgotten what the doctor said about concussions, but perhaps she'd need to take things a little easier.

Letting herself in, she felt better than when she'd left. Some sleep, some food, and then she'd finish up the menu job, get that invoice sent. Between steady work and free rent for a year, her bank account was going to be flush.

When she was done all of that, she could curl up with a good book. Better to get lost in a fictional story than the real thing. Definitely less trouble that way.

Chapter Eleven

THE FOLLOWING DAY allowed for some much-needed quiet time. There was a normalcy in puttering around the house, adding little touches to make it her own. She stacked her favorite books in the office, put her gray chenille blanket on the back of the couch for when she was watching TV. She moved a few of the cupboard and pantry items around based on how little she cooked and what she needed access to. Taking a page from Margie's book, she'd even written out a menu plan for the next couple of weeks according to what she'd picked up at the store.

Her favorite distraction was reading, but every time she dove into her book, a cozy mystery by a favorite author, it brought up thoughts of the real murder lurking in her mind. She was enjoying the whodunnit but couldn't help wondering who did the real thing next door. After spending some time with Mama Cat and her babies, Annie went to the office. With her head hurting less, she had good intentions.

She sent out a few invoices, answered emails from prospective clients, wrote up an estimate for an existing customer. She tucked her hair up in a loose twisty bun, stared at her computer screen and huffed out a breath.

"Who are you kidding?"

She pulled up a Word document and let her thoughts go where they wanted. Maybe writing her blog and working on the event would help her sort her thoughts.

The Sleuth Chronicles
A place to share the love of a good mystery. In any form.

This mystery has all of the elements we love: a not-so-nice victim, several suspects, minimal clues, and a cat with attitude to round things out. This real-life caper needs unraveling.

Our victim is a grumpy car salesman who looks older than he probably was. Likely in his late fifties, he had no friends in the housing complex where he's lived for the last several years. Here are your suspects, murder-mystery lovers.

Okay, what did she know?

Our victim, Gordon Grouchon, was mid-to-late fifties. He spent his days terrorizing his small town when he wasn't trying to fleece them on the price of an automobile. Was it his ex-wife who still raises his blood pressure every time they talk? A vengeful customer? A neighbor tired of this man's antics? Perhaps a neighbor who seems to turn up at the most convenient of times?

Annie stared at the screen a moment. Okay. She'd listed the people she thought could be responsible in real life for Gill's murder, but that was okay. Art could imitate life. But maybe she was going at this wrong. She added a quick note to the blog saying she'd add more suspects and details soon.

For now, she needed a list of questions and a list of *real* suspects. She opened a new document. Who, what, where, when, and why? She only knew two of the five.

Questions	Suspects
How old was Gill?	Bethany—ex-wife
How long had he been divorced?	Raj—he and Gill argued in front of me…he said
What was he arguing with his ex about?	someday Gill would get his
Who's running the dealership?	Margie—neighbor, definitely bad vibes between them
Why was Margie the one to find me?	
Who left the rock?	

When she almost typed *when do kittens look like cats?* she knew she needed a break. Shutting her computer, she went in search of fuel. A can of cola, maybe some chips—which in their purest form were once potatoes—and some dip—dairy. Hello, balanced diet.

Two hard quick raps on her door startled Annie. She padded to the door, her oversized penguin slippers swishing along the floor. Glancing out the peephole, her unease returned. Opening the door, she noticed the man first. He had dark hair and reflective shades covering his gaze. His buzz cut went with his too-slick gray suit. The woman beside him wore a similar outfit but somehow managed to make it look feminine in a way Annie could never pull off. Working from home had changed her wardrobe. This woman's light blond hair was tucked back in a tight ponytail that sharpened her features.

"Annie Abbott?"

She nodded.

The guy held up a badge just like they did on television. Her brain flipped through every cop show she'd ever seen at warp speed. After he tucked it away, he removed his glasses. His gaze was just as dark as his hair.

"I'm Detective Steven Rickers. This is my partner, Detective Meghan Black. We're with Major Crimes. We'd like you to come to the Trenton police station so we can ask you some follow-up questions about the murder of your neighbor." He glanced down at a notepad. "Gill Downs."

Major Crimes. Does Rainbow Falls not have the manpower to solve this? Or did they lack the experience? The sleepy little town probably didn't get a lot of major crimes. She'd answered so many questions the other day, it hadn't occurred to her that more police would get involved.

Her mouth went dry. "Can you ask them here? The Rainbow Falls PD asked me about nine thousand questions on the day of."

The female detective watched her with a gaze that reminded Annie of Mama Cat. Immediately distrusting. Not at all impressed.

"I understand that, ma'am. We'd like to keep things official and have you join us at the station."

Her shoulders stiffened. She wasn't an idiot. They were looking for home turf advantage. "Official as in you're arresting me?"

He regarded her for a moment. "No ma'am. We'd just like to talk to you about an open homicide investigation. We're taking over for the Rainbow Falls PD. They aren't equipped to handle this sort of thing. You can drive your own vehicle and have a lawyer present if you wish."

A lawyer? Nothing in her fictional experience made her think a lawyer was necessary. But backup wouldn't hurt. How about a veterinarian? Or a nosy old woman who was currently watching from her own lawn. Margie waved in their direction, but Annie didn't lift her hand in response.

"Do I need a lawyer?"

"No, ma'am," Detective Rickers said.

"That's up to you, Ms. Abbott," Detective Black said, shooting her partner a displeased look.

"Can I grab my purse and a jacket?" If nothing else, if she went, maybe they'd stop calling her *ma'am*.

"Of course."

Both stepped back. Regardless of their claims that they just wanted to talk, Annie had a bad feeling. She texted Ben because she didn't want to alarm Vivian when she was too far away to help. Hopefully, if things went sideways, Ben knew a lawyer. *Standard procedure,* she reminded herself. *You found the body. It totally makes sense they want to ask some follow-up questions. You were first on scene. You know even the smallest details that seem like nothing could lead to a break in the case.* Yup. She knew her stuff, but it didn't seem to settle her stomach one bit.

HER FIRST THOUGHT when she entered the station was how accurate her favorite shows were. She half expected to see Nathan Fillion on desk duty or walking by in his rookie blues. The air was stale and heavy. There were several metal and wood desks crammed into a fairly small area despite being the bigger of the stations in the area. Police officers and personnel talked over one another. Desktops held state-of-the-art computer equipment, and Annie wondered what the odds were of being able to check out some actual criminal files or their search databases. It would be cool to see a legitimate case file.

Detective Rickers and Detective Black waited for her at the front counter, buzzed her through a gate. They passed a coffee counter and stopped to fill paper cups.

"Want some?" Detective Rickers asked.

She immediately imagined thick, sludge like coffee. "No, thank you."

Detective Black sent her an amused look. "It's not nearly as bad as you see on television."

Annie smiled, her stomach clenching. Finding the body didn't make her guilty. Neither did creating a murder mystery event or loving crime shows. "I'm fine, thanks." Ben was right. That word was becoming highly annoying, not to mention completely inaccurate.

Her phone buzzed in her pocket as she followed them through the bullpen. They passed a couple of closed doors and a couple of open ones showing small offices. Not a plant in sight, though it was brighter than she'd thought it would be thanks to the wall of windows looking out on downtown Trenton. It was only twenty minutes from Rainbow Falls, but from the little Annie saw on the drive, it was a world away.

They were almost to the end of the hallway where Annie sincerely hoped they didn't have jail cells when a commotion turned them all around.

"She's with us!" Margie hollered from the foyer. Joseph hurried alongside of her. "This is her lawyer."

"Friends of yours?" Detective Black looked at Annie.

"The neighbor," Rickers muttered.

Annie sighed. "I didn't even know he was a lawyer."

She watched as Margie gestured frantically toward them but couldn't hear what she was saying. At least she'd lowered her voice.

"Take her back to get started. I'll deal with them," Rickers said.

Annie waved, thinking she'd rather follow Detective Black than "deal" with Margie. Rickers was in for a surprise. Margie was a force. Droplets of sweat formed at the base of her neck when Black led her into an interrogation room. Just being in this room made her want to confess all of her sins. She'd gone from feeling like an extra in a TV drama to feeling like a criminal. The handcuffs attached to the table didn't help.

Detective Black took a seat, giving nothing away with her stony gaze.

Annie noticed she sat with her back to the glass which meant Annie would have to face it. She sat down across from the attractive, stoic faced woman. She leaned her forearms on the table, crossing one over the other.

"You're new in town. Quite the interesting welcome. Sort of weird that your neighbor died inside a few days of your arrival."

Annie pulled in a breath, tried to steady her nerves. She pressed her palms flat on the cool table. "If by weird you mean upsetting, then yes."

Detective Black had a stare that would have broken Annie if she'd done something wrong. Did she always get her guy? She probably had the record for most cases closed. Perps probably feared her. She should partner with Margie.

The cuffs of her white dress shirt poked through her jacket as leaned closer. "You look nervous, Ms. Abbott."

Annie had to bite her tongue to keep from saying, *Duh.* She was grateful she'd grabbed a jacket because the temperature of the room felt like it dropped several degrees. The door opened. Detective Rickers slammed it behind him.

He glanced down at his small notepad, his jaw tight. "According to Margie Tripalo, you're a good girl, and though her paramour—her word, definitely not mine—Joseph went to law school, he is not a lawyer." He pinned Annie with an irritated glare as he closed the book and sat down beside his partner. "Looks like you're on your own."

A place she'd been before. It hadn't ever bothered her, but at the moment, she definitely wished she had a shoulder to lean on. "You said I wouldn't need a lawyer. I don't appreciate being treated like a suspect when I did no more than stumble upon a horrible scene. I walked away with a concussion, a bruised face, and a visual I won't ever forget." She left out the final piece of her thoughts. *And a headache that's making me too tired to deal with jerks who think I'll cower just because they're in suits.*

The two detectives exchanged a look before giving her their attention again.

Detective Black started. "Let's talk about that, Ms. Abbott. What were you doing at Mr. Downs's?"

Annie didn't hide her frustration. They were wasting time and resources interviewing her. "Are you telling me that the Rainbow Falls Police didn't give you my statement?"

Rickers leaned back in his seat. "We have it, but we'd

like to hear it from you."

Seeing no other option, Annie walked them through the story again. Piece by horrible piece. They repeated several of the questions she'd already been asked, going so far as to restate questions in their own wording, as if they could catch her in a lie.

After what seemed like a lifetime but was probably only an hour, Detective Rickers flipped open his notebook again.

"Can you tell us where you were between midnight and eight a.m. the night before you found the body?"

That was a large window of time. "Where I'd assume most people were. Asleep." Which, even she knew, was the worst alibi. Before he could ask the expected follow-up question, she added, "Alone."

"Pretty sweet situation you have. Beautiful home on the water. You make a decent amount of money as a graphic designer but certainly not enough to afford the style of life you'll be enjoying for the next several months."

Mortification clawed at her chest. Gill had alluded to the same thing. She wasn't *using* her parents. Geesh. She was doing them a favor.

She locked her fingers together. "Thankfully, my ability to work remotely made it possible for me to help my parents while they're out living their dream."

"Convenient."

Annie sent Rickers a hard glare. "It doesn't feel that way at the moment. What are you suggesting? That I arranged my living conditions to kill a man I don't know?"

Rickers leaned forward. "People kill for all sorts of reasons. Revenge. Money. Where did you say your parents are?"

Her jaw tightened. "Sailing around the world."

"How hard would it be to get a hold of them?"

"I don't know. I'm sure with a little effort, you'd manage it."

Rickers' eyes darkened. "Did you have a good relationship with them?"

"Yes." She didn't want to elaborate because she didn't like where this was headed.

"When was the last time you heard from them?" Black joined the conversation again.

"What are you suggesting now? That I killed my parents? Then their neighbor?"

Neither of them said a word.

"This is ridiculous." Annie threw her hands up. "You think I hurt my parents? For what? So I could have their house? Surely you have something better to go on than this. Like someone with an actual motive?"

Rickers' smile was not reassuring. "Like wanting to keep a secret about where your parents really are? That could be motive. Maybe Mr. Downs knew something you didn't want him to?"

She shook her head, more frustrated than she ever imagined possible. "Unless you intend to charge me with something, I'd like to go home."

"You're free to go. Just don't go too far," Detective Black said.

Annie stood up, the chair scraping against the floor. When she got to the door, she turned back to see them with their heads close together. They both turned when they realized she'd stopped.

"Something else?" Rickers asked.

"I hope you're better at your jobs than you seem at this moment. If you'd like, I can recommend some great shows that would give you two a few pointers on how to actually behave like professionals. Because while I didn't hit it off with Gill? No one deserves what happened to him. I hope you'll find the actual killer soon."

She paused, then added, "Also, unless you're charging me with something, I can go anywhere I want. Look it up."

It was satisfying to see both of their jaws drop.

Chapter Twelve

L ONGEST. DAY. EVER. Which seemed surreal given not too many days ago, she'd seen a dead man. She'd decided on a hot bath and a book even though it was the middle of the afternoon. Ben had texted several times to make sure everything was okay. She told him she'd fill him in the next day.

After the bath, she phoned Vivian to catch her up. Her friend offered, again, to come to Rainbow Falls, but there was no reason for her to take time off of work.

After consulting her menu, she pulled out the ingredients for pasta, set them by the stove. She stared at the package of noodles, the can of sauce, and the pots she'd pulled from drawers, feeling off.

Needing fresh air more than dinner, Annie went out onto the back deck. She couldn't help but stare toward Gill's property. The sun was still high in the sky, but being close to the water came with a breeze.

A chill wracked her body as she tried to think about who would hurt her neighbor. If the cops weren't going to look for more likely suspects, she needed to think this through.

"Consider the players," she muttered to herself, thinking about who she'd point the finger at if this were an event. Maybe playing it out, continuing to use this real murder as the basis for her group would help her solve it. *Why was Margie there? What brought her into the house?* Had she been there whole time and then just used the opportunity of Annie passing out to play it off as something else?

"That's a stretch," she muttered.

Besides, the woman didn't seem like a murderer. Not that Annie actually knew what such a person would *seem* like in real life. She turned at the sound of shuffling. A large, hooded figure moved slowly up her steps. She squealed, too shocked to cringe at the sound.

Fumbling for her phone, her heart hammered like hummingbird wings. The person stopped walking, pushed the hood back with one hand. In his other he carried a brown paper bag.

"Quit it, dude. I'm not here to hurt you."

Between the *dude* and the realization that he looked too young to shave, Annie's fear came to a screeching halt. She slapped a hand to her chest.

"Who are you? Why on earth would you sneak up on me like that?"

He had the decency to look abashed. "I forgot my hood was on. Chill."

She suspected, based on the teenage tone and vocabulary, she knew who he was. Now if her pulse could settle, she might be able to pull in a full breath.

"Don't tell me to chill. You scared me."

"Sorry."

Annie kept her phone visible in her hand. He still hadn't confirmed his identity.

"You shouldn't sneak up on people." The fact that he could given his height and bulk was a surprise.

"Wasn't sneaking." He gestured with his chin. "You phoning someone?"

"If I need to."

He shook his head, ran a hand over his mouth, muffling his next words. "Everybody's jumpy. I need to talk to you."

"Who are you?"

His tanned face and large build made her think that unless someone was looking right into his eyes, he probably got mistaken as an adult a lot. Now that she could see his face, the hesitancy in his gaze, and now that he'd spoken, he seemed less intimidating.

He lowered his hands. "Tate. I live next door with my pops."

What he'd said just registered. "Wait, you left the rock?"

He nodded. "Yeah. I brought you muffins. Pops said to give you our share as a welcome."

"That was very nice of your dad," she said. She didn't need more muffins.

"Granddad. I call him Pops. He sleeps a lot and is getting over pneumonia so he isn't up to coming to say hi. He will though." He came up the final steps, set the muffins on the BBQ.

Annie's heart settled. "What's your whole name?"

"Tate Murphy."

She nodded. "Annie Abbott. What did you need to talk to me about?"

He shifted back and forth from one foot to the other. The indecision made his youth more apparent. Annie slipped her phone in her pocket.

"Well?"

"I seen someone leaving the house the morning Grumpy Gill was murdered." His voice was low, nearly whispered.

"It wasn't me," she snapped.

"Dude. I know it wasn't you."

"*Annie.* My name isn't Dude."

His lips quirked. "Sorry."

"How do you know it wasn't me?"

"Why would you kill him? You didn't even know him."

With a sigh that was half-exasperation and half-relief, she nodded. "If you can see that, why can't the Trenton PD?"

His gaze widened. "They think you did it?"

Not wanting to talk about it, she said, "They have several suspects." Whether or not that was true, she didn't actually know.

Tate shoved his hands into the pocket of his hoodie, glancing back toward his house then over at Gill's. "I would have seen you go back into your house. This person took off to somewhere else."

Her breath caught in throat. "Did you tell the police?"

Tate looked down at his feet.

"Tate?" If he'd seen the killer, this mystery would be done.

He met her gaze. "No, ma'am." He reached into his back pocket with one hand, pulled out his phone. "I got a picture. It's not good, but I still got it."

She stopped herself from rubbing her hands together but stepped closer as he turned the device. *Let's see the evidence.* The screen was cracked in the corner, like a permanent plexiglass star.

Annie leaned in, squinting. It was dark in the photo, and whoever was leaving Gill's back yard was dressed head to toe in black. The sweater they wore could have been bulky, or it could have been their frame. There was no way to make out a face since the person had their head ducked and was partially hidden by a hoodie.

Annie tipped her head back, met his gaze. "Where'd you take this picture from?"

Tate's eyes were a pale shade of blue, nearly gray. Up close, she could see the subtle sheen of slightly oily skin. What really stood out, however, was the fear in his gaze.

"My room is right up there in the loft." He pointed to the window that faced Annie's house.

"You just happened to be awake at"—she checked the phone. 6:13 a.m.—"six in the morning, looking out your window?"

He was hiding something.

His gaze wandered down again, lifting when she crossed her arms over her chest and tapped her foot.

"I was vaping, okay? Pops says no grandson of his will knowingly wreck their lungs blah, blah, blah. Yet he's down with pneumonia again because he was smoking the real thing back in his day. I'd snuck in. I've been watching him so much I was going stir crazy. I got home, went to the window to vape before bed, and saw this. The person was just leaving. It happened so fast, I snapped a pic and they were gone. Took off toward Joseph's house, and I couldn't see anything else."

Annie considered this as she rubbed her fingers absently over her cheek.

Tate jutted his chin toward her. "That's a nasty bruise."

She smiled. "Turns out Gill's floor was as mean as he was." She felt bad immediately, even more so when Tate laughed.

"Yeah. He was wicked mean. Never had a nice word to say. I told him off once for going at Pops. He tried to get me kicked out of the complex...as if he could do that."

Annie turned to stare out at the ocean, trying to settle her thoughts, which were no calmer than the waves. "You need to tell the police."

"Nuh-uh. No way. I tell the police, they'll tell Pops. He'll be disappointed and think it's his fault. He'll send me back to my ma, and I don't want that. Nobody round here likes me. Well, jury is still out on Margie. Most of them think I'm just looking to steal or wreck something. But Pops doesn't judge me like that."

Annie stared at Tate, torn. "Your pops sounds like a good man."

Tate gave a curt nod that made him seem older.

"A man you'd give up sneaking out on and vaping for," Annie said.

Tate rolled his gaze. "Make you a deal, lady. You don't make me tell the cops, and that'll be my last time for both of those things."

"Just like that?" She tilted her head.

He shrugged, seeming young again. "Felt so guilty anyway. Pops had a coughing spell later that day, and I thought for sure it was my fault. It's not worth it."

"How old are you?"

His eyes narrowed. "Almost eighteen. Why?"

She smiled. His distrust was easy to read. "Just curious. I'm sure it wasn't your fault, but I'd say you should give up the vaping and sneaking out anyway."

"You won't tell the cops what I saw?"

"I need the picture. Can you send it to me?" She held up her phone.

He hesitated. "They'll figure it out. They'll know where it came from."

Not if she was the one who shared it, which she needed

to do. "They won't. I need it, Tate. I won't turn it over just yet, and I won't mention you at all. That's the best I can do."

He turned toward his house, stared at it for so long she wondered if he was going to comply. His shoulders sagged with a heaviness that echoed in her heart. Tate's heavy sigh was her answer. She let out a slow sigh of relief as he Air-Dropped the photo to her. When he took off down the steps and hopped over the fence with an agility that reminded her of a track star, she wondered what his story was. Why did he live with his grandfather and not his mom?

"Like you don't have enough crammed in your brain, you need this, too?" She shook her head, grabbed her muffins, and went inside. Time to visit with her orphaned mama cat and the babies. Funny how she'd thought finding the oversized fluffball would be the weirdest thing to happen to her that week.

Chapter Thirteen

B Y SATURDAY MORNING, her bruise had faded to an icky mishmash of greens, yellows, and dark purples. She'd done her best to hide it with some subtle makeup tricks, but traces could be seen. Hopefully, having her hair down would help draw attention away from her face. If not, maybe Ben would focus more on her cute blue-jean capris and off-the-shoulder peasant-style top.

She worked on a logo for one of her clients while she waited for her friend, Claire, to log on for their chat. Other than Vivian, Claire was her closest friend. Unlike, Vivian, she'd never met Claire in person.

They'd connected at a virtual book club a few years ago and bonded over their mutual love of the book selection the others weren't as fond of. The club hadn't lasted but the friendship had. Now they did a lot of buddy reading rather than joining in with a group. One day, they'd meet up in real life.

Her phone dinged, letting her know Claire was online so she sent her a heads up.

Annie
Heads up, my face is a mess.

Claire
A legit mess, or look at me I'm beautiful without makeup
but I'm going to pretend I'm not?

Annie
LOL. You're probably not going to believe me.

Claire
Lay it on me.

In as few words as possible, Annie summed up her week.

Claire
Oh. My. God. ARE YOU OKAY?

Before Annie answered yes, her computer buzzed with an
incoming call from Google Chat.

She laughed, clicking Accept. Claire's face popped up on
the screen. With her cropped hair and gorgeous bronze skin,
she reminded Annie of a pixie. What she lacked in size, she
made up for in personality and kick-ass writing. Annie was
one of the few people who knew that adorable, seemingly
prim Claire, accountant by day, wrote erotica in her free
time.

"Oh, sweetie. That looks awful." Claire leaned too close
to the camera like that would make Annie seem bigger.

Annie laughed. "Back up. It looks worse than it is."

Claire backed up. "It looks pretty bad."

"I know, but it's actually better than it was."

"It sounds like that sleepy little town woke all the way up when you arrived."

"I feel as though I haven't had a proper night's sleep since I got here. My life in Portland seems boring in comparison to this. I don't know what to do."

"Well, those two detectives sound like idiots. You need to figure out who did this just to best them."

Annie laughed again, glad she hadn't rescheduled. "Something tells me they don't want me digging into their investigation."

"Too bad for them. Maybe if they weren't looking in the wrong direction, you wouldn't have to."

"None of it makes any sense, Claire." She picked up her coffee and took a long swallow, the bite of it settling her nerves.

"You need to check out the guy you said was arguing with him and the wife. I thought it was always the spouse."

"Honestly, I hate to speak ill of the dead, but he was so unfriendly, it could be anyone who crossed his path."

Annie took a minute to fill Claire in on the picture Tate shared.

"I bet if you take that to the police, they won't do anything with it. They probably just want to close the case. Small towns don't get a lot of this. Tell me some of the characters again. I'll write them down and see what Josie can dig up."

Claire's wife, Josie, was a private investigator. When Annie first learned that, she'd thought it sounded fascinating, but in truth, Josie spent a lot of time sitting, waiting, and watching. But she could access channels Annie never could.

"They're not characters. They're my neighbors."

Claire waved a hand at the screen. "Same difference. We're all merely players." She gave a dramatic, mock half bow.

Annie nearly spit her next sip of coffee on the keyboard. The hearty laugh felt good. "I don't know anyone's last names yet. Let me figure that out."

"Fine. But I mean it. You can't wait around for these cops to pin the murder on you just so they can say *case closed*."

Sometimes Annie thought the only person more obsessed with crime scene shows than her was Claire. It was just one more thing the two had in common.

Her doorbell rang. "I have to go. Ben is here."

"Oh. Take a picture and send it to me."

She shook her head as Claire's fingers tapped on the keyboard. "No way."

"Never mind. It's on his website. He's yummy enough to get an animal for."

Annie laughed again. "You like women."

"Sweetie, that doesn't mean I'm blind. Message me later, okay?"

"You got it."

"Stay safe."

Annie nodded before disconnecting. She hoped she wouldn't need the reminder. As she walked to the door to let Ben in, she made a silent wish that today would be completely uneventful.

Chapter Fourteen

ANNIE BREATHED IN the ocean air, filling her lungs with the sweet, salty scent. Just a completely normal day in her new life. With a hot guy who'd seen her at her worst. More than once. Ben walked beside her, telling her tidbits about the different vendors while introducing her to a number of people. She didn't miss the subtle stares and even a few glares from a handful of women whose gazes lingered longer than polite on the town's vet.

"I think I might need to watch my back after today," Annie said when the woman who sold them a bag of mini donuts gave her dagger eyes.

Ben looked down, grabbed a donut from the bag, and popped it into his mouth. "What do you mean?" He spoke around the treat while they walked.

Annie smiled up at him, passed him a napkin for the sugar on his lips. "In case you haven't noticed, I'm receiving some unfriendly looks just for being at your side."

He chuckled but stopped when he realized she was serious. Looking back toward the donut truck, he waved. Annie followed his gaze. Sure enough, the woman was still glaring at Annie. Her long, straight hair was pulled forward on both sides, framing her scowling—yet still attractive—face. Annie looked back at Ben and lifted her brows.

"I can feel her gaze penetrating my skin even now," she whispered.

Ben laughed, putting a hand on Annie's back to guide her forward. "You're imagining it. Chrissy is just wary of newcomers."

"Whatever you say." A thought occurred to her that hadn't before. "It must be hard to date in a town this small. You'd trip over your exes." *Exes are great suspects. Maybe the killer for my murder night should be the ex. Or is that too predictable?* She needed to update the blog. She was still waking up with mild headaches, and with everything going on, she'd let it slide. *Tonight.*

Ben wiped his fingers on his legs, then shoved both hands into the pockets of his dark jeans—which fit him *very* well. Not that she was staring. She was just really observant.

"Definitely. Though, I was gone for a while so by the time I came back, the girls I dated had grown up, moved on."

Annie glanced back at Chrissy, then looked up at Ben. "She an ex?"

He ducked his gaze, shrugged. "Prom date." He mumbled the two words.

Annie laughed loudly. "Thank goodness you said we were sharing the donuts. Had I gotten my own she probably would have powdered them with arsenic."

Ben bumped her with his shoulder, making her laugh again. "Stop it."

"Aw. Dr. Ben is bashful." He looked down at her, and their gazes held, the moment suspending between them. This look, these few seconds of tense air, rushed heartbeats, and deeper breathing were things she hadn't felt in a really long time. It was unnerving to feel so much from just a look. It was nearly impossible to describe it in words.

Music pumped through large stand-up speakers, adding a fun ambiance to the sunny day. The grassy area where the market was set up overlooked the water. It was a gorgeous view. Sailboats dotted the ocean, making her think of her parents. Maybe she'd walk to their boat slip and just check it out. It wouldn't make her miss them less, but it would be cool to check out the pier and docks.

"You okay?"

She nodded, carried on walking until they stopped at a little trinket vendor who sold pretty bracelets. Annie looked through the selection while she told Ben about the detectives and their thoughts.

By the time she finished, he looked ready to throw the donuts. "That's ridiculous. Idiots. We'll talk to Ryan and see what he says. Come on."

He took her hand, but Annie dug in her heels. "No way. I'm not going to another police station. Today was supposed to be normal." This was a stark reminder that being entangled in a real-life crime held none of the entertainment value of a fake one.

Ben squeezed her hand, then released it. He pointed to the far end of one of the rows of tables. "Ryan sets up his pickle stand next to my gran's table."

Her shoulders relaxed. "Of course he does. Because we're in Mayberry." *Mayberry with an edge.*

Unoffended, his smile just widened. "Exactly."

Making their way to the end of the row, Annie's nerves fluttered unevenly in her chest. She didn't know if it was from the idea of meeting Ben's grandma or talking to the cops again. *Just one cop.*

Her memory of meeting Officer Ryan Porter was hazy at best. She remembered the thick eyebrows but not the friendliness of his dark eyes. She recalled his height but not the muscles his T-shirt revealed. His laughter rang out as he chatted to the woman beside him.

The woman had to be Ben's grandmother, but she didn't look old enough to have fully grown grandchildren. Her cropped haircut reminded Annie of Claire's. It suited the woman's slender, youthful face. The silvery locks perfectly styled and paired well with the dark-blue blouse and jeans she wore.

"Benny," she said, catching sight of them.

Ben walked forward to kiss the woman on the cheek.

"Benny," Ryan mimicked.

"Bite me," Ben replied, ducking out of the way when his

grandma tried to smack him for his response.

Annie laughed, stepped forward with her hand outstretched. "Hi. I'm Annie Abbott. Your grandson saved me from a feral cat this week."

Ben shook his head, muttered under his breath, "Wimp."

"Desiree, but my friends call me Des. It's a pleasure to meet you. Feral cat?" Desiree looked at Ben.

"Gill's cat went into labor. Annie got scared."

"Hey." She sent Ben a mock glare, not bothering to show him the scratch was still there, not quite healed. "She was really mean."

"I forgot he had a cat," Ryan said.

"It's been living in my parents' garage," Annie said. She shifted her feet, unsure of what to say to Ryan.

"How are you doing? Seeing a body can be awful. You holding up okay?"

Annie blinked, caught off guard by the sincerity in his tone. "I am. Thank you for asking."

"The Trenton detectives have been jerks about everything." Ben put a hand on her shoulder, squeezed.

Ryan's jaw tightened. "Yeah. They took over before we even left. Pushed us aside like a bunch of looky-loos. That Rickers guy and his partner are both trying for promotions. I've only met them a few times, but I'm never sure if they're secretly dating or plotting to kill each other."

Interesting. At least she wasn't the only one who got a bad vibe from them. Annie looked at the goods on Desiree's table. Fresh produce was displayed in colorful groupings. Fruits and vegetables packed up in small and large portions made choosing difficult.

"Terrible thing. Gill wasn't a nice man, but it's just awful. If you need anything, Annie, you come see me. I didn't know your parents well, but they were lovely every time we ran into each other here. I hope their cruise is going well."

Not quite a cruise, but Annie just nodded. "Thank you."

Ryan crossed his arms over his chest. "Try not to worry about the detectives, Annie. There wasn't much evidence at the scene, so they'll be tripping over themselves trying to come up with theories."

With a tight smile, she nodded. Annie thought about Tate and wondered if she should take a chance and show Ryan the photo. She didn't think it was enough for the other two to dismiss her as a suspect. Plus, she didn't want them to find out about Tate and give him a hard time. He seemed like a decent kid, and Annie didn't want to cause problems for him or his grandpa. A couple walked up to his stand and asked about his pickles, pulling his attention away.

Looking through the produce, Annie chose a generous amount, promising herself she'd make up for all the muffins she was going to eat in her new home. Speaking of which, her turn was on Monday.

Math wasn't her strong suit, but she recognized the discount when Ben's grandma rang up her purchases.

"Ben's going to bring you around for dinner in the next

couple of weeks," Desiree said, passing her the bagged produce.

Annie looked at Ben. "He is?"

His smile was genuine. "Absolutely. If you're up for it."

Laughing, she took the bag. "My social calendar is wide open. Other than work, exploring the beach, and kittens in my garage, I don't have much going on." *Just a real murder investigation tugging at my curiosity while I make plans to host a fictional crime from the comfort of my living room.*

"What is it you do for work, dear?" Desiree said.

"I'm a graphic designer. I used to work for a large firm in Portland, but I've been on my own for a while now."

"Annie's work was featured in *Around the House*," Ben said.

She knew her eyes popped open like a cartoon. "How did you know which magazine?"

Ben ducked his gaze, focusing on the table. He shrugged. "I Googled you."

Annie's heartbeat sped up, but before she could say anything, Desiree laughed. "In my day, you got to know a girl first, Benny."

Annie couldn't comment on the shade of pink Ben's cheeks turned because her own went hot. "Is there a bookstore around here?" Her voice was a little pitchy when she asked, which seemed to add to Desiree's amusement.

"What to Read is on Center Street. Ben, you need to show Annie around."

Worried he was being locked into place by his grand-mother's not-so-subtle suggestions, Annie shook her head. "Oh, that's okay. I'll find my way around. I planned to do that anyway. I need to find nine more coffee shops. I'm determined to visit each of them."

Desiree and Ben exchanged a glance, then laughed.

Looking back and forth between them, she finally asked, "What?"

"You live a couple doors down from Margie. She's got a whole system for visiting each of the shops that she will, no doubt, impress upon you as she orders you around in a slightly terrifying yet endearing way. For a while, she wanted us to do our book club at different locations. It wasn't easy convincing her otherwise." Desiree reached out and patted her shoulder. "Good luck, dear."

"Thanks. I think."

As they walked away, waving to Ryan as they did, Annie wondered, not for the first time, what she'd gotten herself into by coming to this little town.

Chapter Fifteen

B EFORE HEADING DOWN to the beach on Sunday morning, Annie made a few tweaks to her website. She uploaded some images from Pinterest as "inspiration" for the characters, listing quirks and characteristics that readers and participants could use as clues. She'd thought of telling Ben—even inviting him to join—but decided the full level of her dorkiness could be revealed at a later date. Better safe, and all that.

She answered questions in the Facebook group and posted a link to the clues, saying she'd update everything again soon. She'd choose one of the group members to take part in a few days, giving them one of the roles.

Once she wrapped that up, she was able to finish off two freelance jobs for repeat clients. All in all, she deserved some fresh air.

Annie moved out of the way so the little kid on the bike didn't run her over. The mom, who was chatting on the phone with her hair blowing in her face while trying to control her German Shepherd, mouthed "sorry." Annie smiled and waved.

The pier wasn't busy today. Not that she had a frame of reference, but she assumed given the little cove of hidden shops she'd discovered, along with cobblestone pathways, benches, great views, it was typically crowded.

The pocket of shops was a delightful find. There was a florist, two ice cream shops, a bakery, two tourist shops, and a waffle restaurant. When she'd taken the stairs down to the beach today, she'd decided to explore all the way to the docks.

She waved at an older man who was holding a fishing rod off of one side. There were two piers. One of them had a little restaurant in the middle of it. According to the sign, they served the best burgers and curly fries in all of Washington. Annie would definitely be verifying that. Making her way off the pier, she turned to the right, away from the shops to head for one of the docks.

When she stepped onto the one with a canteen-like outbuilding, she came face-to-face with Ryan. Annie grinned.

"Okay, how many jobs do you have?" She stepped up to the counter. The sign on the wall behind him offered everything from bait—both live and dead—to harbor cruises and ferries to the other close by tourist islands.

He wore a ball cap backward. "Just one, technically." His worn sweater looked cozy. Next time she walked the beach, she needed to remember to dress warmer. Even with summer fast approaching, the nip in the air amplified closer to the water.

She held up her fingers as she listed them. "Police officer, pickle seller, and now, what? You're a tour guide? A salesman?"

"He's a good son," an older gentleman said, entering the area from a side door.

Ryan gestured. "This is my dad, David. He's the former chief of police. When he retired, he bought this place." Holding his hands out, he turned from side to side. "In all its glory."

The resemblance was easy to see in the crinkle of the older man's eyes and smile. Though his dark hair was a match to Ryan's, his was sprinkled with a generous helping of gray.

"You work your whole life punching a clock, you get to choose what makes you happy," David said. "Though, maybe I should have spent more of my life teaching my kid some manners." He held out a hand. "What's your name, dear?"

Ryan winced. "Sorry. Dad, this is Annie Abbott. She's John and Amanda's daughter."

They shook hands. There were shouts from some of the boats around them along with the background noise of people talking nearby.

"It's nice to meet you, sir."

David nodded his approval, poking Ryan in the shoulder. "Hear that? Sir. Her parents raised her right."

Ryan gave his dad a mockingly defeated expression. "Guess they spent more time with her than you did with me."

Annie laughed. "Don't put me in the middle."

"Speaking of great retirement plans, your parents are off on their worldwide adventure, right?" David leaned his hands on the counter.

"They are. I'm living in their home for the next year."

His expression changed. "Heard about Gill. Sorry you had to see something like that." He turned his head toward Ryan. "Any news on the investigation?"

Annie noticed the way Ryan's jaw tightened, the way his lips flatlined. "They're not playing nice. Rickers and Black are all about secrets and setups. It's starting to get to me. It happened in our town."

David shook his head, patted his son on the back. "I've been saying since I was chief, we need a Major Crimes unit. I think, eventually, it would be more beneficial to combine the two stations. We're only twenty minutes from Trenton. Pooling resources is the best way to serve the community."

It was obvious Ryan disagreed. "Or our current chief could trust that we can do our job. He didn't need to call in Trenton PD right away. Now everything is wrapped up in red tape."

A beep sounded, pulling David's attention. Pulling his phone out of his pocket, he glanced at the device. "That's my timer. My harbor cruise starts in ten minutes. Be sure to put the closed sign up when you go."

Watching a grown man roll his eyes at his dad's reminder

was amusing. Ryan saluted. "No problem."

"Nice to meet you, Annie. Stay safe." David left out the side door again, heading toward one of the larger boats moored at this dock. People were milling about behind a roped off area. They must be his passengers.

Annie turned back to Ryan. "You always help out?"

"Usually just when my mom is away."

"Your mom okay?"

He glanced up from his phone. "Oh, yeah. She went to visit my aunt in Seattle for a week. If you can imagine, sometimes this town gets boring."

Annie laughed, leaned against the counter. She started to respond when her phone rang. She was more of a texter than a conversationalist so the ring surprised her. Pulling it out of her back pocket, she frowned at the screen, turned it to show Ryan before answering.

His gaze went fierce as she slid her thumb across the screen. "Hello?"

"Ms. Abbott?" The detective's voice was curt.

"It is."

"Detective Rickers. We met the other night." He paused, like maybe she needed time to remember.

She rolled her eyes. "I'm aware. What can I do for you?"

"Your truck is in the driveway, but you're not answering your door."

Straightening away from the counter, she glanced around. "I'm not home. Why are you in my driveway?"

Ryan came out through the side door of the building, joining her in front of the shop. He pulled a cord that brought down a protective cover for the shop window.

"How long until you're home?"

"Why?"

Ryan attached a lock, then came to her side.

Irritation warred with worry. Why were they back? What did they want now?

"This would be better in person."

She was really starting to dislike this guy. "What is this about?"

He sighed loudly into her ear. "We have a warrant for your computer."

As soon as he said it, all the pieces tumbled into place like dice being rolled across a table. She swore quietly. She knew what this was about. And it wasn't good.

Chapter Sixteen

Ryan hurried after her as she pocketed her phone, taking the pathway through the shops and eateries.

"Why would they have a warrant for your computer?" He caught up to Annie no problem. She might be tall, but he had a foot on her, about the same as Ben. She sort of wished he'd stayed behind for this even though she appreciated the support. A concussion and a bit of idiocy had stopped her from seeing this before it hit her in the face, and she wasn't eager to tell Ryan the why.

"Probably a misunderstanding." He wasn't stupid. He wouldn't buy that, but she couldn't worry about that yet. She glanced his way. "Ben knows a lawyer?"

Ryan pulled his phone out, started texting as they walked at a clipped pace.

"Let's not eat the meal before everything is ready," he said absently.

The statement caught Annie off guard, slowing her down a step. "I really am in Mayberry. Are you secretly ninety-two?"

He gave her a tight smile. "No. But my nan is close to

that, and it's one of her favorite expressions."

They walked the rest of the way in silence, Ryan texting. She wasn't sure who he was talking to, but the hard set of his jaw suggested it had something to do with Annie or warrants. *This isn't a big deal. So you used Gill as a character. They won't find it amusing, but this hardly gives them reason to convict you.*

They hit the top of the steps that led up from the shops and turned left to head toward the complex. There was a side entrance with a code that let them into the complex from the street. Annie entered the numbers, hoping they wouldn't pass Margie or Joseph.

"Have they even been back to Gill's house since his death?"

She pursed her lips in thought. "Not that I've seen."

Ryan mumbled something under his breath. "They didn't even take their time combing through the crime scene. What do you want to bet there's evidence sitting around Gill's house that the two hotshots didn't bother with because they think they know it all?"

Annie didn't know how to answer that. She was more concerned with explaining a simple misunderstanding. *One that, if it doesn't make you look like an idiot, makes you look callous.*

Fortunately, he didn't seem to need an answer. "When they arrived, I was combing through Gill's financials. I bet they haven't even gotten a warrant for his bank accounts."

He shoved both hands through his hair. "I'm sorry. I shouldn't be going on like this. I just don't like feeling helpless. Or left out."

She winced, hoping he'd forgive her for the part she'd omitted. Though, to be fair, she hadn't given any consideration to how her murder mystery event would look until the moment he mentioned her computer. "I understand that. No reason to apologize. Those two definitely know how to put a person on edge."

"I'll say. And speak of the devils. There they are."

Rickers and Black were leaning against their large, black SUV, doing nothing but pulling attention from a couple down the lane who were openly staring and chatting back and forth to each other. They noticed Ryan and Annie, turned back to their gardening.

Annie hurried forward, irritation increasing her speed. "Detectives. You have a warrant?"

Like carbon copies of each other, they looked to Annie then to Ryan.

Black tucked her hands in her pockets. "*Officer* Porter. I didn't realize you and the suspect had a relationship."

It was a wonder steam didn't pour from Annie's ears. "Unlike you two, most of this town has been friendly to me. There's no reason to insinuate anything else."

Rickers cleared his throat. He pulled a paper from the inner pocket of his suit jacket. "As I mentioned, the warrant."

Ryan reached out, snatched it from his hand. Ricker's brows shot up. "It hasn't taken you long to make *friends* or enemies, Ms. Abbott."

The fact that she didn't display the level of temper she felt should have been all the proof these two needed that she wasn't the killer. Because if she was…

"It's legit," Ryan said.

"You thought it wouldn't be?" Detective Black asked.

"Easier to get where you want to be by cutting corners. Isn't that the Trenton PD motto?" Ryan's stiffened beside her.

Rickers stepped toward him. "Careful, *Officer.*"

Annie pulled her keys out of her sweater pocket. She felt like a naughty kid. Like Tate not wanting to get caught for vaping. "My computer won't tell you anything." Heading for the steps, she tried to smooth out her nerves. *Stay calm.*

"You forgot to tell us about your hobbies, Ms. Abbott."

When she turned back from opening the front door, the two detectives were staring at her with muted glee. Ryan had his cop face on. She couldn't read him.

"What are you talking about?"

Ooooh no. I should have told him.

Rickers glanced at Ryan. "Did you know she described the victim on a murder blog before his death?"

Annie dropped her keys. "Murder blog?" She nearly shrieked the words.

She bent forward, grabbed the keys, looking up to see

Ryan's shocked expression.

"Wait. That's out of context. Murder blog. What a ridiculous thing to call it. It's a *blog*. I'm part of a Facebook group. We like mysteries." She wasn't helping herself.

Black stepped onto the porch, crowding Annie. "There's no mystery about the fact that you perfectly described the victim of a *murder*. You made your feelings about Mr. Downs quite clear. Now, we'll take your computer, and I strongly *suggest* you are available for questioning once our techs have gone through it."

Mad at them and at herself, she tried to ignore the look of surprise on Ryan's face.

"Why can't you look through it here? I'll show you the blog, my Facebook group, and past events."

"Too little, too late, Ms. Abbott." Black came as close to smiling as she was likely able. "Do you want me to grab it for you?"

Annie went to her office, Black following her, and grabbed the laptop.

Tears struggled to break free. "This is my livelihood," she said, the implications of what was happening truly hitting her square in the gut. What on earth had she been thinking? That this was a game? That she could treat it like a puzzle without any recourse?

"We'll have it back to you soon enough," Rickers said. "Unless, of course, we find something significant and you no longer need it."

"You're intimidating Ms. Abbott, and I want you to know I will report it to your superiors."

"You have no intention of rising through the ranks, Officer Porter? Because questioning *your* superiors isn't the best route."

Ryan shook his head. "Intimidating me won't work. You have what you came for. The next time you speak to Ms. Abbott, it'll be through a lawyer."

She could have sworn both detectives smirked. They'd barely pulled out of the driveway when Ben pulled in. Margie and Joseph must have been waiting in the wings because Annie saw them heading her way as the SUV of doom disappeared through the entrance gates.

"You called Ben?"

Ryan looked at her, his anger visible in the hard set of his jaw. Ben got out of his truck at the same time Margie and Joseph stepped onto her front walkway.

"Ben will connect you with a lawyer," Ryan said.

Her stomach roiled like a ship caught in a storm. Oh God. She was sinking. This time, she'd sunk the boat herself.

Ben took the front steps two at a time, reaching her in what seemed like seconds.

He pulled her into a hug that she gratefully accepted, running his hand up and down her back. "What the hell is going on?"

"That's our question, too." Margie spoke over Joseph's winded breaths.

Annie pulled back from Ben but stayed close, grateful for both his support and his warmth. A chill had reached beneath her clothes, traveling over her skin.

"Annie's going to explain that to us right now," Ryan said, gesturing to the open door.

She met his gaze, stepped closer to Ben. *Okay, then. Full-on cop mode.* She had no idea what that meant; if he was on her side; if the police could really use a harmless hobby against her; or why, once again, Margie had perfect timing. But she knew she could trust Ben. At least, she hoped she could. If he knew a lawyer, she had to.

Chapter Seventeen

FOUR SETS OF eyes stared at her with a range of judgment. At least, it felt like judgment to Annie. She turned her gaze to focus on a graduation photo of herself that sat atop the mantle next to other pictures of her and her family over the years.

"You blog about murder?" Ryan's voice was strained.

Annie twisted back to look at him. "No. Of course not. That's not what it is. Have you guys ever been to dinner theater or one of those evenings of murder?"

She avoided Ben's face and looked toward Margie and Joseph. *Come on, Margie.*

Margie tapped her chin. "I went to one where I was the killer. It was a boatload of fun, but that was years ago. I did teach drama for two years at the high school. We hosted a dinner theater night to raise money. It was a big hit. Joseph, maybe we should get the community center to host one."

Thank you, Margie!

Joseph patted Margie's hand. "Great idea, love."

"Can we focus, please?" Ryan paced the room, hands shoved into his pockets. "You used Gill as a character in a fictional blog that turned out to be true. That doesn't look good. On the other hand, it's not as if you said how and when he was murdered. It's a loose connection at best. They'll take a look, check your browser history, emails, and hard drive. Once they find nothing, they'll give it back and be done."

Sounded good. In theory. Except for the whole browser history thing. "They can't build a case on my internet searches, can they?" It hit her, in that moment, that this wasn't as fun when it was real. There was no veil or curtain to shield the gritty, unpleasant parts of this. She couldn't cut to commercial or rewrite the ending. This was real.

Ben groaned. "Why? What did you search?"

Annie's shoulders sagged. "Look. I like crime shows. I obviously don't have the stomach for it as you all know, but when we plan these events, I look stuff up to make it sound realistic. It's for fun. I want people to enjoy the events when it's my turn so I sometimes use real-life examples of things that have happened. So, yeah, I research when I'm planning. I read murder mysteries, I blog about them, chat about them with friends. There are weirder hobbies, I'm sure."

Ryan gave a groan of frustration. "I like cop shows and thrillers, too, Annie. I just don't write about it using a real-life jerk who happened to wind up dead."

Okay. That was her bad. She'd used items from the news in her last event, but this was closer to home and she should have thought it through more clearly. Of course, she had no idea they were going to see her as a suspect.

"It's not like I knew he'd end up dead. I didn't do it, so regardless of what they think they have on me, it won't do them any good. What we need to do is find the real killer."

Margie clapped her hands together. "You're preaching to the choir, dear. You're not one of those city girls who takes other peoples' ideas as their own, are you? Because I did say we ought to dig into this ourselves." A hint of a smile played on Margie's lips. Joseph looked at her like she'd come up with a cure to end world hunger.

Wouldn't hurt to have a man look at her like that, but Annie figured this latest hurdle would be her third strike with Ben. Not that it mattered right now. She needed to be more concerned with not getting blamed for murder than dating.

Ryan stopped pacing. "No one is looking into anything except me. You'll all stay out of this."

Ben caught Annie's gaze. "You can trust Ryan."

"And us," Margie said, a hint of indignation in her voice.

"That's right, you can." Joseph smiled at her.

It wasn't about trust. She was the only one in the room being looked at for murder. She was in this whether she wanted to be or not. Ryan couldn't stop her from poking her nose in. After all, the only one whose nose would get locked up was hers. That meant, regardless of Ryan's warning to back off, she was in this all the way.

ANNIE WAS NOT only in a stare down with a cat but the cat was winning. She couldn't stop thinking about the idea that the detectives hadn't bothered to do a thorough sweep of Gill's house. What if Ryan was right and evidence of his killer was just lying around to be noticed? The picture Tate showed her kept running through her mind. Someone had been there. She'd gotten wrapped up in trying to convince Ryan she wasn't some weird murder-blogging chick and didn't share the picture. Plus, he'd been really adamant about her not getting involved.

"It isn't breaking and entering." The cat—rumor had it her name was Shelby after the classic vehicle—meowed in argument.

"I'm going to get *you* some more cat food and some of your things. Don't you have toys or something?"

Shelby glanced down at her kittens, as though she thought Annie was a fool of epic proportions.

"Fine. You have no time for toys. I get it. They're starting to look more like you," Annie said, scratching behind Shelby's ear.

Shelby looked up and meowed again. The kittens tried to nestle impossibly closer.

"Should we name them after cars like you?"

Shelby said nothing. To be fair, she was bathing her babies. Annie wanted to go next door and take a peek around.

If the detectives wanted to wrap up the case with minimal effort, they wouldn't dig too hard. But maybe there was something they didn't look at, something they missed. She had the most to lose if they didn't do their jobs properly. Between the picture and whatever she might find tonight, she could prove it wasn't her and she might even be able to help them, steer them in the right direction.

Shelby hissed at her kittens, pulling Annie's attention. The cat looked up and glared at Annie.

"Hey. I didn't do this to you. You made your bed," she said, holding her hands up in surrender. "Listen, I'm going to go. I won't be long. Do you have a favorite squeak toy or anything? I'll grab it."

Shelby moved away from the hungry kittens, stood up and swished her tail. Hopping out of the bed, she used the boxes and shelves as her own parkour course and made her way to the top of the workbench.

"Fine. Be like that. You're not the one looking at jail time," Annie said. She refused to judge herself for arguing with a cat. *Strange times, strange measures and all that.*

"Call Ben if I don't make it back," she said on her way out of the garage.

It was late. Ben had stuck around after the others left. He didn't seem put off by this new revelation about her and even admitted to a few quirks of his own. He liked to skateboard, had a closet full of items purchased from late-night shopping shows, and he'd listened to more than a few crime podcasts.

Best of all, he hadn't walked away. All attraction aside, he was proving to be a good friend. At the moment, he was her only friend. Shelby might be warming up to her, but Annie suspected she had a long way to go with the finicky feline.

After eating grilled cheese for dinner, Annie used her phone to send an email to her clients saying things would be delayed by a few days due to a family emergency. She ordered an iPad online. It'd be here tomorrow, but for now, she didn't have a way to work on projects.

Claire messaged, suggesting she *follow the money*. Murder typically had one—or more—of three motives. Money, sex, or power. Which of those three had ended the man's life? Annie wondered if there was something in Gill's belongings or house that would point at Raj. She didn't want to immediately assume the worst of her new neighbor, but heck, she also didn't want to go to jail.

With the cover of night having her back, Annie stepped out onto her front porch. She channeled her inner-wannabe-sleuth and decided to act like she belonged.

Glancing around at the other homes, she saw most of the windows were dark. In and out. She'd told Shelby she was going to grab some of her cat things. That would be her cover if she got caught. Steeling her shaky resolve, she walked to Gill's as she had the morning she found him, taking the driveway and the path. She hadn't given any thought to how she was going to get in until her hand reached the doorknob. It turned.

"Lucky," she whispered. Or one more oversight by the detectives.

Slipping in, she closed the door behind her and tried to calm her rapid breaths. Her stomach turned at the lingering stench of days' old bacon. Breathing through her nose, she focused on the swift rate of her pulse, counting in an effort to tame it.

Pushing off the door, she shuffled into the living room, giving her eyes a few seconds to adjust to the dark. The moonlight slanted through the window just enough to give a hint of visibility. His coffee table was littered with car magazines. Looking—but not touching—she saw the name on the address label. GILL'S CLASSIC CARS. She needed to look up the dealership and see who was running it.

In the corner, beside the recliner she'd sat in days ago, she noticed the cat bed. Shelby didn't really need a bed, though maybe she'd be more comfortable. She picked it up, put it by the door, and then headed for the back of the house, which was the same layout as hers. She'd start with the bedroom and office because she wasn't entirely sure she could go into the kitchen.

The office was not nearly as nice as her parents', but that could have been because of the mess. Papers, binders, car manuals, and envelopes littered every surface. A computer sat on the desk, but Annie didn't think she had enough tech skills to do any digging there. Instead, she used the sleeve of her shirt to open the bottom, largest drawer. Surprisingly, it was set up with folders all labeled and alphabetical.

Annie dug through, belatedly wondering if she should have worn gloves. Would they already have swept for fingerprints already? Ryan didn't seem to think they covered all of their bases here, but she'd worry about that later.

One file label read LOANS. She opened it, pulled out some papers to scan them. He'd been in debt. Not surprising. Who wasn't? But it was interesting, given how he'd accused her of being a freeloader. From the look of the papers, he'd taken a mortgage out on the dealership. The bank letterhead seemed legit, so it wasn't like he'd borrowed from a loan shark or something who then offed him for not paying. *Jeez, Annie. This is real life, not a novel.* After snapping a picture of the paper, she put everything back, closed the drawer, frustrated because she didn't really know what she was looking for.

A receipt on the desk caught her gaze because it had Gill's handwriting scrawled across. It was for flowers. Gill had sent someone flowers? She looked closer, saw he'd written TO BETHANY—WE WILL GET TO THE OTHER SIDE TOGETHER on the card. The other side of what? Life? She needed to find out more about the ex-wife and who had she supposedly turned against Gill. Did she inherit the dealership?

She froze. *What was that?* Annie held her breath. Had she

heard the door? Phone in hand, she dialed the first two numbers for help, as she had with Tate. She tiptoed away from the desk, peeking out of the room. When she heard nothing, she tiptoed toward the living room. Annie didn't know if her scream was from stubbing her baby toe on the wall or seeing a dark, shadowy figure.

A flash of white caught Annie's gaze as the person moved, shoving something into the pocket of a dark sweater or cloak.

"Who are you?" The voice was ragged and raspy. And female.

"Who are you? I only need to press one number to get the police here," Annie said, hoping her voice sounded more threatening than she felt.

Something about the woman kneeling on the couch felt familiar. She stood slowly in *sky-high leopard-print* heels. Shopping bags. The Lexus.

"You followed me at the grocery store." Annie pointed at her. "Who are you?" Her eyes adjusted, and she saw the answer herself. "Ginger. You live at the front of the complex. You followed me at the store."

"Yes, I'm Ginger. I wasn't following you. I was curious, that's all. I thought I'd say hi but changed my mind. It was nothing."

It'd felt like a lot more than nothing to Annie. "What are you doing in Gill's house?"

Now that she could see better, Annie noted the woman

wore a black, fur-style jacket. Whatever she'd tucked into the pocket stuck out a little. The white practically glowed against the coat. Between that and the shoes, Annie felt very under-dressed for this little mission.

"I could ask you the same."

"Gill's cat made my garage into a delivery room for her kittens. I was grabbing some of her things," Annie said, gesturing to the door.

To her surprise, Ginger's expression softened in the pale light. "Oh, I wondered where Shelby had gotten to."

"You knew Gill had a cat?"

The woman straightened her shoulders, an unnecessary show of dominance given the heels put Annie at a disadvantage height wise.

"I knew many things about Gill." Her breath hitched.

"That doesn't explain what you're doing here." Annie stepped forward, fighting back the knowledge that this woman could be a killer.

"It's personal." She looked away, her hand going to her pocket again.

"I'm sure Detectives Rickers and Black would be curious what personal business you have with Gill to be skulking around the dead man's home close to midnight."

Ginger hissed out a breath. "We were having an affair okay, Nosy Nelly. Not that it's anyone's business, but we…" She trailed off.

Annie stepped closer, swallowing down the ugly thought

of Gill having an affair with anyone. "What?"

Ginger stepped closer, and Annie saw the sheen of tears in her eyes. "We were fooling around—one thing led to another. I left a personal item here and didn't want the police to find it."

Said the killer. Annie backed up a step. "What personal item?"

Ginger's expression hardened. "You'd think a concussion would make you more cautious."

Wowzers. She's got more attitude than Shelby. Maybe you ought to tread carefully. "How did you know about the concussion?"

"Please. Everyone knows everyone's business here."

Except for the affair apparently. Or was Annie the only one who didn't know? Unless she was lying through her perfectly whitened teeth. It was hard to picture Gill having enough…affection for anyone to engage in an affair. Wait. Was this woman married?

"Are you married?"

"Are you a cop?" Ginger sighed loudly. "No. I'm not."

"Then why the secret? How do I know you're not lying about Gill and you?"

Ginger sank onto the couch, dropped her head. "You don't. That's the thing. I've been so tangled up in all of the lies, I'm not even sure what's true anymore."

Against her better judgment, Annie sat on the edge of the recliner, waiting for Ginger to continue.

She lifted her head, and now that her eyes had adjusted fully, Annie saw the pain in the woman's gaze, even beneath the heavy makeup.

"Bethany was my friend. I didn't mean to fall in love with Gill. He was using me. I came to get these," she said, pulling something out of her pocket.

Annie reared back when she saw the flash of white cotton scrunched in her fist. *Underwear?* "Ew." She slapped a hand over her mouth.

Ginger's gaze darkened. "Oh, grow up. He was a very proficient lover." She shoved her underwear back into her pocket while Annie fought off her nausea.

"Not to point out the obvious, but *scorned lover* kind of makes the top of the suspect list," Annie said. She continued to grip her phone, the final number ready to be pressed.

"You're right. Except I didn't want him dead. I wanted him to miss me. I've been staying with my son. I came home the afternoon of his murder, only to find out he was gone. I couldn't even ask questions because I don't want to wreck my friendship with Bethany."

Not sleeping with the woman's ex-husband seemed like a no brainer. Friendship 101. Annie held her tongue. She hadn't seen the Lexus around in a while, but it was hardly her focus.

"Did the police question you?"

She nodded. "I have an alibi. Do you?"

Annie nodded, unsure where to go from here.

"We need to find out who did this, Annie. As much as I don't want to believe it, I think it was someone close by. Raj has a terrible temper. So does Joseph."

She'd witnessed Raj's—though she wouldn't have labeled it as such. More like a vengeful streak. Or tone, at least. As for Joseph, he didn't strike her as having a mean bone in his body.

"Did you share your thoughts with the police?" She'd skipped over the whole "we" thing.

"Of course. But many people hated Gill. Whoever did this was strong. It had to be a man. I heard it was an act of passion or extreme anger."

Annie could attest to that. She'd read the same thing time and again. Knives were a close-up weapon. Usually, stabbing was fueled by anger and, in some cases, a twisted sense of passion and love.

"Why would either man kill him?" She wanted to find out more about Bethany but didn't know how to ask.

Ginger looked around, her gaze sad. "Who knows. Maybe it was Bethany, but that seems like a stretch. But...if she found out Gill was sleeping with me?"

Seemed to Annie that Bethany might want to kill Ginger for that bit, not her husband.

"Tell me you'll help me. I'm not young like you are. Gill's death has flattened me, and I can't share that with anyone. No one cares how the jilted lover feels."

Again, Annie thought the jilted lover might feel like getting revenge in the form of a knife in the back. She'd play along for now but ask Ryan about Ginger's alibi.

"We should go." Annie stood.

"Not through the front. Joseph sometimes sleepwalks after midnight. Let's go through the back."

Annie didn't know what to do or think. Was this woman a killer? A devastated lover? A con artist? She'd followed her in the store but seemed nearly docile when Gill said hello to her that one day.

"Lead the way. Just let me grab the cat bed."

Though she'd come for clues, Annie couldn't force herself to look toward the spot she'd found Gill. She kept her gaze trained on Ginger's back as the woman slipped open one of the French doors and exited onto the back porch. Annie was just thinking how she'd fall flat on her butt if she wore Ginger's heels when the woman did exactly that, hitting the dusty little path to the fence with a hard thud. Her hands clenched at the dirt and she moaned low in her throat. Annie hurried toward her.

"Are you okay?" She whispered the words, glancing around to make sure no one—like Tate—was watching.

Ginger nodded, her gaze filling with more tears. "Just hurt my pride. Which I guess is a good thing because after Gill, I didn't think I had any left."

Despite the situation, Annie laughed quietly. "Come on, let me help you up."

The woman's fingers remained clenched and her movements were stiff. "I'm fine now, dear. Thank you."

They let themselves out of the yard, standing in the small path between Annie and Gill's house.

Ginger sighed. "I know people thought Gill was awful, but he had a softer side. He didn't deserve to die this way."

Annie wasn't sure about the softer side—though she'd caught a glimpse of it that one day—but she agreed with latter statement. No one deserved this.

"We can help each other. You obviously want the truth, too, or you wouldn't be here."

Ginger had a point. Plus, Annie was doing this anyway. Ginger knew more than she did about Gill and the people in his life.

Annie gave a very subtle nod. "I think it's time all of the neighbors got together. What day works best for you?"

Chapter Eighteen

ANNIE SMILED AT the pharmacist, pushing the list of items she didn't want to look at across the counter. "These are for my neighbors. Apparently everything is on file and ready for pickup."

The older woman laughed and let her glasses slip down to the end of her nose as she read the list. Her hair was the kind of feathered style that made Jane Fonda famous.

"Margie called me last week and told me there was a new Tuesday girl in the rotation. Annie, right?" She tapped her glasses back up so they sat on her nose properly.

"Yes, ma'am." She winced. She hated being called ma'am, but it was polite and this woman didn't have a name tag.

"Eleanor, dear. I'll grab these for you."

Annie tapped her fingers against the counter, keeping her head down. She didn't feel like talking to anyone, which wasn't like her, but in the last few days, she felt like she'd done a lifetime's worth of talking. About the same thing on repeat.

"Here you go," Eleanor said. She placed six white bags,

all stapled and labeled in front of Annie. "Do you have anything you want to put on file for when it's someone else's turn to pick up?"

She shook her head before the word "no" flew out of her mouth. She did her best to smile around the brusqueness. "I'm all good."

"I'm sorry you found Gill. That had to be terrible. He used to visit my son's coffee shop frequently, and there wasn't one time he didn't cause a problem with someone."

Annie put the white bags into her oversized purse, making the connection. "Your son owns Just Coffee?"

Eleanor smiled, parental pride shining in her gaze. "Simon prefers simplicity."

Hmmm. Barista and owner. No wonder he felt comfortable putting Gill in his place.

"He was very nice when I met him," Annie said.

"He's a sweetheart. And newly single."

Feeling her cheeks warm, Annie nodded. "Oh. Well, that's nice. I should go deliver all of these."

"Don't forget the muffins," Eleanor called as Annie hurried away.

Right. Six stupid dozen muffins. One trip to the library for books she'd drop off to a neighbor she hadn't even met yet.

As she ran the errands, she wondered about Gill. If he went to Just Coffee regularly, maybe the rest of his schedule was predictable. Which meant retracing his steps should be fairly easy.

In the last episode of *Frontline Blues*, her favorite cop show, they'd traced the twenty-four hours previous to the victim's death. Knowing the moments that led to his final breath could be the key to solving the mystery.

Annie returned to the complex, jumped in and out of her car a literal half dozen times, dropping flats of muffins— they'd know they weren't homemade, but too bad— prescriptions, and, for one neighbor, a nice selection of romance and mystery books.

Raj was outside washing his car as she carried his muffins and prescription. He turned the hose off when she approached.

"Morning, Annie. You're off to an early start."

Annie laughed, her gaze lingering on a wide Band-Aid between Raj's thumb and pointer finger.

"No choice if I wanted to get all of my chores done."

Setting the hose down, he took the items from her. "That's fair. How are you doing?" His tone went somber.

She shrugged. "I'm okay. Just trying to figure out what happened. Are you okay?" She gestured to his hand.

He glanced at it, and she couldn't read whatever it was that flashed in his gaze. Worry? Frustration?

Raj smiled too wide. "Damn cats, right?"

Annie looked toward his house as if she expected a cat to come strolling out. When she turned back, Raj had put some distance between them. "Thanks for this. Now you're off the hook for a while. I should get back to this. I need to get to work. You take care of yourself, Annie."

Solid brush off, neighbor. As she went back to her truck, she made a mental note to ask Ben if Raj had a cat.

ONE OF THE best parts of being an adult was no one could tell you what you had to eat. Well, unless it was Margie and she was pushing muffins on people. Annie sat down with a bowl of tortilla chips and a nice salsa she'd found at the market. She stared at her notebook where she'd written Gill's name surrounded by people with motive for killing him.

Even she could see the motives were weak. A knock on the door elicited a long, irritated groan that bordered on a growl. Annie slapped her notebook shut, checked her phone. She was due at the coffee shop soon. Maybe it was one of her neighbors.

Bingo. Margie stood much as she had last time, far enough away to be seen through the peephole.

"Hi," Annie greeted, a smile on her face as she took in the woman's outfit.

"Hi, yourself." Margie let herself in, amusing Annie. Today she paired a neon-pink blouse with a pair of wide-bottomed gray pants. Her hair had a streak of pink that matched the shirt, while her make up was more subtle today but no less stunning. Between her and Ginger, Annie felt like she needed to up her game just so she wouldn't look drab next to the older women.

"Come in." She shut the door behind Margie, following her to the kitchen.

"How are you holding up?"

"I'm bored and want my laptop back." In the kitchen, she went to the fridge while Margie took a seat at the table, opened up the folder she was holding. "Juice?"

"What kind?"

"Strawberry kiwi or orange."

"Orange, please."

Pouring them both a glass, Annie went over to chat with her neighbor. It seemed easier to give into the woman's will. Despite being pushy, Annie *liked* her. She didn't want to believe the worst. Could she have a dark side? Could Margie have killed Gill? It didn't sit right that she'd just happened to be there. *Ask her why she was. Ease into it.*

"Why did you tell the police Joseph was my attorney the other day?" She picked up her juice, took a sip.

Margie shrugged. "He went to law school. Never finished, but that doesn't matter. He knows the lingo. Gets me all frisky, it does. Nothing like a man who can use the term *exclusionary rule* and know what he's talking about."

Annie laughed, hoping to sidestep any details. "He definitely knows more than me—because I have no idea."

"Well, we were worried they were taking advantage of you. We wanted to make sure whatever you said couldn't be used in a trial."

Her mirth died in her throat. "Let's hope it doesn't get there."

"Let's. I'll feel better once they give you your laptop back."

She started to say agree, but Margie carried on. "What have you figured out so far? I've got a list going. I've brought it to share with you. Now, on Tuesdays, we head to Cuppa. It's my favorite of the coffee shops, but we try to be equitable and switch around. We'll have about six members of the Homeowners' Association there. Ginger said you wanted to meet everyone else."

Annie picked up the top paper on Margie's pile. "Are you friends with her?"

Margie snorted. "In the same way I'd be friends with a bear or a cobra. Just to get on their good side."

"Do you think she could have killed Gill?"

"No. It would require too much effort, and she might break a nail. That woman considers a day without a pricy lunch or a twenty-dollar cocktail wasted."

Interesting. Maybe the woman and Gill were well suited. On the other hand, if Margie was a killer, she would have been quicker to point the finger at their neighbor. Of course, she was in the clear at the moment since Annie was suspect number one.

Margie unfolded her list, showing Annie that she'd written down Raj and Tate down as possibilities with notes about why. According to her bullet points, Raj and Gill had argued extensively and heatedly about Gill clipping Raj's car. Gill claimed it didn't happen. Raj had a picture showing Gill's paint on his car. It seemed like a long shot to Annie, but apparently the two got physical more than once with each other.

"Seems like an unfair fight. Raj is what? Twenty years younger than Gill?"

Margie leaned closer. "Yeah, but they both have tempers and Gill is enough to make anyone lose theirs."

Hmm. "Guess his cat has a temper, too," she said absently.

"He doesn't have a cat," Margie said, then scoffed. "Cats get up on counters. You haven't seen Raj's custom-designed quartz countertops."

Annie's eyes widened. Then whose cat scratched him? She pushed that aside for a moment, taking the opportunity Margie offered.

Good segue. "How did you come to find me in his kitchen?"

Margie was pointing to something on the page about other fights the two men had when just her gaze lifted to Annie's. "The door was open. I was doing my laps around the complex. I do a minimum of six each day. It's why I'm shaped like a younger Sofia Vergara."

Annie bit the inside of her lip hard so she didn't chuckle at the idea that this woman thought she looked younger than the *Modern Family* actress.

"What about Joseph?"

"He's a little slower than me, but I think it's because his mind wanders. He's about the sweetest man I've ever met, but I'll tell you, it just takes something shiny to distract him."

At this point, Annie had no reason and all the reasons to suspect everyone around her, but the truth was, it could easily be someone outside the complex.

"Aren't we going over this at the coffee shop?"

An impatient sigh left Margie's lips. "Yes, but Raj is joining today, and I can't exactly have his name down on a suspect list while he's there, can I?"

"No. I guess not. Why Tate?"

Margie leaned back. "Have you met him?"

Nodding seemed like the safest answer. No details accidentally spilled.

"It's a weak suggestion, I'll admit. But he has a history of violence. He was thrown out of the last two schools he attended before coming to live with Bob. That's his granddad. The parents are split. Bob's daughter is too wrapped up in her own drama to parent that boy properly so he'd been allowed way too much freedom."

"Has he been violent while he was here?"

"Not that I've seen. He's protective of his pops though, and there was some bad blood between Bob and Gill. Tate doesn't do himself any favors, walking around with that hood over his head half the time. Hard to trust someone when you can't see their eyes." Margie folded her arms across her chest. "I've seen lots of kids like him. Get under that tough shell, and there's a sweetheart. We just haven't seen it yet."

Annie thought of Gill. Whoever killed him stabbed him in the back. Perhaps an act of passion, but even if it wasn't, it showed cowardice.

As if she sensed Annie's mood, the elderly neighbor reached out a hand and squeezed her arm. "Are you doing all right? Between seeing the body, my God, I don't know if I'll ever wipe that from my mind. I don't know how police officers and related officials do this all the time."

Annie shook her head, trying to clear the dark visuals from her brain. She gave the list back. "It's hard to forget. I keep thinking I'm fine, and then it pops up in my brain. It doesn't help that I'm worried about being charged for doing something I can't even stomach thinking of."

Margie squeezed again, then lowered her hand. "We won't let that happen. I told your parents I'd keep an eye on you, and I always keep my word. Why don't you take a walk on the beach? I bet your laptop will be returned in no time. We'll meet this afternoon and get some answers. Rumor has it Shelby's taken up residence in your garage with some kittens."

Annie nodded. "Yeah. We've reached some mutual footing. I provide her food and stay out of her way; she doesn't scratch me."

Gathering her papers, Margie stood. "Grumpy cat suited him well. Wonder if Mira will take her home. I'm surprised she hasn't been by yet."

"I think I need a character chart to keep everyone straight. Who's Mira?"

"Gill's daughter. They were close once, but she hasn't been around in a long time. They had a falling out when Mira refused to work for Gill."

Annie tucked that piece of information away with the rest of it. She'd considered herself pretty good at figuring out the killer in shows and books before the reveal, but this was proving more complicated. Guess that was the difference between a fifty-minute episode or a three-hundred-page book and real life.

The more she learned, the less she felt like she knew. Her gut told her it wasn't Margie but, really, how could she possibly know? All Annie could say for certain was it wasn't her.

Chapter Nineteen

ANNIE ARRIVED AT Cuppa earlier than the scheduled time. Ben's grandma wasn't joking when she said Margie would have things all mapped out for them. A group of them visited every shop each month, rotating among them to make sure each of the businesses benefited from their caffeine addictions. Margie organized several groups both in and out of the complex. Annie couldn't even imagine what the woman's home calendar looked like.

She still had about an hour before the group from the complex were due to show up. After Margie left, Annie got a call from Ben's lawyer friend who agreed to chat with her via Zoom the next day. He was away at the moment, which wasn't helpful, but at least he could update her on her rights. The call left her antsy and needing to get out of the house.

The waitress came over to see if Annie needed anything else. She'd already polished off a large latte and a delicious lemon scone.

"Good, aren't they?" The waitress pointed at the empty plate, then picked it up.

"Delicious. Are they baked in house?" Annie kept her

notebook closed as she spoke to the woman.

Her auburn hair was done in two braids that looked charming rather than juvenile. She wore a pair of boot-cut jeans, Converse high-tops, and a loose T-shirt that read CUPPA. It was cuter for the fact that the *u* looked like a cup. It was nice to know there were lots of people her age around town. If she spent too much time in the complex, she might feel older than her years.

"They are. My sister is an amazing baker. I always joke that she's the baker, I'm the brains. Between the two of us, we seem to do okay even with all the other coffee joints in town."

Annie probably didn't hide her surprise. "You own this place? You're so young."

A wide smile stretched across her face. Little freckles dotted her nose, adding to her youthful appearance. "My sister and I are thirty-two this summer. Twins. We have our mom to thank for looking young. Sometimes we get mistaken as triplets. I'm Ashley." She held out her free hand.

"Annie. I just moved into town."

Ashley cheeks brightened. "I know. Your parents came in every Saturday morning. They took their time drinking their coffees while your mom read and your dad did crosswords. I heard about Gill. I'm friends—or I used to be—with Mira, Gill's daughter. I'm sorry you were the one to find him."

"Wow. Everything you hear about small towns is true. Thank you. It was awful."

165

"Ryan says the lead detectives are looking at you as a suspect. He's madder than a chicken on fire."

Annie's brows scrunched as a visual of that popped into her head. In that case, the chicken would have every right to be pretty irate. "I guess if it's something that doesn't happen much, no one knows how to approach it. The good news is murder isn't a common thing. The bad news is I'm worried they'll pin it on me because I was the one who found him."

There were only two other people in the quaint little shop that was styled to look like the office or cozy living room of someone's home. Wingback chairs were set up to allow for easy conversations. There was a big table at the front that looked as if it belonged in a rustic farmhouse. Dark wood shelves lined the walls, filled with books that could be taken if one was left—like a large-scale miniature library. The front counter was rectangular, the glass case showing a number of delectable goodies. The rich woods and warm atmosphere made Annie think it would be hard to top as a go-to spot.

Ashley slid into the seat across from Annie. "I'm sorry. That's scary. I can't even imagine. Ryan and I have been friends forever, but once he puts on that uniform, I get stupidly nervous. I've never broken a law in my life, but being around police makes me think they're going to catch me for something."

Annie could laugh at that as she was sure the other woman intended. "I've never even been pulled over for speeding, so this is all new to me. Between the murder, Margie's strict schedule for the complex, and work—which I can't do because the detectives took my laptop—I'm feeling a little more on edge than usual." Wow. She hadn't meant to unload all of that.

"Margie is friends with my grandmother. She means no harm. If you tell her you have other obligations, she'll schedule someone else in your spot for the muffins, the carpooling, and even the coffeehouse rotations. She's in our book club. You should totally join. We don't let her take over though."

That was a lot of information. "I've certainly met far more people than I expected to in the first week or so."

Ashley lowered her chin. "Heard you met Ben."

Annie groaned and rolled her gaze. "Please don't tell me you're in love with him. First, we're just friends, second, he helped me out."

Ashley waved a hand in the air, dismissing Annie's words. Her wide smile told her she knew what kind of attention Ben received. "Please. Ben is friends with my older brother. Same with Ryan. The three of them together are clueless as to how they make the townies swoon."

She'd picked up her cup but paused on the way to her lips. "Townies?"

"Those of us born and bred right here in Rainbow Falls. There isn't a woman who went to school with those three, who isn't already married, that isn't wishing she were the one. Some of the guys, too, but that's not going to happen."

"You're not under the spell?"

"Nah. Once you've burped the alphabet in a contest against a guy—and won—they take you off the dating list. Which works out fine for me."

It felt so good to laugh. This was what Annie hoped for—to ease into a new life, create new friendships, and get to know her new home.

"I guess that's a risk you take."

The door swung open. Two elderly men came through. Ashley waved to them.

"We have a games night every second Saturday. Steph— that's my sister—and I close up early. Everyone brings an appetizer, and we just hang out here, play some games. You should come. I'll tell Ben to bring you, okay?"

Annie nodded as Ashley rose. "That sounds wonderful actually."

"Perfect. Let me know if you want more coffee."

"I will. Nice to meet you."

Giving herself a few extra moments of blissful normalcy, Annie sipped her coffee, watched people walk by the front window and relaxed her shoulders into the cozy chair. She could imagine reading here, being friends with Ashley. Things would work out. The cops would find the real killer, and Annie's life would go back to the boring state it had always been.

She flipped open her notebook, wishing she had her laptop. When she got it back, she should probably switch some things around on the blog. She'd written her own thoughts along with some of the things she'd gleaned from Margie's notes. There was likely no chance Ryan had any inside information from the detectives, but Claire had told her to send some names, so that's what she'd do.

Annie reviewed her chart.

Who wanted Gill Downs dead?			
Suspect	Connection	Motive	Questions/Notes
Raj	Neighbor	Frequent fights/car damage	Does anyone else have issues with him? Did he go to Gill's argue then get scratched by Shelby, which sent the cat to my parents' garage?
Margie	Neighbor	?	Was she really just walking by?
Ginger	Neighbor/ Lover	Spurned lover	Would she have the strength and gumption to kill him? Margie said she was pampered.
Bethany	Ex-wife	Insurance? Found out about Ginger?	How did she feel about reconciling? Was it Mira that Gill said his ex had turned against him?

It wasn't perfect, but it was a start—some names to give Claire's wife. It was better than the list the Trenton detectives had started. To her knowledge, she was still the only one on it. Maybe she should drop by the police station and talk to Ryan herself. She should show him the picture so he wasn't blindsided by anything else. Maybe he could get her laptop back for her. One thing was for certain: It couldn't make things worse. Could it?

Chapter Twenty

A LINE OF sweat formed at the base of Annie's neck. She was hyper aware of how heavy her breathing was at this particular moment. It was taking a lot of energy to play it cool.

Ben's gaze held hers, the intensity drawing her in, fueling her with renewed energy. "You still want to do this?"

She adjusted her grip, nodded once because she didn't trust her voice.

"You sure?" It was easy to recognize the teasing glint in his expression.

"It's your move."

"Okay. Bend your knees. On three."

Annie braced.

"One, two, three."

They both lifted the stupidly heavy, deceptively awkward treadmill and made their way down the hall, around the corner, and into the guest bedroom. Getting it up the few steps to the porch had nearly done her in.

When they set it down, Annie bent in half and leaned against the wall. "I think moving it in here counts as a month of workouts."

"Maybe we should get you some weights," Ben said, not hiding his laughter.

Annie tipped her head up, glared at him from her hunched position. "Careful. I haven't fed you yet."

Ben held both hands up. He wasn't even sweating. Jerk. "I'm teasing. Are we having chicken and chocolate again?"

Pushing off the wall, she shook her head. "You're a little mean. I don't know why I like that."

They stood in front of each other, their gazes locked. She was acutely aware of her heavy breaths and the way he was looking at her. The corner of his mouth tipped up in a sexy almost-smile. Annie bit her lip to stop herself from blurting out something she'd regret. Instead, she moved around him and headed for the kitchen where they were not, in fact, having chicken and chocolate.

Ben followed behind. "That's not an answer."

At the fridge, she turned and sent him a smile over her shoulder. "I've got steaks marinating, a beautiful salad, and potatoes perfect for baking." Grabbing two sodas out of the fridge, she passed one to Ben.

He took it, popping the top and taking a long swallow. "Sounds delicious."

"Do you mind if I shower quick?"

Their gazes locked over the words, and for one heartbeat, the air went out of the room. She thought she was overheated before. *No more heavy breathing.*

"Not at all. You did just work out." His voice was gruff.

Annie laughed. "You're a smartass."

He nodded with a mocking expression of disappointment. "It's best you learn this now."

She took another swallow of her drink. "I won't be long."

"Want me to get the potatoes in while I wait?"

She'd started past him but stopped when he spoke. Now she was all caught up in how good he smelled. *And you smell like you just ran forty miles on that treadmill rather than moving it thirty feet.*

"That doesn't make me a very good host."

Ben reached out, moved the strands of hair trailing across her forehead back behind her ear. It was such a casually sweet gesture. It made Annie feel warm and tingly inside.

"I'll put the potatoes in and get the grill ready."

Annie shrugged. "If you insist. You can whip up a cake, too, if you want."

"Don't push it."

She headed for the shower, happy despite the circumstances surrounding her life right now. Her meeting with her neighbors today didn't prove much. Only that all together they were one noisy bunch. They talked over one another, a mixture of old stories, new plans, and veiled accusations. It had yielded nothing more than seeing a piece of their personalities.

Stepping under the hot spray, Annie grabbed her favorite

shampoo to wash her hair, then left the conditioner in a few extra minutes. Might be nice for Ben to become intoxicated with the way *she* smelled. Seemed fair. It was getting more difficult to stay within the *just friends* zone.

Ben had texted early in the day about dinner and checking on Shelby. They were going to name the kittens tonight. She couldn't—*wouldn't*—keep them, but she was excited all the same. It wasn't the only phone call she'd received that day, but she didn't want to think about the other one right now.

Though she didn't want to keep Ben waiting, she took a few extra minutes to moisturize her face, put some product in her hair so it dried softly in large waves. A touch of mascara and some lip gloss were her go-to for makeup. She dressed as casually as he had—jean capris and a loose-fitting, flowy, pale-blue tank top.

Checking herself in the mirror, she was happy with what she saw. She'd decided not to put any expectations on their relationship. He made her laugh and showed up when she needed him. Two excellent qualities in any human. For now, she was just going to enjoy spending time with him rather than obsessing over the fact that the detectives had left a message saying they needed to talk.

Ben was at the table when she joined him in the kitchen. He'd found some chips and dumped them into a bowl. She sat across from him, not realizing what he was looking at right away.

"Doesn't look like you're taking Ryan's suggestion to stay out of it." He pointed to her charts, his tone free of judgment. When he looked her way, his eyes went darker. "You look good."

The huskiness of his tone sent a shiver over her skin. Annie nibbled on her bottom lip. Nice that he'd noticed, but not the right thing to focus on. How much did she say? *Of all the people you've met here, he's the only one you're sure you can trust.* Although she had good feelings about Ryan and Ashley as well.

"I can't stay out of it when I'm right in the middle. Black called. They're stopping by tonight to ask more questions and hopefully to return my laptop. I can't leave everything up to them."

"That's fair. Ginger and Gill were lovers?" He didn't hide his distaste.

"That's the rumor. But I'm not sure. I got the sense she was really sad about his death. But I could be wrong. Raj feels like the most likely suspect at this point. He didn't lie about having a cat, but his hand is all bandaged from a supposed scratch and he doesn't own one."

Ben listened as though she was making perfect sense. "No. He doesn't. I'm pretty sure the couple in unit eight, Rebecca and Anya, have two. They don't bring them to my clinic though."

"I haven't met them, but I did drop off a stack of library books for them today." She sighed, the weight of having more questions than answers, feeling heavy. "It could be any of them."

"Or it could be none of them. You haven't checked out Bethany. And what about his business partner?"

Annie's fingers itched to write down more information. "Who is it? Do you know who inherits the dealership?"

Ben shook his head. "I don't know who inherits, but Conway Leese is his partner. The funeral is Saturday. Speaking of which, did you want to attend together?"

"Do you think it's okay if I go?" She'd been worried about that.

"I don't see why not. You haven't been charged with anything."

Aiming for humor, she muttered, "The night is still young."

Ben smiled but reached over to cover her hands with his. Patting it twice, he went back to her notes. "Something will turn up." He cleared his throat, and she knew he was working up to something. Looking at her through lowered lashes, he hesitated a minute. She braced.

"I found a couple of Murder Mystery games on my phone. They're…interesting." He lifted his head, met her gaze square on. "I also looked up a company that hosts mystery events. That's the sort of thing you like, right?"

She nodded uncertainly. Slowly. "Yes."

"Okay. So, if you were planning this, thinking of the suspects—which I guess you were," he said, tapping the list she'd made. "How would it play out?"

Annie beamed at him. She couldn't help it. His attractive quotient just doubled. "No judging?"

He laughed, leaned back in his seat, and gestured for her to tell him. "No way. There are definitely weirder hobbies, and in the interest of full disclosure, I'm a sci-fi fan."

She groaned mockingly as he picked up a chip, which he then tossed at her, making her laugh.

"Come on, Sherlock. Lay it on me."

"It has to be something more than just anger. Gill made people mad all the time. Close up, with a knife suggests someone snapped. They were at the end of their rope. Possibly passion, which means Ginger isn't ruled out. But in the back makes me think *coward*. It seems pretty weak to stab him with his back turned."

"Or smart. Someone with less upper-arm strength would have struggled to attack him face-to-face."

She tapped her finger on the table. "Good point. Okay, but why? He knew something or did something or was planning on doing something that would so terribly impact another person, he was murdered for it."

Ben glanced at the chart. "Raj has a temper, but he's a good man. Some people think it's silly, but animals tell you a lot about a person and when he brings his dog in, the other dogs take to him well. Besides, both Gill and Raj have money. If Gill lied about hitting Raj's car, it would piss him off, but Raj wouldn't kill over it."

"People kill for all sorts of reasons. Also, Gill was in debt."

His brows furrowed. "You going to tell me how you learned that?"

When she shook her head, he continued. "Raj would have gotten in a fist fight with him, even taken it too far, but a knife in the back seems like a stretch."

Annie's shoulders sagged. "I think so, too. Honestly, my gut says it was a woman."

He looked down again. "So, Bethany, Ginger, or Margie."

"Or Mira, the daughter."

Ben frowned.

Annie grinned. "Don't tell me you dated her."

His grin did funny things to her insides. "Stop it." He nudged her foot with hers.

Because she could feel her cheeks warming, she did. "I feel like Margie is so organized she wouldn't have killed him unless she wrote it down first."

Ben laughed, then stopped. "I shouldn't laugh about murder."

Guilt gnawed at her gut. "I shouldn't joke about it."

His gaze softened, his feet still touching hers as if he liked being connected. "I guess whatever helps us get through, right? Let's switch topics. Tell me about your work. Or something you like to do outside of sleuthing."

Annie got up, surprisingly comfortable with leaving her

notebook in front of him. She started pulling out the fixings for salad.

"Well, I really love sleeping in. Like, I could gold medal in it."

"Good to have dreams."

"I love the water. I'd like to try kayaking. My parents have two in their garage."

"I noticed. It's fun. It can be tricky on the ocean, but there's lots of great spots around here. We could go."

She smiled. "I'd like that."

Ben came up beside her, using a paper towel to wipe down the produce she washed. "Ash said she told you about the games night. You're in?"

"If you're okay with that."

He gave just a hint of a smile. It made her want to work for the full-on grin. "I was going to invite you."

They were quiet a few minutes before he spoke again. "You leave behind any broken hearts in Portland?"

A sharp laugh escaped. "No. Certainly not like the trail you've left in Rainbow Falls."

He bumped her hip with his. "Funny."

She shook her head. "I haven't had a relationship in a while. Casual dates here and there. I'm not big on dating apps, which is how a lot of people connect these days."

Ben's chin dipped lower. "I prefer in person. Body language and facial expressions matter. Hard to tell if there's chemistry just by swiping right."

Her heart puffed up with adoration. "Can I keep you?" The words were out of her mouth before she thought it through.

Their gazes locked, but Annie broke away first. "Don't answer that."

"You make me smile, Annie Abbot."

They finished making the salad as they chatted about her work, books they liked, movies, his patients, and swapped stories about their college lives. They shared dinner, their conversation moving from one topic to another with the ease of old friends. Annie was thinking the night was pretty close to perfect by the time they finished up dinner and were heading back out to name the cats.

"I'm vetoing Snowball and Midnight right off the top."

"That's fair," Ben agreed as they put their shoes on. "You want car names?"

She grabbed a sweater, as the evenings cooled considerably. "Yeah, but there aren't many cool car names. Mustang? Corvette? Honda?"

Ben laughed, pulling the door open for her. "I think…Oh, Mira."

Annie was looking at him when he spoke. "That seems weird. Naming it after—"

Ben cut her off by pointing to the door. A dark-haired woman with thick-framed glasses stood on Annie's porch. She was short, dressed in a style Annie could only call goth.

The woman looked from Ben to Annie. "Are you her?

Are you the one who found my father?"

Annie's heart came to a screeching halt. "Yes."

Then she braced, grateful Ben was at her side because she had no idea if this woman was going to introduce herself or attack.

Chapter Twenty-One

IN A WAY, Mira Downs *did* attack; she tackle-hugged Annie. She felt the woman's sobs wracking her body even before she heard them.

Ben's gaze clashed with Annie's as she patted the woman's back. He shrugged.

Mira pulled back, swiped at her tears with the long sleeves of her scratchy, wool sweater. "I'm sorry. I've been holding that in since we found out."

Empathy swelled in Annie's chest. She couldn't imagine finding out something had happened to her parents. "Don't apologize. Please. Come in."

They led the sniffling woman to the kitchen where Annie did what she knew her mother would—put on the tea kettle.

It wasn't until Mira sat down that she really took notice of Ben. "I'm sorry. I'm completely interrupting."

Ben shook his head, sat across from her, and set a comforting hand on hers. "Not at all. In fact, if you want some relatively good news, your father's cat, Shelby, had four healthy kittens. We were just about to go out and check on them."

Mira laughed. It was watery but real. "He loved that damn cat more than me or my mother. Probably disowned it when she got knocked up. Is that why she's here?"

Annie's gaze widened. "I'm new to the area so I don't actually know what brought Shelby to my parents' garage."

"Right. I met your mom once, I think. When I stopped by to see my dad, I usually arrived or left mad, so I wasn't always in the mood for chitchat."

Which was something she couldn't say at the moment because this girl was talking as though she was being fast-forwarded.

"Would you like a cup of tea?" The kettle sounded even as she asked.

Mira nodded, pulling a Kleenex out of her purse. "That would be great. Thank you. You're Ben, right?"

He nodded. "Yes. I think you were a few years behind me in high school."

Mira ducked her head. Annie barely heard her response. "Five. My friends and I had such huge crushes on you."

Annie bit her lip, forcing herself not to look at Ben. She'd be able to tease him later even without checking to see if his face turned redder than his grandmother's tomatoes.

"Uh. How's your mom?" Ben asked.

"Heartbroken, angry. I guess that's what you're left with when a person you're always at odds with dies. I thought we'd have time. That we could keep spinning around in the same circles and one day we'd figure it out. Smooth things out. Now we never will. I'm still so angry at him, but now when I feel it, I feel guilty, too."

Annie brought tea over, then found a little pitcher for milk and grabbed the sugar bowl. She brought them to the table as well, wondering if she should put out some muffins.

"I think anything you're feeling is acceptable and understandable, Mira," Ben said in that soft, smooth doctor voice that probably soothed animal parents every day.

"Maybe. But regardless of how I feel or felt about my father, he didn't deserve to be murdered." Her curly hair bounced with the energy in her voice. Her fingers curled around a teacup, which she added nothing to before sipping.

"You're absolutely right." Annie took a seat beside Ben on the bench.

They sat a moment, each of them sipping their tea. Annie was happy to see Ben added a healthy dose of sugar to his as well. He glanced at her, knowing she'd noticed.

You should be thinking about this poor young woman in front of you and not tea. "Will you be staying at your father's?"

Mira set her cup down. "Yes. I'll start packing his things. My mother can't do it. She broke her foot two weeks ago and has been bedridden, which is driving her bonkers."

Annie had to stifle her laugh. She didn't think anyone outside of the Mad Hatter's tea party said *bonkers*. It was oddly charming. Pressure built in Annie's chest. This was a terrible way to meet someone she could see herself being friends with. Mira removed her glasses, huffed on them, then cleaned them, using the sleeves of her sweater. She had to be sweltering in that thing.

Annie started to say something but realized what Mira said. "Your mom is bedridden?"

Mira nodded. "Well. Not entirely. But she's out of commission. She fell off of a stool trying to get a platter down from the cupboard. She's an awful patient. I've been staying with her to help."

Which means Bethany is officially off the list. There was no way she stabbed her ex-husband. Would Ginger have known that?

Tears trailed down Mira's cheeks again. "Maybe if I'd been on better terms with my father, this wouldn't have happened."

"You can't know that. What-ifs will drive you…" Ben said, pausing with a sweet smile, "bonkers."

It lightened the moment, which made the next words out of Mira's mouth hit twice as hard.

"I know who killed my father."

Annie choked on her tea.

Chapter Twenty-Two

BEN RUBBED SLOW circles on Annie's back. "You okay?"

She nodded, her eyes watering. "Yes. Just caught me off guard. What do you mean you know who?"

Mira's expression flipped like a switch. Sad one second and harsh the next. "I mean there's only one person who wanted my father gone."

Oh, sweetie. That's not true. Annie felt guilt for thinking it, but that just wasn't realistic. People *hated* Gill. He was nasty. An unhappy man who took pleasure in spreading his anger. Every person she'd spoken to about him—even Ginger, who supposedly loved him—said the same about her neighbor.

Ben shot Annie a glance, then turned toward Mira. "Who?"

"Conway Leese. He wanted my father out of the picture. They argued several times, and once, he even threatened my dad. I knew he was going to snap, but I never expected this."

"Have you told the police this?" Annie wrapped her fingers around the cup to warm them up.

"Yes. But they said he has an alibi. Except I know he's

lying." Mira stiffened her shoulders.

"How?" Annie met her hard glare.

"Because he's a liar."

Not exactly foolproof. "I'm sure the police will follow any viable leads." Annie sure as heck hoped so because at the moment, as far as she knew, they were only traveling down the roads that led to her.

Mira's shoulders seemed to sag. "I should go. I need to face going into his house before I lose my nerve."

"We could come with you," Ben said.

Mira smiled, but it was so sad, Annie's heart tweaked. "Thank you, but I think it's better if I do it alone."

"Would you like to see the kittens sometime soon?" Annie asked as she stood.

"Yes. I would. Thank you for the tea and for being so gracious."

"It's literally the least I could do. I'm so sorry for your loss, Mira."

Her lips twisted. She stood up and ducked her gaze. "Most would say it's not much of a loss."

Moving around Ben, Annie put a hand on her arm. "He was your father. Of course it's a loss."

Mira looked up, and Annie could see the gratitude in her eyes. "Thank you." They walked to the door before the woman spoke again. "I can't do anything to repair my relationship with my dad. I want to do this. I want to see his killer brought to justice. I can't do it alone."

The words weighed Annie down like cement blocks. She let loose a deep sigh. "You're not alone." *Unless she's the killer.*

Mira nodded, then opened the door.

Turned out the evening wasn't over and definitely wasn't getting any better. Detectives Black and Rickers stood on her doorstep. The upside was they held her laptop in a large, sealed plastic bag.

They seemed surprised to see Mira and Ben at Annie's side. Rickers recovered first. He arched his brows, looking at Mira. "Ms. Downs. Seems like an odd place to be hanging out."

Mira stepped back. "Why is that?"

Detective Black sneered just a little. "Most grieving daughters wouldn't want to spend time with their father's suspected killer."

Annie let out an unnatural squawking sound. "Hey. You can't just say that. I didn't do it, and you can't prove anything." She was glad she had a meeting with the lawyer. She'd need to ask him how to respond to the detectives' unfair statements.

"Is that so, Ms. Abbott?"

"It looks like you're returning the laptop. Which means you didn't find what you needed. Do you have a warrant to arrest her?" Ben asked, his tone taking on a hardness that surprised Annie.

Detective Rickers looked him up and down. "Here again,

Mr. McIntyre?"

Ben stiffened.

Annie was still stuck on the fact that they didn't answer the question. Was she going to jail? She should grab a sweater. It seemed like it'd be a cold place. Or maybe they wouldn't even let her have a sweater. Would she have to wear a jumpsuit?

"No warrant, but we do have some questions."

"Are you heading to your father's house?" Detective Black asked Mira.

She nodded, then looked at Annie, eyes wide.

"Let me walk you there." She took Mira's arm, leaving no room for argument.

"Were you leaving?" Detective Rickers asked Ben, stepping forward.

Annie took a step to block his way. "I didn't invite you into my house, and without a warrant, you have no right to bully your way in."

He smiled. He actually smiled. Annie had never been in trouble with the police, but she desperately wanted to slap this man. It might be worth the charge.

Rickers stepped back. He didn't make any moves to hand the laptop back. Annie wanted to snatch it from him. "I can question you out here just as easily."

Ben stepped closer to her as if he could share his strength or warmth. She was grateful he didn't just leave. Annie saw Mira stealing glances back at them as Black walked her to her dad's.

"What's this about?" Ben asked.

You might want to pay attention to this part, Annie. She looked at the detective who was looking back and forth between them, clearly trying to figure out what they were to each other.

"I'd like to ask you about some substantial deposits into your bank account, Ms. Abbott."

She thought about that for a second. She'd received the final portion of one advance for finishing up another smaller scale magazine spread. Her mother had deposited money for household expenses for the year, so that was substantial. She received an advance for a new job the other day. What else?

"What about them?"

"I had no idea graphic design was so lucrative," Rickers said.

Warmth flooded Annie's cheeks. "I do well enough."

"You have a wide range of clients?" He took his little notepad out.

"Yes."

"Care to tell me about a sizable deposit from JTT Enterprises?"

That was Josie's private investigation company, Just the Truth. She'd revamped Josie's social media, website, and done a series of ads for her. It was a great job, and she'd actually received several referral clients as a result. But what did it have to do with anything?

"It seems to me that you're the detective, you should be able to figure that out on your own." Annie crossed her arms over her chest. It showed their lack of effort and detail that they couldn't find the answer to their question.

"Did someone pay you to kill Mr. Downs?"

A groan of frustration left Ben's throat. "Are you serious?"

Annie shook her head. "You think I moved into town to kill a stranger for money?"

"You were paid by a private investigation company." Rickers dropped the words like a mic. He stared at Annie, no doubt waiting for her to freak out.

"For a graphic design job. I helped her revamp her image. After you two finish blaming the wrong person and messing up this case, your department can use my services to do the same thing."

His lips clenched into a hard line, his nostrils flaring. Then, as though she hadn't bothered him at all, he tilted his head to the side. "We haven't been able to reach your parents. All activity on their credit cards and social media has stopped."

Black joined them, hitting the Pause button on Annie's temper.

"You did say they'd reach out, didn't you?" Black wasted no time getting in on the conversation.

"They're sailing around the world. I'm guessing the Wi-Fi is spotty." Annie couldn't temper her glare.

"For a woman looking at being arrested for murder, you're awfully flippant."

"For detectives who are supposed to understand procedure, you're awfully far over the line, edging into harassment," Margie said, joining them as if she'd just magicked herself beside them. She was pumping her arms, marching in place as she glared at the detectives.

"Ms. Tripalo," Detective Black said with a wary tone.

"Annie, perhaps you should get yourself a lawyer. I do believe these two are grasping so desperately at straws they might pick up a stick and say that'll do."

Both of the detectives' jaws dropped open, and Annie bit her cheek hard so she didn't laugh.

"I have a Zoom meeting with Ben's friend tomorrow. He's a lawyer, and he's advised me that I have rights. Something you should know," Annie said. Ben smiled at her.

"We're trying to find justice for the victim and his family, Ms. Tripalo, and it would be in your best interests not to interfere." Detective Rickers towered over the woman, but she didn't even bat her perfectly curled eyelashes.

"It would be in everyone's best interest if you took this investigation seriously and looked for the killer. I've watched enough *Law and Order* to know that a person has to have motive. Why on earth with Annie kill Gill? Now, had she known him as long as the rest of us had, she might have been tempted, but for all she knew, he was just having a couple bad days."

Whoa. Margie was going to bat for her. Which meant the attention could shift, and she wouldn't do that if she'd offed Gill, would she? Didn't seem smart. And Margie Tripalo was all kinds of smart.

"To answer your question, no, I wasn't hired to kill Gill. I didn't kill him. I didn't know him. Have you talked to Conway Leese? His business partner?" The picture. She needed to show them the picture. She pulled her phone out of her back pocket.

Detective Black's lips curled back. "We know how to do our jobs."

Annie, Ben, and Margie stared at the detectives. *Not from where I'm standing, you don't.*

Ben and Margie's gazes whipped to Annie. Shoot. She'd said that out loud.

"This is ridiculous." Annie threw up her hands, her irritation stomping out most of her rational thought. "Mira Downs is convinced that Conway killed her father. If you have nothing else to ask me, I'd like to end this meeting. Can I please have my laptop?"

"We may have some more questions for you. You'll be around?" Detective Black said. He handed over the device.

"I'm living here now, so yes."

Detective Rickers put his notebook away, patted his pants pocket, and pulled out his phone. "One more thing, Ms. Abbott?"

"What?" She spoke through clenched teeth.

He turned the phone toward her so she could see the screen. "Any idea who this might be?"

Sun on the beach. As swear words went, it was weak, but so was her pulse. The screen showed the photo Tate had shared with her. Her heart hammered off beat but nearly stopped when she saw how ghostly white Margie went. Ben leaned forward to get a better look.

Annie did her best to keep her face expressionless and gave them the truth. "I have absolutely no idea."

Chapter Twenty-Three

"IS IT POSSIBLE it's you?" Detective Black asked.

Annie wondered if a person could be in contempt in front of a police officer the same way they could in a courtroom. If she knew with absolute certainty that she wouldn't be fined or jailed, she would have shared her thoughts with Detective Black.

"Of course it's not her," Margie spat, her pallor still alarming. "I'd like the name of your supervisor. Maybe he or she would be interested to know that the city's money is being wasted on wild goose chases rather than actual detective work."

Ben cleared his throat. "Look, tensions are high. If you have nothing else, Detectives, it's been a long day."

"What's the nature of your relationship to Ms. Abbott?" Detective Rickers asked.

Margie threw her hands up, saying the words Annie was thinking. "None of your business. We're done here."

Annie turned and started to leave but thought better of it. "Margie, are you all right?"

Margie met her gaze, anger flashing like a wildfire in the

older woman's eyes. "I'm fine, dear. You take care of you. I've got some things to do." With that, she turned and power walked toward her house.

"Ben, are you coming?" Annie asked.

She felt the heavy, accusatory gazes of both detectives as she and Ben walked toward the garage. When she reached the door, she turned around. The detectives were headed to their vehicle.

"Detective Rickers?"

He turned when she called.

"Who gave you that photo?"

"I'm not at liberty to say. Do you recognize it?"

Annie gave him a weary smile. It took effort to summon it up. "I'm not at liberty to say."

Ben snickered beside her. When they entered the garage, all of her bravado evaporated and she fell against the door, using it as a prop to hold her upright.

"You okay?"

"The world has turned upside down. I feel like I'm stuck in a bad novel. One of those ones where you're thinking, *Wait, this makes absolutely no sense. What the hell is the author doing?*"

Ben stepped closer, looked at her like he was seeking permission. Straightening, she stepped closer. "If you're asking if you can hug me, the answer is a hard yes."

He wrapped his arms around her, and she let her head fall to his chest, listening to his heartbeat. It wasn't about attraction or defining statuses. It was about comfort, and boy, did Annie need it. She hated admitting that, even to herself, but it was the absolute truth. Her world was imploding, and she couldn't find the button to stop it.

"Things will be okay." Ben smoothed a hand down her hair, and she wanted so badly to believe him. But she didn't. "Maybe we should talk to Ryan."

Tears pricked her eyelids as she stepped back. "If it's okay with you, I'd rather not. I don't think I could handle another person who could control my fate believing the worst of me. I know he's your friend, but I just need time to sort through things."

Ben nodded, his expression cautious and concerned.

Swallowing the lump in her throat, she forced another smile. "Let's name the cats. Then I have some calls to make."

They sat down on the garage floor. Shelby looked up at them with disdain.

"We've been busy," Annie said in their defense.

The cat looked away, licked her babies as they nuzzled against her. She let out a deep purr.

"That sounds like a judgmental purr," Annie muttered.

Ben laughed. "I think she's just happy."

Shelby looked at Ben with obvious cat love. Annie scowled. "Hey, I'm the one feeding you."

Ben shook his head, petting Shelby. "Stop looking for trouble. You have enough of it."

She poked his shoulder, her fingers itching to pick up

one of the cats. "She started it."

Ben's laughter startled Shelby, but she seemed to forgive him easily. "I'm guessing their names will change. You still want to do this?"

Annie looked at Ben, staring at his profile as he stroked Shelby with exquisite tenderness. "Yeah. I feel like we should. The names can just be for us. You said they'll need to stay for a while, right?"

He nodded. "Six weeks minimum. They should open their eyes sometime next week. You've got an even split; two boys, two girls."

Annie didn't want to know how he knew that, especially since the websites she'd read said don't touch them. Of course, Shelby would let Ben get away with a lot more than Annie.

"Well, the boys' names seem obvious."

Ben stared at her. When he clearly couldn't guess, she shared. "Sherlock and Watson."

Ben laughed. "I should have guessed."

She nodded. "You really should have."

Annie watched the kittens squirm and nestle into a multicolored ball of fluff as Ben thought about girls' names. When a few minutes passed, she turned and caught him staring at her. Nerves fluttered under her skin like mini pulses.

"This is harder than I thought."

"It is," Annie said, breaking their stare first.

"Uh, okay. Dorothy and Blanche."

Annie sucked in a breath that caught around her laughter, and she started to cough. When she regained her composure—which she seemed to lose around him far too often—she tried to school her features.

Ben's cheeks were slightly pink. "My grandma watched *The Golden Girls* when I was growing up, and now that I've shown her how to use Netflix, she's back into it."

"I think it's sweet, though I worry we're setting one of them up to be a bit promiscuous. That was Blanche, right?"

"She's just secure in her sexuality," Ben said, clearly fighting his own laughter.

"The cat or the character?"

"Both, I think."

Shelby joined them again, brushing up against Ben's leg. Annie couldn't say she blamed the feline. He was awfully nice to cozy up to. *Like you don't have enough things on your plate at the moment?*

Ben nodded firmly. "Then it's settled. To us, they'll be Blanche, Dorothy, Sherlock, and Watson."

Annie nodded, a strange clutch in her heart making her fingers clench. She wanted one of them. Well, she actually wanted all of them. *You're just feeling emotionally attached. It'll pass.*

"You okay?" Ben touched her shoulder.

She nodded. "I am. Or I will be. I have the Zoom call with your friend, and I also have a friend of mine—the private investigator—looking into a few things. I was going to tell them about the picture."

She explained how she'd first seen it. Ben let out a low whistle. "This just keeps getting more tangled."

Annie swallowed down the unexpected lump in her throat. "There's still time to run."

Ben tucked a strand of hair behind her ear. "I'm not much of a runner."

After an awkward moment that made her stomach somersault, they stood, dusted themselves off. She walked him out to the driveway where he'd parked his truck, then did the whole standing around thing, unsure why her emotions were boiling over.

"I'll pick you up Saturday for the service?"

She nodded. "Sure. If I'm not in jail by then."

Ben didn't laugh at her joke. "Don't do that." He stepped closer, kissed her cheek. "Everything will be okay."

When he pulled back, she gave him a smile. He'd been so great. The least she could do was fake her belief in his words.

"Thanks for dinner."

"No problem."

"Guess it's my turn. My grandma wants you to come, but I was wondering if we should wait until things settle a bit."

She gave a humorless laugh. "I should do it as soon as possible before—"

"Annie." The one word cut off her negative thought.

"Right. Positive thinking only. Let me know. My schedule is wide open. Other than Saturday. Between the funeral and games night, I'm all yours for the day."

His eyes brightened. "It'll make one easier and the other more fun."

She waved as he pulled out of the driveway. Annie rubbed her hands up and down both arms. She sighed, looking toward Tate's house. What had he done? And why? He'd been so opposed to sharing with the police. What changed his mind?

Annie shook off the feeling of being watched and headed for the house. It was time to find out some information about the people she'd met. Before she fell too hard for any of them, she needed to rule them out as murderers.

Chapter Twenty-Four

ANNIE MADE HERSELF another cup of tea before logging back on to Zoom. She was happy to see Claire's face just for the familiarity.

"You okay?" Claire asked. "You look like you're carrying the weight of the world on your shoulders."

Annie's tears pricked again, but she refused to cry. She had no reason—yet. Filling Claire in on the latest, she watched as her friend got madder and madder on her behalf.

"Seriously. Those two detectives sound like complete jerks. Josie did some digging. I'm emailing you the information on the names you sent."

Annie opened up her email. "I unfortunately need her to check out one more. Tate Murphy." Her gut said it wasn't him, but at this point, she needed to explore every avenue.

Claire wrote it down while Annie scanned the notes Claire sent.

Raj Adhar: 54; mortgage broker; financially stable; married twice, both divorces amicable; six parking tickets, all paid; no history of violence; belongs to several business organizations; no red flags

Bethany Rail: 64; retired secretary; married once, divorced four years ago, estranged from husband, restraining order filed against him but never served; one child; no history of violence or red flags

Ginger Bennett: 61; formerly in public relations; married three times, first husband died of unknown causes, inherited substantial amount of money, donated a large chunk of it to various charities; three children—two sons, one daughter, three grandchildren; former beauty queen; several overextended credit card debts, but owns her home outright

Margie Tripalo: 59; retired high school sewing teacher; involved in various organizations including city council, chamber of commerce, several retired teacher associations; ran for local office four years ago, but pulled out before voting; one marriage, widowed fourteen years ago; suspected member of several radical protests against for climate change, but never charged with anything

Mira's words came back to Annie. "Even if it didn't show Bethany as squeaky clean, I met her and Gill's daughter tonight. Bethany has a broken ankle, so she's out of the running anyway. Looks like Raj should be, too."

"What about the daughter?" Claire said something to someone off camera.

"Do you have to go?" Annie felt bad for taking up her friend's time with futile searches.

"Not just yet. The daughter?"

Annie shook her head. "I don't think so. She said she's positive it's someone named Conway Leese, his business partner. I'll scroll through his social media, but she didn't have any concrete reasons for thinking it was him. Not that she shared, anyway."

Claire jotted it down. "I'll ask Josie to check him, too. We'll figure this out. What did the lawyer say?"

That meeting had gone reasonably well. "To write everything down, to not speak to them again without legal counsel. He gave me the name of someone about a half hour from here who can stand in for him until he's back, if I need. I'm sorry I'm dragging you into this."

"Are you kidding? This is setting me up with plot bunnies for months. Besides, you're my friend and the first person who reads my stories before they're ready for the world. I can't risk you going to jail. Who knows how the Wi-Fi is there?"

Annie laughed when she didn't think she could.

"Now. Onto other things. How's Dr. Hottie Pants?"

"I'm not calling him that, and neither are you."

"You're no fun."

Annie told Claire about the Ben portion of the evening.

"Sounds like the beginning of a beautiful friendship," Claire said.

Annie hoped so. Regardless of anything else, Ben was providing her a shoulder she needed now more than ever. "He's a good guy. He named the cats after Golden Girls."

Claire choked on her cocktail. "You sure he's into women?"

"Hey. His grandma loves the show. It reminds him of her."

"Okay. Statement retracted. Listen, I know you have eight thousand things on your plate, but is there any chance you could read over my last few chapters before I send them to my editor? I'd really like to get some feedback before I do."

No matter how many things she had on her plate, she always said yes to her friends. "Of course. It'll be a welcome distraction. Send now, and I'll curl up in bed with your words."

Claire gave her a naughty grin. "You might wish you weren't alone by the time you finish."

Annie laughed again, harder this time. "I'm a big girl. I know how to take care of myself."

Her friend's expression shifted, growing serious. "I hope so. Make sure you do."

Annie nodded. She'd do her best.

LUCK OR HAPPENSTANCE—OR maybe bad luck and awful karma—found Annie outside putting the garbage cans next to the road when Tate rolled in on his skateboard. With his dark hoodie over his head, his baggy pants, and the dark scowl, she could understand why first impressions of him tended not to be great.

He chin-nodded a hello to her, clearly intending to head straight into his house.

"Hey. Come here for a second," Annie called.

Tate hopped off his board, flipped it up into his hand with one kick. "What?"

Annie stopped herself from rolling her eyes. "Seriously? That's your response?"

"I didn't do anything," Tate said, his shoulders hunched.

Annie closed the gap between them. "Who said you did?"

He looked at her like she'd swallowed one too many drinks. "Everyone. Nothing happens here that I don't get blamed for."

That hardly seemed true. "I could argue against that seeing as I'm the one being blamed for killing Gill."

Tate's dark, sleepy gaze widened. "No sh—" He cut himself off.

"None. I thought you said you didn't feel comfortable sharing that picture."

Tate shifted, avoiding her gaze. "So?"

So? So!? Is this kid for real? Annie clenched her fingers. "Detectives showed up at my door asking if it was *me*."

She didn't think his gaze could get any wider, but he proved her wrong. "Listen, I didn't mean nothing. I just…I had no choice."

"Who did you share it with? Detective Rickers or Black?"

"Who?"

Annie held his gaze until she was sure he wasn't messing with her. He didn't seem to know who they were, which meant he shared with someone else. Who?

"Did you send it to the police? I'm just trying to figure out how they got it."

He shrugged, clearly hiding something. Annie felt as though she was trying to catch someone's attention over the roar of waves. A futile endeavor.

"Tate? Everything okay, son?"

An older man with an oxygen tank on a roller ambled out onto the porch. He looked winded, even with the machine.

Tate's demeanor changed immediately. Softened. His expression filled with concern. "Pops. What are you doing up?"

The man started to cough, then held up a hand. "I'm fine. Can't spend my life in bed. What are you doing there? Who is that?"

Tate shot her a pleading glare, but she didn't know for sure what he was asking. "This is Annie. Our new neighbor. Annie, that's my pops, Bob."

Bob waved. "Nice to meet you, dear. You settled in okay?"

"Nice to meet you, too, and yes. Tate brought me the muffins the other day. I was just thanking him again."

Bob nodded, moved backward into the house as his gravelly voice called out to Tate. "Time to come in, son."

Tate shot Annie another look she couldn't decipher. "Look, I didn't do anything to get you in trouble. I know what it's like to be blamed for something you didn't do. I wouldn't play that game with someone else. I gotta go."

She watched him walk away, sure of only two things: His grandfather was off any possible suspect list, and Tate Murphy was hiding something.

Chapter Twenty-Five

A NNIE WAS DETERMINED to put murder out of her mind and get to know her new hometown. The funeral was the day after tomorrow, and she wanted this chunk of time to feel like herself again. Unless the police showed up again, the murder didn't exist. Today, she was just a girl who'd moved to town almost two weeks ago and had yet to find all ten coffeehouses.

Heading out from the gated complex, she was grateful she didn't have to stop and chat with any neighbors. The perks of having a work from home job when others didn't. Losing her laptop for a couple of days hadn't put her behind.

If anything, she just became more in demand. Vivian's boss, a nightclub owner where she did publicity and marketing, wanted to hire Annie for some rebranding. She'd enjoyed her conversation with Vivian that morning. She'd caught her friend up on all the events of late and realized she knew more neighbors here than she ever had in Portland.

The main road outside the gated complex was busier than a lot of other areas in town due to its beach access. Annie took the sidewalk that wove a path parallel to the ocean. She could see people down in the sand flying kites and chatting with others. No one was in the water that she could see, but there were boats dotting the blue. After looking at a map, she knew if she took the first side street, she'd be able to wander down to the marina. Not today. Today she'd find the coffee shops, visit the bookshop, and get her bearings.

Annie loved living in Portland. With the bookstores, the restaurants, and easy access to everything, she'd felt very connected. The seagulls squawked overhead, dive bombing creatures she couldn't see. It surprised her that she felt connected here as well. In a completely different way. Stopping at the crosswalk, she took in the scenery. The Marina diner was just down to her left. Spotting an aging sandwich board sign just past the diner, she grinned when she read the words: MARINA COFFEE. *One.* She knew if she kept going, she'd hit the high school, elementary school, and Gill's dealership.

No thoughts of Gill. The light brought the traffic to a stop, so Annie could cross. The people in the cars waved and smiled, so she returned the gesture, giggling a little to herself. Small towns were a bit weird. But she could get used to weird. Portland had its share.

The other side of the street had a few houses that probably got tired of the traffic in the area. She was grateful her parents' home was not only gated but set back from the road, unlike the ones that faced the street.

Going from memory, she made her way to Center Street. Seeing the row of shops was exciting. She planned to check out each of them thoroughly, though maybe not all today. Wondering if the street came alive at lunch hour when people had a break, she waved to an older couple walking a large dog as she passed.

Shelby and her babies had been in good spirits this morning. Well, the kittens had been *loud*. They might not be able to see just yet, but they had no problem getting to the spot they wanted, even if it meant climbing over another's head. Would Mira want them all at Gill's house as soon as they could be moved?

No Gill. Harder than she thought. Annie passed a real estate office that was closed; a small clothing boutique that was open; and stopped outside Tiny Trinkets, which appeared to be a souvenir shop. From where she stood, she could see Just Coffee.

That one, the Marina, Cuppa, and the Perfect Cup. *Four out of ten. Almost halfway there.* The bookstore, What to Read, with its window display of new releases beckoned her in. She didn't need much of a nudge.

Opening the door, she smiled at the little jingle that announced her arrival. A counter with computer tills sat in the center, surrounded by tables and book racks taking up most of the floor space. Along each of the three walls—the fourth one being the entrance and a wall of windows that displayed more books—the shelves were lined from ceiling to wood floor with books. For a small store, it was well stocked. Annie decided to start from the outside left and work her way in.

"Welcome to What to Read," a woman said behind her.

Annie startled, turned and pressed a hand to her chest. "Oh, I didn't see you there."

The woman had short blond hair and a cherub-style face with rounded cheeks. Annie was terrible at guessing ages, but she figured they were in the same range. "My bad. I was grabbing more bags from underneath. I'm Kasey. Let me know if I can help you find anything."

Annie nodded, grateful she didn't get the expected, *Are you new around here?*

The first wall held biographies, memoirs, and history books. Moving along, feeling the contentment slip over her like a glove, she reached the back wall. New releases, staff picks, and award winners. Annie spent some time in that section before moving to the final wall, which was romance and mystery, her go-to genres. She picked up Candace Havens's newest book in the Ainsley McGregor series. Annie didn't usually need a reason to buy new books, but if anyone deserved a break from real life, she did.

"That's a great one," Kasey said, joining her at the wall to shelve the books in her arms.

After chatting about the series for a few minutes, Annie picked up a couple of other books and headed to the checkout.

It wasn't even quite dinnertime, but her stomach grumbled. Her culinary choices in direct sight included the bakery or a sandwich shop, but her heart was set on Cuppa, so her stomach would have to endure a bit of a walk.

Cuppa was fairly busy. Almost all of the chairs were taken, but there were a couple free stools at the counter. Annie slipped onto one, setting her purse and bag in front of her.

When Ashley looked her way and said, "Be right there," Annie smiled and waved.

Ashley did not. She continued making the order she was working on, passed it to the customer without a smile, and then came to Annie. "What can I get you?"

Annie was caught off guard by the abrupt greeting. "I'll have a London Fog and a cinnamon apple muffin. Are you okay?"

She narrowed her gaze. "I'm fine. Why?"

It clicked then. Annie laughed. "You're Stephanie."

The woman looked at her like she was a few cards short of full deck. "I know."

Annie laughed again. "I'm sorry. I met your sister the other day. She was really nice and invited me to a games night this weekend."

Stephanie's smile finally made an appearance. "That makes more sense. Ash is the friendly one. Everyone says I have resting bit—"

"Annie!" Ashley came out from the swinging door that separated the work and kitchen areas.

"Nice to meet you, Annie. I'll grab your order," Stephanie said, tapping her hand on the counter.

"How are you?" Ashley asked when she reached the counter.

"I'm good. I think I just creeped your sister out though. I thought she was you."

Ashley laughed. "Trust me, there's no way to count how many times that's happened. Steph, you have her order?"

"On it, social butterfly." Stephanie winked at her sister.

"You guys are a lot busier than many of the shops I've passed today," Annie said.

Ashley leaned on the counter. "We're off the main strip, which locals like. Especially as the tourist season picks up."

Someone approached the counter, pulling Ashley's attention. "I have to help. You coming Saturday?"

"I am. Looking forward to it."

Ashley started walking toward the customer but turned back. "You coming alone?"

Now why on earth were her cheeks getting hot? "With a friend."

Ashley's snort of laughter caught the attention of others, and Annie knew she resembled a Maine lobster at the moment. "Guess who her friend is, Steph?"

Steph brought over Annie's order, set it in front of her. "Hmm. Let's see."

"Ben," Ashley said, not giving her sister any time.

Stephanie's gaze widened. "Uh-oh. That should make Chrissy take the train straight to Crazy Town."

Annie groaned. She wanted to drop her head to the counter, but she focused on her drink instead.

While she ate her muffin, sipped her tea, she got filled in by Ashley and her sister about the women who were crazy about the "Triple Threat Trio." According to the sisters, this was the name assigned to their older brother, Levi; Ben; and Ryan. All three had been popular in high school and returned to the small town successful, single, and sexier. A triple threat.

When the sisters got busy, Annie's brain did what it always did—wandered. What had Gill been like in high school? Was he a charmer? Did he have friends? Grow up in Rainbow Falls? Could someone from his past have wanted him dead?

"What are you doing tonight?" Ashley asked, pulling her out of her thoughts.

Annie smiled, realizing she'd totally zoned out. "Reading." She lifted the bookstore bag.

Ashley glanced at her sister, who gave a subtle nod. Leaning across the counter, the barista whispered, "Stick around."

Annie laughed. "Why? Am I being initiated?"

Ashley's grin was too wide. "Sort of. We like you. You're good people, and you need a break from all this murder stuff."

Brows pushing together, Annie stared, trying to figure out of the woman was messing with her. "Thank you? I like you, too."

"We have a special meeting on Thursday nights. It's fun. I think you'll enjoy it."

Annie wondered if she was supposed to agree without learning details. "Is it legal?"

Stephanie snorted with laughter behind them. "She should definitely come."

"What is it?"

"You'll see. You love to read, so you'll fit right in. It's our version of a girl's night."

Annie checked her phone. The shop closed in twenty minutes. She didn't have other plans. And truthfully, what other trouble could befall her? She'd kind of hit the mother-lode of bad luck this week. Whatever the sisters had planned might be fun. Plus, she needed some friends.

"Will I be sorry?"

Ashley grinned. "You'll see."

Chapter Twenty-Six

ANNIE DIDN'T OFTEN lie to herself, so she admitted to the nerves bubbling up as Ashley and her sister set out snacks, closed the blinds on the front windows, and then disappeared into the back.

If she was being initiated into something dark or twisty, at least there were snacks. She sipped the iced tea Ashley left, listening to the voices coming from the kitchen.

She stood. *Right. Because that'll save you. No one ever gets in trouble standing up.* What was the big secret? Why hadn't she pushed to find out what it was she was sticking around for tonight?

Ashley grinned—she'd tucked her hair up in a messy bun, so Annie knew it was her. She walked to the front of the store, followed by Steph and...*Margie.* Another woman came behind them. Ben's grandma. What the actual heck was happening? Images of weird ceremonies, chants, and that scene from *The Proposal* with Betty White dancing around a fire came to mind.

"Come sit," Ashley said.

The women sat around the long rectangular table teens

seemed to prefer. The snacks and drinks sat in front of them as they all settled in. Annie tapped her fingers against the table.

"I'm so excited you're joining us. This is an exclusive club, you know," Margie said.

Ben's grandmother smiled at her so warmly, some of her nerves faded. "I'm still not sure what we're doing."

"Technically, we're a book-slash-wine club," Ashley explained. "We have a couple more members, but they're busy tonight. Basically, we read books and, if we're feeling frisky, try to emulate them."

"Fan fiction?" Annie asked. Nerves returned, making her fidget with a napkin. She picked up her drink, sipping slow as a distraction.

"Oh, I love that term," Margie said. "It works. This week we read a new one by our favorite erotic writer."

Annie swallowed the iced tea wrong and started to choke. Her eyes watered.

"You're not one of those prudish city girls are you?" Margie thumped a hand on Annie's back.

Annie shook her head, her eyes continuing to water.

Desiree patted Annie's hand. "Now, Margie. Don't be judgmental. Girls, you should have explained to Annie what tonight was all about."

Clearing her throat, she tried to smile. "I think I'm figuring it out."

Stephanie shot Ashley a frustrated glance. "You didn't

tell her the details?"

Ashley looked contrite, folding her hands on the table. "Sorry. I wasn't trying to trick you. I really do think you'd enjoy this club. You don't have to do the fan fiction or even read any of ours. But when we put our minds together, we're pretty awesome at weaving a story." She glanced at Steph who nodded again, before fixing her gaze on Annie. "We want to help you figure out who killed Gill. Like the Women's Murder Club but different."

"Oh. I did love that series by James Patterson. We could be The Women's Sleuth Club. The Bookish Sleuths. The Undercover Murder Club. The Wine Sleuths—"

Desiree cut Margie off with a laugh. "That one won't incite too much faith in us."

"The Undercover Murder Club sounds as if we're the killers." Stephanie picked up a dessert square, broke off a piece, and popped it into her mouth. Annie's lips twitched.

Margie picked up her wine and drank down half the glass. "Best way to inspire faith is to catch the killer. Which is why none of us have any faith in Tweedledee and Tweedledum."

At this point, Annie honestly couldn't say if those were the woman's nicknames for the detectives or if she was really referring to the *Alice in Wonderland* characters. Annie was Alice. This was another dimension, complete with food and drink, quirky sidekicks, and a whole lot of feeling like she was upside down.

"So? You in? Can we help you? Nothing ever happens in this town. You're the catalyst. Let's figure this out together." Stephanie crossed her arms over her chest.

Catalyst? That didn't sound great. Neither did working alone. Annie picked up her wine, took a fortifying sip. "Sure. It can't possibly make things worse."

Margie and Desiree clapped in unison. Margie asked, "What will we call ourselves?"

"What about Undercover Sleuths?" Steph asked.

Annie left it to them to decide the name. She felt equal twinges of amusement and affection for all of them.

In the closed café, the lights low, Annie felt like she was telling campfire stories to girlfriends as she told them everything she knew. Except for the nagging worry that Margie recognized whoever was in Tate's photo, she filled them in. The problem with letting people in was they each had their own opinion.

"I'm in shock about Ginger. I can't imagine her and Gill getting it on," Margie said.

"Could you maybe never say those words again?" Stephanie asked, making Ashley snort some of her wine through her nose, which made Annie and Des laugh.

They were talking about murder, yet somehow, Annie felt lighter than she had in a while. These women were strong, funny, and independent. Annie really, really liked them. She liked this town. The only downside so far was someone she knew—possibly someone in this room—was a killer. She was certain it wasn't someone from Gill's past. Something current had come to a head, pushed things forward, and someone in Gill's present-day circle had snapped.

"This took strength," Desiree said quietly. She was the most reserved of the group by far, but she wasn't afraid to share her opinion.

"Which makes me think Tate. But that's so hard to imagine," Ashley said. Her lips puckered up in thought.

"I don't think we're ever ready to imagine a murderer among us." Stephanie topped up the wine glasses.

"Definitely not," Annie agreed. For her, it sucked, but for these people, it was likely someone they'd known for a long time was to blame. It could be a friend of theirs if it was Mira or Bethany. Ginger didn't seem to have as many friends, but they all seemed connected in some way.

Ashley got up, went behind the counter. Annie figured she was grabbing more snacks—not that they needed them—when she came back with a chalkboard sandwich sign.

She set it up on one of the tables, used pink chalk to put Gill's name in the center. In blue, she wrote their suspects.

"Make sure you erase that before writing up tomorrow's specials," Stephanie said.

Annie laughed. The sisters might look identical, but Stephanie was the sarcasm to balance Ashley's sweetness.

"Money, sex, and power. That's what it's all about. Put a

little line to each person from Gill, Ashley," Margie said. "We'll put an *M*, *S*, or *P* beside a possible motive."

It was easy to get swept up in the evening like she would a night out with friends. If she stopped thinking about the fact that this was *real*, she could look at it differently.

"It's possible it's someone we haven't thought of," Annie said, getting up to add Conway Leese's' name to the board.

Stephanie put her feet up on one of the chairs, crossing them at the ankles. "Conway is a nice guy. He's obsessed with Mira. Maybe they're in it together?"

Ashley sent her sister a hard look. "Mira wouldn't hurt her dad."

"I know you like to think there's goodness inside every-one, A, but the truth is there's darkness, too." Stephanie's words were soft, but her meaning was clear. She didn't think anyone was exempt from being a suspect. Including Margie or Joseph. Would Margie kill for him? Would he do the same for her?

Annie wondered what the woman thought of her. Surely, if people thought she was the killer, they wouldn't have pulled her into the fold like this? Unless this was their way of seeing if she *was* the killer.

Putting the chalk down, Annie let out a deep sigh. "We're going in circles now. I think we should call it a night." She didn't like where her thoughts were taking her.

"Are you okay, dear?" Desiree stood up, started gathering plates.

"I'm just tired. I want this to be over. Thank you for this. It means a lot to know all of you have faith in me, that you believe I wouldn't do something like this."

She let the words lie there like one of Steph's desserts, tempting them to take a bite. To show their hands.

"Of course we know you didn't do it. Now, if you'd known him as long as any of us, you might have had a reason, but this just doesn't make sense. We can't leave it up to those two detectives. We'll figure this out, Annie. Don't you worry." Margie moved to Annie's side and patted her arm.

Despite her neighbor's assurances, she knew worry would be her constant companion until they found the truth.

Chapter Twenty-Seven

ANNIE TWEAKED THE design she had up on her screen. A new rock-climbing company had hired her to create their logo and do all of the branding. It was a fun challenge to create just the right look for a brand-new company.

She pulled up her blog, her fingers hesitating over the keyboard. Taking a deep breath, she started typing.

> It is with great regret that I've decided to postpone my turn for the Evening of Murder. I've reached out to Jamilla, who ran our fantastic For the Love of Murder in February. She's going to pick up where I left off. Personal reasons are pulling me out of this one, and for that, I apologize.

She added a few details, ignoring the pang of regret. When she pressed Post, she felt like a feather tied to a rock. Something light weighted down by something she couldn't shake. This was for the best. There'd be other events. When she wasn't a suspect herself.

Giving herself a short break, she went to check the cats. Not for the first time, she wondered if she should bring them indoors. The way the kittens slept on top of each other, a tangle of paws and fur, made her smile. Shelby lifted her head when Annie crouched down.

Annie took a minute to stare, then said quietly to the cat, "You did really good."

Shelby made a small murmur of agreement. Standing, Annie pulled her phone out to text Ben, to ask about moving them. Before she pulled up her text messages, her phone rang.

Sliding a hand over her screen when she saw her mom's number, she reminded herself to play it cool. They had absolutely no need to find out about Gill's death.

As the connection froze a second, she realized she'd actually managed a mental break from thinking about it all day. Once she got done with this call, she'd go back to it.

Her mother's face flashed on the screen. "There you are."

"Hi, Mom," Annie said, overcome with emotion she tried to keep in check. They were clearly docked somewhere. Annie saw the wall of a building, heard the clatter of dinnerware and voices. She glanced at the cats once more before leaving the garage and heading into the house.

"Annie, are you okay?" Her father pressed his cheek to her mother's so they could share the screen.

If they'd just move it back a bit, they wouldn't have to smoosh.

"Of course. I miss you guys."

"Not for long," her father said. "We're coming home."

"What?" Annie didn't mean to shout the word.

"The police phoned us. They said you're wanted for murder. What on earth is going on?" Tears dotted her mother's cheeks.

Annie groaned. So much for not telling them.

After grabbing a can of cola and getting settled in the deep cushioned chair in their living room, Annie walked her parents through the events of the last two weeks, consistently steering them away from the topic they both wanted to discuss. Every time they veered back to Gill, she assured them the police were about as capable of solving the mystery as Shelby. When they asked who Shelby was, Annie took satisfaction in knowing they hadn't just moved the cat in without saying a word.

"So, we have Gill's cat and kittens living in our garage, his daughter is next door, and he's dead. My word, honey, I think you've drummed up more drama in two weeks than the town has seen in the last decade." Her father's voice was somewhere between amused and stressed.

"It's not my fault, Dad. But while we're on the topic of me living here, it would have been nice to know I was immediately being signed up for muffin duty, coffee shop visits, and prescription detail."

"It's good for you, sweetie. Gets you socializing more. Besides, you took over our home—it makes sense," her mother said. "Of course, if you don't want to do any of those things, all you need to do is talk to Margie."

Annie started to respond with her thoughts on how well

that would go over with the captain of their complex when she had a thought. Her parents would know details about each of their neighbors.

"Any chance you think Margie or any of the others have enough of a temper to get rid of Gill?"

Her mother's small gasp made her wince. She didn't mean to throw it out there like that. "Sorry, Mom."

"You think someone in the complex did this?" Her father's skepticism was loud and clear despite what sounded like a party atmosphere in the background.

"I don't, Dad. I just know it wasn't me. Everyone has their secrets. Ginger says they were sleeping together, Margie showed up out of nowhere, and Raj couldn't say the man's name without fuming."

"None of those things make someone a murderer." Her dad wasn't wrong.

"I think you should leave the detecting to the detectives, Annie. This isn't a game or one of those shows you love. This could be quite dangerous."

She hadn't even told her mother she was digging. "I have my doubts about the detectives' ability to…detect. I'm just thinking about the puzzle piece of it all to keep my mind busy and off of thoughts of the actual body."

"I'm so sorry you had to see something like that, honey." Her dad's tough voice came across emotional.

She really missed them. But not enough for them to come home. "You guys can't come home. We had a deal. I don't have anywhere to live."

"But you need us," her mother countered.

"Always. But that doesn't mean you need to come home. Please. I promise I'll contact you if I need you."

She waited, biting her bottom lip, knowing that whatever choice they made, they wouldn't necessarily be swayed by her.

"Fine. As long as you *promise*." Her dad's tone softened.

A promise meant something in their house. It should always mean something, but in a fast-paced, technological world where options were constantly evolving or changing, they didn't always get seen through. Annie never said *promise* if she thought she couldn't meet the obligation.

They talked for a few more minutes before Annie said goodbye. She tried returning to her work, but there was too much energy coursing through her.

Deciding fresh air could cure all, Annie left the house, ready to explore a different piece of town. She wanted to see where Ben worked. He might be the only person she could run her Margie-and-Joseph worries by. Margie was always in the right place at the exact right moment. And her face when she'd seen the photo? Surely Ben caught that.

She also wanted to bring him a thank-you for all of the help and support he'd given her since she arrived. Deciding nothing said thanks better than delicious food, she stopped at the bakery she'd passed over the day before.

More than Cake was an adorable store that reminded

Annie of something from another era. The décor could have been inspired by the malt shops of the fifties. The wide windows were filled with a delicious collection of display desserts. She wasn't sure if those ones were edible or for show, but she certainly hoped they sold what she saw there. She wanted one of each.

She pushed open the brightly painted red door to be greeted with a plethora of delicious scents. Vanilla, cinnamon, and chocolate were the strongest.

"Welcome to More than Cake," a short, pleasant-looking woman said. She wore her gray hair in a bun. Her rounded face showed the lines of a life well lived and enjoyed. "I'm Hazel. I own and run the place. What's your name?"

Smiling, Annie reached out her hand as Hazel came around the long display case counter. "Annie Abbott."

"Ahh, yes. You're John and Amanda's girl. They were so excited about that trip. Are they doing well? Have you heard from them? I can't imagine living at sea for a year. Of course, I've never been outside Rainbow Falls, so that's not saying much. Terrible thing with Gill. Are you holding up okay, dear?"

Trying not to show her surprise at the onslaught of words, Annie nodded. "They're doing well, and yes, I'm okay. I just hope they find whoever killed him sooner rather than later."

Hazel smoothed down her red-and-white apron. "That might take some time. Especially if they're making a list of people who didn't like that man. He was some kind of mean—I'll tell you that. Not like his business partner. There's a good man. How those two came to work together is beyond my imagination."

Huh. Annie wondered how well Hazel knew Conway. Mira seemed pretty certain her dad's business partner was not worthy of Hazel's praise. "I've never met Mr. Leese. I heard about him from Gill's daughter."

"Oh. That poor girl. I should take some goodies to her and her mom. They must be hurting something awful. Doesn't matter what we all thought, he mattered to them. Look at me rambling like I've never had a customer before. What can I get you, Annie?"

She went back behind the counter, giving Annie a few minutes to decide. The display case was full of cream-filled delights; old-fashioned donuts; ginormous cookies; and, of course, cupcakes. The tartlets caught her gaze, but she didn't know what Ben liked. She ended up going with what Hazel called the Rainbow Assortment Pack.

"The funeral is tomorrow. I'm wondering who they have catering it. I thought Bethany might ask me to, but I know she's hurt. She may not be taking care of things for the service or the wake, but I sure hope it isn't all falling on Mira. She's had enough heartache, that one."

Annie left the adorable shop with a bag full of goodness and a head full of questions. Hazel had made her wonder so many things. At the top of the list was Mira's heartache.

What was that all about? More importantly, did it have anything to do with a fallout Gill had mentioned? That had to be who he was referring to when he said Bethany had poisoned her thinking.

"I'll bring her something tonight and see if she needs anything," Annie muttered to herself. She couldn't imagine what the young woman was going through.

Chapter Twenty-Eight

ANNIE STROLLED THROUGH town, finding herself at Ben's grandparents' place on the edge of town—almost at the beginning of it, really. She saw the coffee shop she'd seen that first morning. She'd try it another day. The McIntyre property was the last on the street and quite large. A large, old-style farmhouse sat on a slightly raised hill. The green lawn was perfectly manicured. It looked like a storybook version of a homestead. Large trees dotted the property, offering the kind of shade that would be perfect on a sunny day. The wraparound porch with an actual wooden swing hanging from the rafters was enviable. She could imagine reading or writing on that very spot.

An old weather vane sat on top of the house, turning softly. Perhaps they'd get some rain. She couldn't wait to watch the ocean in a storm. To the right of the house was a detached rectangular building with its own little porch. A rustic-looking wooden sign read MCINTYRE VETERINARY CLINIC. On the porch, two dogs lay side by side, both black, white, and brown in coloring with very floppy ears. They lifted their heads, looking sort of like animal versions of grumpy old men. One of them huffed a sound that might have been a bark, but there was no energy behind it. They both lowered their heads again.

"Clearly, you two aren't guard dogs," Annie said, holding a hand out for them to sniff.

The door to the clinic opened outward. A woman in high heels, a skirt, and a shimmery top stepped out, a cat in her arms. Her hair was tied up with a silky-looking white scarf, and she wore huge sunglasses. She looked like an undercover celebrity.

"I'm telling you, Benny, you don't charge enough. I insist you accept my dinner invitation. Chrissy will be there. We'll have a wonderful meal," the woman said.

Annie arched her brows when Ben's gaze met her own. She wondered if she was imagining the happiness in them when he looked her way.

"I assure you, Ms. Robins, it's unnecessary."

"I'm going to match you two up one of these days. I might have to go around you and tell your grandmother you're dodging our invite."

"Tell you what," Ben said, putting both hands in the pockets of his jeans. "If you can convince Grams to come, I'll be there."

"Done," Ms. Robins said, a wide smile on her red lips. She noticed Annie belatedly as she stepped down the first of the stairs. Dropping the frames of her glasses a tad, she eyed Annie up and down. "You're supposed to bring an animal as a cover, dear." The words were whispered in passing.

Ben waved as she got into her Lexus SUV, which Annie hadn't even noticed was parked to the side of the clinic in the small four-car lot.

"She's a treat," Annie said with a smile. "Let me guess. Chrissy's mom?"

"You're good." Ben said. He stood close enough she could smell his cologne and the scent of soap.

Annie dug her heels into the dirt so she didn't lean in and sniff him.

The dogs rallied again, lifting their heads, giving a few weak barks. Ben glanced back at them with amusement, then looked at Annie. "You've met Mac and Cheese?"

Annie snorted with laughter, which apparently excited the dogs. They roused themselves and scurried down the steps to say hello. She knelt to say a proper hello.

"Are those really their names?" The sun blocked her vision when she glanced up.

Ben crouched beside her, and their knees touched. "Of course. I don't kid about animals or my favorite foods."

Their gazes locked, Annie trying to figure out if he was messing with her. "There's no way growing up here, on *Little House on the Prairie*, your favorite food is mac and cheese." Though, looks could be deceiving. She wondered if Ben knew about his grandmother's book-slash-wine-slash-murder-solving club.

Standing, Ben held out a hand to help her up. That little

flash of *yes, please* darted through her system again. "Don't knock mac and cheese. You keep forgetting that I was away at school. Grams could only send so many care packages, you know."

When she pulled her hand back, it continued to tingle. The dogs hefted themselves back up onto the porch and collapsed with the effort. "Of course. I think you may have been a bit spoiled."

"Still am. But I appreciate it. Grams said you joined her book club?"

Annie coughed. Okay. So, he knew about part of it. Ben gave her a funny look so she tried to cover it. "Yeah. I sort of got roped in. I didn't know what I was sticking around for at first. It's, um, an eclectic group."

Ben smiled. "They like to try new things."

You have no idea, buddy.

He gestured to the building. "You want to see the clinic?"

Tipping her head back, she smiled at him. "I do. That's why I came." She held up the bag. "And this."

"That's a More than Cake bag. Are you trying to win my heart, Annie Abbott? Because the only thing better than mac and cheese is baked goods."

She laughed, deciding to leave that particular question alone. For now. "I couldn't make a choice, so there might be one of everything."

Ben opened the door of the clinic, letting Annie go first.

"Are Mac and Cheese yours?"

"No. I live over the garage here for now. I'm planning on buying my own place soon. I don't want to get an animal until I'm settled."

"That makes sense. This is adorable." She looked around the homey waiting room. A long L-shaped counter took up most of the space. Cozy chairs with dark-blue padding made another L in the left-hand corner of the square room. Magazines and books sat atop a dark wood coffee table. Pretty plants—ones Annie would most certainly over- or under-water—decorated some floating wall shelves. There were two hallways, one directly ahead and one to her right, both behind the counter area. There was a large mural on the wall behind the longer side of the counter. It showed animals of all sorts playing in a yard that resembled the one outside.

"Grams painted that," Ben said, taking the bag from her hand.

"It's beautiful."

"She's talented, for sure. Come on back."

Annie followed behind Ben. "Do you have more patients today?"

"Not for about a half hour."

"How long has Chrissy's mom been trying to pair you two up?" She hadn't meant to ask, but now it was out there.

"Since I got back. She's persistent. I'll give her that."

"People want to see their kids happy," Annie said.

There were doors along both sides of the hallway. When

they reached the end, the space opened up again. To the left was a door marked STAFF. To the right was a room, enclosed in glass from halfway up the wall to the ceiling. The operating room behind the panel was so clean it sparkled even from a distance.

"There's an overnight room through the doors there." Ben pointed to the small hallway that went past the operating room, leading to double swinging doors.

"It's much bigger than I would have guessed from the outside."

"My grandparents have added on more than once. When they first opened, it was the waiting room area and one small exam room down the hallway to the right of the door. If we went through the double doors there, we'd end up making our way back to the front."

He gestured to the staff-room door. Couches; a television; and brightly painted, beautiful art on the walls made it a welcoming room. There was a small table against the wall, a sink, fridge, and dishwasher in the far corner. Ben held out a chair for Annie at the table, then set the bag down. He grabbed plates and forks from the kitchen area and joined her as she pulled their goodie box out.

Annie opened the lid of the box to reveal the delicious treats inside.

"You really did get one of each," Ben said with a smile.

She nodded. "I wanted to thank you for everything. There's been a whole lot of everything."

He held her gaze, his smile slipping. "There really has. You're holding up remarkably well on the outside. Are you doing okay?"

What was it about someone asking if you were okay that made a person feel *not* okay? She nodded, swallowed around the lump in her throat.

When she reached for a fork, Ben took her hand. "You're not alone here, Annie."

Her lips twisted in her attempt not to cry. Finally, she said, "I know. Hence the treats. It's the least I could do."

Ben laughed. "All I did was answer the phone. Do you want to choose first?"

"No. Your treat, you choose first."

He eyed them all with more than a little longing in his gaze. "I say we split everything."

Chuckling, Annie said, "Maybe not all today. Throwing up isn't on my to-do list."

Ben winked at her, stirring feelings inside of her that she wasn't prepared to deal with. "Wimp."

As they each took half of an oversized eclair with chocolate cream overflowing from its middle, Ben pointed his fork at her. "So? While I've been working, what trouble have you found?"

"Hey. I don't find trouble."

He broke off a large chunk with his fork. "You're right. Sorry. What trouble has found you since we last spoke?"

She wanted to argue but, really, what was the point?

"I think Margie and/or Joseph are hiding something."

He listened as he chewed, making the odd tingle-inducing noise when he particularly enjoyed a sample of one of the treats.

Wiping his fingers on a napkin, he shook his head. "Joseph is a solid guy. And Margie is fantastic. They're pillars of the community. They spearhead every festival and event. I did see she went pale, but I have no idea why."

Annie leaned forward. "What if she thought she recognized the person in the photograph. What if it was Joseph and that's why she left so quick?"

"Joseph has no motive. You said yourself that motives are usually sex, money, or revenge. I just don't see it. There's got to be another explanation."

Maybe. But Annie had no idea how to figure out what that was. Instead, she filled him in on the other things she'd learned in the last two days, leaving out the part where his grandmother, her neighbor, and a couple of his life-long friends were helping her investigate Gill's death.

Chapter Twenty-Nine

T HE DRIZZLY WEATHER suited the somber mood of the funeral. Annie and Ben sat at the back of one of the rooms the funeral home offered for their services. Last night, she had gone to see if Mira needed anything, but the woman wasn't home. From where they sat, she and Ben were able to watch people arrive. Their legs touched from knee to hip, and Annie realized she was grateful not to have come alone.

He looked good in a suit, but the muted sadness in the air took away from her ability to truly admire him. Along with that sadness, there was another energy coursing through the room. She wondered if Ben felt it. If she believed in such things, she'd say it was a negative, almost angry aura.

Margie and Joseph walked in arm in arm, waving to Ben and Annie. Ginger wore one of those black hats with the netting across the face. If it had been a play, she'd clearly cast herself in the role of grieving widow even though Bethany had already been wheeled in to sit at the front of the room near the casket.

Annie was surprised to see that Gill's ex-wife was a tiny woman who looked as if she could be blown over with a strong wind. For some reason, she'd assumed whoever married Gill would have had to have had some sort of presence. But when Mira introduced Annie to her, the woman looked timid. Almost frightened. *You have no idea how she's processing the grief.* Even without the broken ankle, however, she didn't seem like she could sink a knife into a breast of chicken, never mind her ex.

Ben leaned toward her ear, his breath fanning over her skin. "Are you mentally cataloging suspects?"

Her lips quirked. "Am I that obvious?"

"Unless you're looking for a better-looking date to this thing, I can't see any other reason for your eyes to be continuously scanning."

Annie had to bite back her laugh. She lowered her chin so their conversation stayed private. "Maybe I'm just seeing how many women's gazes are shooting daggers at me for showing up with you."

Ben tapped her knee as the director of the funeral home tapped the microphone.

Annie felt a pang of guilt for enjoying sitting so close to Ben. But one thing about sitting at a funeral on a Saturday morning—it reminded people how short life really was. And how easily it could be taken away.

As the director spoke of housekeeping items, turning off cell phones and the like, a noise startled most people into turning around.

Annie watched as a man around her age stumbled

through the door, clearly inebriated. His blond hair stuck up at odd angles, and his dark suit was wrinkled, the dress shirt pulled almost entirely out of the pants on one side. Even drunk, it was easy to see he was handsome. Grabbing on to one of the pews, he steadied himself. An usher came to his side, but the guy shook him off.

"No. Leave me alone. Where's Mira?" His words were slurred.

"Who is that?" Annie whispered to Ben.

"Conway Leese."

Annie's jaw dropped. *This* was Conway? Gill's business partner? She felt like people did when they read a book, pictured a character in their head and then had that image spoiled by the movie. He looked nothing like she expected. Of course, she'd expected someone older, rounder, more jowly. Mira hurried down the aisle, her black dress elegant and ornate. A little too much, in Annie's opinion. She looked like she was in a black wedding dress.

"Mira," Conway said loudly.

Everyone was looking at them.

"You need to leave," Mira spat.

Ryan stood from where he'd been sitting a couple rows ahead of them, joining Mira.

"Hey man, let's go grab some coffee." Ryan put a hand on Conway's shoulder.

Conway pulled away. "Don't want coffee. I want Mira. That's all I ever wanted."

"This is not the time or place," Mira said, her voice cracking.

Conway's shoulders slumped so far, Annie thought he might sink to the ground. Ryan grabbed him again, holding him up.

"Please, Mira. Talk to me. Let me in. You know I'd do anything for you."

"Get out. Get out of here and out of my life." Mira turned and walked away from him.

Ryan started to walk Conway out, but the man shook him off, straightened up, almost as if Mira's words had sobered him, and walked away.

Ben sighed. Annie turned to face him as Ryan went back to his seat.

"What's wrong?" Annie asked, her gaze darting to the doors.

"I think I know you pretty well already."

She met his gaze, tension thrumming through her blood. "Why's that?"

The funeral director apologized for the interruption.

"Something tells me you're going to miss the service," Ben whispered.

One side of her lips tipped up. "Someone should check on him."

"I could do it," Ben said, his smile amused.

"You knew Gill better than me. You should stay. I'll meet you after."

He shook his head, squeezed her hand, and Annie snuck out of her row and quietly left the room.

The funeral home was two floors. She found Conway sitting on the steps up to the second. Seeing that he'd found himself a spot, she detoured to a room set up with cakes and snacks. Grabbing a cup of coffee, she brought it to the man.

He looked confused when she handed it to him.

"Hi. I'm Annie. I lived next door to Gill."

He took the coffee looking so defeated, Annie's heart clutched. She wasn't cut out for real life detecting—she felt too much. She couldn't be detached, never mind picturing any of the people she met as stone-cold killers.

"Gill. That bastard is still ruining my life," Conway said, the coffee sloshing a bit in the cup. He took a sip, then a longer one.

Annie was struck by the anger in his voice. It changed his face to one that could much more easily be viewed as lethal.

"You were his partner?"

Conway huffed out an angry laugh. "Partner in name. Really, I was his lackey. His scapegoat. All I ever wanted was to show Mira I'd do anything to be with her. That backfired, didn't it?"

She couldn't help wondering if anything including killing her father.

"Why does Mira think you killed him?" He was drunk. If she was going to dig for answers, she might as well start at the right spot.

His gaze widened. Annie braced when she saw the flash of anger. They were in a funeral home with people thirty feet away. He wasn't likely to kill her for asking.

"She thinks it's all about money. I never wanted the money. I wanted her. I've done everything I can to prove that to her. She's determined to believe that my love isn't real."

What Annie noticed, aside from this man's strong, unpleasant breath, was that he didn't deny killing his partner. He didn't sound outraged at the idea or try to defend himself.

"There's no other man who would do what I did for her, and this is how she repays me?" He stood, the coffee spilling as he set it on the stairs. "She'll be sorry for this. I'm not about to wreck my life any further just to get pushed away."

He stumbled down the stairs, and Annie hoped that he wasn't driving.

"Wait," she said, grabbing his arm. He turned like he'd forgotten she was there. "Do you need a cab?"

He pulled his arm away. "I walked. Everyone walks in this goddamn town. What's the point of having a car dealership? Especially one that Gill was sinking."

Conway stormed away, pushing the door open with both hands. It bounced off the wall outside and fluttered closed with a contrasting slowness.

Annie sat back down on the stairs. *Well. That was interesting.*

The rest of the morning passed without incident. Annie watched the interactions between Ginger and Bethany with more than a little interest. For two such good friends, there seemed to be an air of dislike or at least distrust between them.

Though she wasn't hungry, Annie nibbled on a miniature cinnamon roll while Margie, Joseph, and Ben chatted. She couldn't stop looking around, watching the way people interacted. She didn't even realize Joseph and Margie had left when Ben tapped her shoulder.

"You want to get out of here?"

Annie looked around. They'd shown up, paid their respects. There was no reason to stick around. "Yes. Let me just run to the restroom. I feel like my fingers are sticky. I'll meet you by the door."

Ben gave Annie a sweet smile. "Sugar does tend to make things sticky."

Heat flashed in his gaze, resulting in a spike in her heart rate. *So wrong time and wrong place.* "Meet you at the front."

She hurried away. When she turned the corner for the restroom, she heard quiet, angry voices.

"I'm not doing this with you right now, Joseph."

From where Annie stood, just out of sight, she could see Margie with her hands on her hips. She and Joseph were standing facing each other.

"He's gone. He was the only one blocking us from what we want."

"It's too soon, I'm telling you. It'll look suspicious."

Joseph's arms lifted and dropped in what Annie could only characterize as exasperation. She'd been there with Margie herself so she could understand Joseph's feelings.

"I've been asking you forever. Now there's nothing standing in our way and you're still making excuses. Maybe this isn't about Gill. Maybe it's that you don't love me the way I love you." He started to walk away.

Margie grabbed his hand. "That's not true, and you know it. Let's just let the dust settle."

"Fine. But with him out of the picture, nothing is stopping us but you."

"Just a little longer."

Annie watched as they embraced, her nerves bouncing like those little rubber balls she'd played with as a kid. She backed up slowly and headed for the exit.

Ben stood waiting for her with a smile. He took her hand. She didn't have time to think about that before his brows furrowed and he looked down at hers.

"Your hand is still sticky," he said with a wide grin.

Annie glanced behind her, then squeezed Ben's hand and tugged him out of the funeral home. "There's a reason for that. I'll tell you in the car."

Chapter Thirty

ANNIE WAS A little surprised by the excitement she felt looking at the kittens with their eyes open. She took a few pictures, sent them to Ben and her parents. Using the markings, she was able to identify each of them. Sherlock had one completely brown ear while the other was a blend of brown and orange. The bridge of Watson's nose had a tiny white mark that resembled a star. Blanche's tail had flecks of white, and Dorothy was solid orange.

"They're growing up," Annie said to Shelby, who stopped bathing them to look at her like she was Captain Obvious.

"I need to get Mira over here. Do you remember her? Do cats remember like dogs do? Do dogs remember?" Annie shook her head, got up off the garage floor. "What do I know? Anyway, I need to bring her over here, but how would you feel about me keeping one?"

Shelby locked her feline gaze with Annie's. There was judgment in it. Annie slipped her phone in her pocket. "I'd be a perfectly good kitty parent."

Shelby meowed loudly, making Annie point out the obvious. "You're alive, aren't you?"

Turning her attention back to the kittens, Shelby dismissed the conversation.

"You'll see," muttered Annie on the way out the garage door. Going up the stairs, she was thinking about whether to wear her jeans or a pair of capris to the games night. Ben was picking her up in a few hours. He'd been as surprised as she was about the conversation she overheard between Margie and Joseph.

She stubbed her toe, hard, at the exact moment she'd mentally chosen jeans. Cursing, Annie looked around before looking down at what she'd run into. A decent size rock, sort of the size of the one Tate had left for her last week, sat on her porch mat. She picked it up, her gaze wandering over the complex. It was mid-afternoon, no one was around. People had all gone their separate ways from the funeral home. She hadn't seen Raj there, but his car wasn't in his driveway. Margie's and Joseph's were in their respective spots, but no one was outside. She looked over at Bob and Tate's house. The curtains were all drawn.

Looking down at the rock, she saw the message written: *Keep digging before the wrong person is arrested.*

Annie's pulse skipped rapidly. She gripped the rock tightly. It barely fit in her hand. Walking down the stairs, she went to Tate's house, hesitated a moment but knocked on the door.

It took a few minutes before the door was pulled open.

Tate's granddad looked worn out. His breathing was choppy and somewhat raspy.

"Oh. Hello, dear. Can I help you?"

Crap. Cover story. She assumed Tate would answer. "Hi. I had a couple heavy boxes in the garage I need in the house, and I wondered if Tate could help me move them."

Bob looked out the doorway like the boxes would be right there, then back at Annie. "Would help you myself, but those days have passed," Bob said with a smile.

Annie smiled back but didn't know what to say. "Is Tate around?"

"You just missed him. He went out with friends. I'll tell him when he gets back."

"Okay. Thank you. Do you need anything?"

"No, dear. Thank you for asking. How was Gill's funeral?"

The rock felt heavier than it had a moment before. "It was respectful and well attended."

Bob shook his head, coughed, taking a minute to clear his throat, which made Annie wince. Did she ask if he needed a drink? Some oxygen?

"I'll tell you," Bob said around his cough. "That man was unhappy. I hated seeing him throw everything away. We were friends once."

"Oh?" What had ended the friendship?

Bob nodded, looking past Annie like he could see what used to be. "He was a good man a long time ago. Made a series of choices that flipped his life upside down." Bob's gaze came back to Annie's. "That happens to everyone. The problem for Gill was he didn't accept responsibility for any of it. Had he done that, faced his part in the ways his life went wrong, he could have turned things around. Saved his marriage, his relationship with Mira. He could have repaired so much. Imagine letting twenty years of friendship go over a few thousand dollars. Makes me sad when I think of it."

Had he owed Gill money, or the other way around? Was Tate trying to protect his pops? Was that what the note was about? *If it's even from him.* She really needed to find out more about Mira. What had caused the woman's heartbreak? Conway or her father? Both? This was becoming so convoluted, especially since she now strongly suspected Margie and Joseph of covering something up.

Heaviness clogged Annie's lungs. Gill had been an awful person. It made it easier to accept his death. But the truth was he'd also been someone's friend once. Someone's husband and father. Whoever killed him needed to be found. Annie shifted the rock into her other hand. She didn't know if it was Tate who sent the rock, but one thing was for sure: The message was right. She needed to keep digging.

But not tonight. Tonight, she was going to pretend she was just a girl with a simple life, no deadlines, and all sorts of possibilities ahead.

Chapter Thirty-One

B EN HELD THE car door open for Annie to step out. She took the hand he offered but dropped it as soon as her feet were planted on the cement.

"You okay?" He shut the door behind her.

"I am. I don't know what's wrong with me. I feel a little keyed up. I'm not walking into an inquisition about your love life here, am I?"

Ben chuckled, walked along the sidewalk beside Annie. "I'm allowed to make and have new friends, Annie."

She gave him a sideways glance. "I've been in situations before where other women didn't like me because of perceived notions."

"You intrigue me," Ben said, stopping on the sidewalk, just down from Cuppa. He stood close, facing her. He wore a plaid shirt over a white T-shirt and a pair of jeans. He looked like an ad out of *Small Town USA* with just the right amount of charm and sex appeal.

"Why's that?" She stared at the sidewalk.

"You swing back and forth between confidence and uncertainty."

Her gaze lifted. "Doesn't everyone?"

Ben shook his head. "Not necessarily. I think you do—more right now than I'd guess normally—because you feel like everyone is watching you."

She laughed. "I am the new girl."

"You've already made a good impression on people." Ben watched her closely.

"Maybe. But it feels dependent on the choices I make going forward. Do I keep digging, Ben?"

He didn't seem to move, but he *felt* closer. Taking her hand in his, he bent his knees so they were eye level. "You don't have to do anything you don't want to. I think we should tell Ryan about the rock."

Annie's jaw tightened. "I'd feel better if I talked to Tate first."

Ben pulled his hand back, ran it through his hair. "The kid has a history of unpredictability. I know Ryan's spent some time with him, but he doesn't say much. Like everything else in this place, most of what I know is based on one part truth and ten parts gossip."

Something caught her gaze just over Ben's shoulder. "I think we're adding to the gossip part right this minute."

Ben looked back over his shoulder. Chrissy and another girl were going into Cuppa. It was obvious where Chrissy's attention lay. Ben lifted his hand, then turned back to Annie.

"How about we forget gossip, murder, and everything else unpleasant and just have fun?"

She took a deep breath. "That sounds like an excellent idea. But if Chrissy offers me food or drink, I'm not taking it."

Ben laughed, moved to Annie's side so they could head toward the shop. "I like a woman who knows how to watch her own back."

As they entered the coffee shop, Annie noted the different feel. It was more crowded than she'd seen it with customers, but because the people here were all friends, it felt more relaxed. Just a night with friends. Her gaze caught Chrissy's. *Friends and a few dirty looks.* She could handle that.

Ashley came over. Annie knew it was her because she grinned and greeted her right away. "I'm so glad you came. Hey, Ben. You ready to lose?"

Ben rolled his eyes, then glanced at Annie. "I'd say Ash is a poor loser, but the truth is she's a poor winner, too."

Ashley slapped Ben's arm in a playful way. "Like you're one to talk. I believe you're still the reigning champion of rage quitting."

Annie's brows went all the way up. She stepped away from Ben dramatically. "Uh-oh. Something I should know?"

Ryan showed up with a tall glass of something dark with ice. "Don't worry, Annie. I'll keep him in line."

She noticed how close Ryan, in jeans and a T-shirt, stood to Ashley. She also noticed the way Ashley's gaze was drawn to him.

Tucking her smile away, Annie looked at Ben. "Why doesn't that comfort me?"

Ben slapped Ryan on the shoulder. "Looks like she's got your number already."

Ashley pulled her toward the counter to get her a drink. Apparently, Long Island Iced Teas were the drink of the night. Steph made Annie one, and although it wasn't her beverage of choice, she wasn't driving so she said yes.

Doing her best not to glance over her shoulder, Annie wondered if Chrissy was giving her death glares. As if Ashley could read her thoughts, her new friend leaned toward her.

"Chrissy doesn't usually show. She came with Steph's friend. I'd bet money she heard you were coming."

Annie sipped her drink, keeping her head down. "I'm not looking to cause drama."

Ashley stood close enough to nudge her hip. "Come on. Where's the fun in that? It's time she realizes high school is over, life moved on, and she's not the Belle of the Ball anymore."

Annie turned toward Ashley. "Hard feelings between you two?"

Ashley frowned. "Long story."

"I'm not going anywhere," Annie said with a smile. Not for at least a year.

"Let's have lunch next week. We're closed on Sundays."

Annie smiled. Despite everything else swirling like a twister around her, this was what she was looking for. What she craved. People. Friends. Ashley seemed like a perfect start. Well, Ashley and Ben, but she didn't have any conflicting feelings for Ashley.

"That sounds great. Come to my place. I'll make you lunch."

Ashley straightened, turned. "I'm in."

"Okay," Stephanie said, standing on a stool so she was a bit taller than her already tall stature. "Here's how tonight works. We draw numbers, you get your number and go to the assigned table. Every game has a minimum of two players, maximum of four. The winner from each game will compete in a four-person game. There's lots to eat, be good sports, refill your own drinks, and if anyone beats my sister, please brag loudly."

"Hey!" Ashley wadded a napkin up, tossed it at Steph, making everyone laugh. She looked at Annie with a sheepish expression. "You lose your temper one time."

Ben appeared at her side, pretended to cough into his hand. "Every time." The words were mumbled around the cough but clear enough to make Annie smile.

"I'm not sure I'm cut out for this cutthroat world. Isn't it just card and dice games?"

Ben gave her a mock glare. "There's no *just*, Annie. You need to take this seriously because when I win, I'm going to need you to praise me the whole ride home."

"I could do that without the games," Chrissy said, coming up to Ben's side, putting her hands on his arm.

Annie bit her lip, felt Ashley's hand on her shoulder. "Let's grab our numbers."

Ben shot Annie a *don't leave* look, but she just waved and smiled, leaving Ben to his own devices. And Chrissy.

"That was a little mean," she whispered to Ashley.

"I love Ben like a brother, but the man needs a backbone. He hasn't been interested in her since high school. It's time he told her. And her mother."

Since Annie wasn't stepping on someone else's territory—*ever*—she couldn't help but agree. Right now, she and Ben were friends. If it went somewhere else, he needed to make sure he didn't have a bunch of women pining away for him thinking they had a shot.

Luck, or maybe a bit of twin trickery, paired Annie with Ashley for the first game. It was a card game she hadn't played before. There were two groups of two, two groups of four. The groups of four were playing board games. Ben was paired up with his friend Levi—the twins' brother, Chrissy, and the woman she'd come with. Steph was paired with a friend of Levi's and two other women. Ryan was at the table next to Annie and Ashley, also playing a two-person card game with a woman named Taylor. Annie wondered if the groupings changed each week.

After giving a few moments to go over the rules at each table, a timer was set and the games started. Annie had no idea what she was doing, but Ashley took pity on her and walked her through several of her mistakes. There were nine rounds of the game they were playing. Someone had clearly given serious thought to which games and activities could be played because the timing worked perfectly. Ryan and Annie lost at exactly the same time.

Ashley slapped her cards on the table. "Sorry, newbie. No beginner's luck for you."

"No wonder people don't come back," Steph said from her table. She laughed around the words.

Ashley ducked her head, glanced at Annie. "Sorry. I really am a poor winner. But I'm still fun. I promise."

Annie could only laugh. She didn't have much of a competitive streak, and she had fun even with the losing. There was a ten-minute break between the games once everyone's first game was done. The final game was set up in the middle. Annie could almost see the gears turning in Chrissy's head. She'd miscalculated in her win because now Ben was back beside Annie as they took a seat on the high back chairs set up at the back of the store. Levi introduced himself and sat across from them, a beer in hand. A few others joined them while Ashley, Chrissy, Levi's friend, and Taylor took the center table for the playoff.

Annie sank back against her seat, lifting her cola to her lips. She'd switched after one. "This is very serious."

Ryan nodded, grabbing a handful of chips from the table in front of them. "Ashley's always been this way. She did track when we were in high school, and the coach had to teach her how to win graciously."

"To be fair to my sister, she smoked every opponent. It's hard not to get a big head when you're that good," Levi said.

Steph leaned in to grab a couple chips. "You say that because you're the same. I spent my time baking, and those two spent it competing over absolutely everything."

"You have any siblings, Annie?" Levi asked.

She shook her head.

"Lucky," Levi and Stephanie said at the same minute before laughing. It was easy to see that these people, not just the siblings, had a great rapport and bond.

Annie was close to Vivian, but she'd only kept in touch with high school friends on Facebook, and even then, it was more because it seemed rude to deny a friend request.

She couldn't imagine growing up in one little town and living there her whole life, although she didn't miss the big city like she'd thought she would.

She listened to them tell stories about high school and college. They moved their way up the years, talking about what they all did now. She'd never had this—the ease of old friendships and knowing people from the time she was young. It felt like something she wanted to be part of. Especially when Ben's hand quietly slid over hers, linking their fingers.

The moment snapped when Ryan called her name. His tone was enough to make her body tense.

"What's up, man?" Ben said, his tone serious.

"Tate got arrested for the murder of Gill."

Annie sucked in a sharp breath, staring up at Ryan, whose gaze burned into her own.

"I was his one phone call, but he asked me to bring you with me to the station."

She pointed at her chest. "Me? Why?"

Ryan fixed her with a hard glare. "That's what you'll explain to me on the drive there."

Chapter Thirty-Two

ANNIE'S NERVES FELT like livewires snapping to attention all along her skin.

Ryan frowned down at her as they walked into the station. "You look like you're walking to the gallows."

Annie narrowed her gaze. "Not exactly my favorite place. Last time wasn't fun."

"Well, this time, you're not on your own. They better have a damn good reason for holding Tate."

Annie put a hand on his arm when she saw the way his fingers clenched. "I don't get it. Why did he call you?"

Ryan stopped just before they reached the counter where she could see Detective Rickers watching them.

He turned so they had a semblance of privacy. "We'll get into it after we get out of here, but I have a feeling we need to start working together."

Annie gave a humorless laugh. "Just so you know, figuring out the killer on paper is a lot easier than in real life." She should have shown him the photo. If Tate phoned him for help, it was probably Ryan he showed. But why? He didn't seem to trust adults so why a cop?

"Did you two want a room for privacy? We have some in the back," Detective Rickers called out.

Under her breath, Annie asked Ryan, "Can I get arrested for telling him how much I dislike him?"

Ryan laughed. "No. But I'd advise against it." He nudged her toward the gate Rickers had swung open for them to pass through.

Rickers smirked. "Aren't you two cozy?"

Ryan nudged Annie with his arm before she could give the response she wanted. Instead, she smiled at the detective as if he was her favorite person in the world.

"Did you get your hair cut?"

He eyed her suspiciously. "No."

"Hmm. Looks like you did. You look great. Almost…smarter."

Ryan covered a laugh with a harsh cough. "Annie. I'd like to leave here with both you and Tate. Don't make that more difficult."

Detective Rickers glared at her. "Listen to your pal."

She sealed her lips shut and followed Rickers to the same room she'd been in once before.

He hadn't shut the door before Ryan asked, "Where's Tate?"

"With my partner." Rickers held Ryan's hard glare, neither of them flinching.

"Does he have a lawyer?"

Rickers smiled, took a seat. Annie stood on the other side

of the table watching Ryan.

"Seems his public defender is running a little late." Rickers leaned back in his seat.

"Is this how you run things in Trenton? Skirt the rules? Pick on women and children who have nothing to do with the actual crime?"

"You seem awfully invested in our young friend." Rickers looked at Annie. "Have a seat. Why don't you tell me why Tate was so interested in talking to you."

"I'm not telling you anything without a lawyer present."

Ryan came over, grabbed the chair, and sat down. He leaned his forearms on the table. Annie's heart rate hiccupped. This felt like one of those good guy-bad guy moments in the movies right before chairs went flying.

"What do you have on Tate?"

"Seems he sent our friend a message tonight," Rickers said, staring at Annie.

Ryan looked her way. "Annie?"

She sank down into the chair, focusing only on Ryan. "Ben and I were going to talk to you after I talked to Tate. He had a picture on his phone that he showed me a week or so ago. Someone leaving Gill's house. He got my attention by leaving a rock with a message on it. Today, I stubbed my toe on another rock with a new message, but I wasn't positive it was from him."

"You didn't think to tell the police about clandestine meetings with a teenager, Ms. Abbott?"

Annie turned her face to smile at Detective Rickers. "I just did."

He scowled. "You're skating on thin ice."

"She's not though. And neither is Tate. The truth is you have nothing on anyone. You're so worried about showboating, you two are missing clues and whoever killed Gill is working you like puppets. You're no closer to the truth than you were when you walked in and took over."

Go, Ryan.

Detective Rickers leaned in, his nostrils flaring. "Listen to me, *Officer.* You have no idea what's going on behind the scenes. You aren't privy to that sort of thing at your level. But here's what I do know: Tate Murphy was seen in Gill's house. Gill owed Bob Murphy five thousand dollars. All that oxygen gets expensive. Between the money owed, the kid's prior offense, and the eyewitness report of seeing him on the morning of the murder, we have enough to hold him."

"He's seventeen." Ryan's jaw looked tight enough to shatter.

Annie's brain was tripping over the new details.

"Guess you're not as close as you thought. Our young friend is eighteen as of a few days ago."

Ryan's hands curled into fists on the table. "Did you press charges?"

"No. Not yet. We're going to hold him for the forty-eight hours though."

Annie's heart twisted. "Can I talk to him?"

Both men looked at her. She steeled her shoulders. "Listen, I'm not going to tell you how much I dislike you because Ryan advised against it. But let's suppose you actually want the truth here. Let's pretend you really want to see the right killer brought to justice. Let me talk to Tate and see why he reached out to me through Ryan. Why he may or may not have left me another note."

Detective Rickers watched her carefully like maybe if he stared long enough, she'd break.

"Fine. I'll send him in. I assume you're staying, Officer Porter?"

He left, closed the door behind him. Ryan growled out a curse word. "I think I'll take my detective exam just to spite him."

"Ryan, I'm scared for Tate. I saw Bob today, and Tate wasn't home. He mentioned that he and Gill used to be friends. How much do we know about Tate?"

Ryan set his gaze on Annie, and she saw the fear in it. "He didn't do this. Everyone judges him by his previous choices. He's a good kid. I'm sure of it, Annie."

Annie believed him. Or, at least, she believed he meant what he said. The problem was when feelings got involved, perceptions got skewed. Annie knew Tate had a knack for sneaking out. He could have found time to hurt Gill. Though she didn't see him as a killer, she did see him as a young man who'd do anything for his pops. Especially if he felt he had no other choice.

Tate shuffled through the door in cuffs. Annie bit down on her cry of outrage and stood up to greet him.

She stared at Detective Black. "Is it really necessary to cuff him?"

"That's what we do with suspects, Ms. Abbott."

Annie stepped closer to the woman while Ryan took Tate by the arm. "I have a very close friend who excels at her job in publicity and media management. She'd know all the right channels to get out a story about two detectives who think they're above the law. People should know how you treat people—*children*—in your custody. I'm sure the city of Trenton and beyond would love to see a behind-the-scenes picture."

Black glared at her so hard Annie wondered if she was casting a curse over her. She stalked to Tate, unlocked the cuffs. She left without a word, and Annie turned to see Tate rubbing his wrists.

"Are you okay?"

The kid shrugged, but she saw the fear in his eyes. He looked away. "Fine."

"What the hell is going on, Tate?" Ryan said.

"I didn't do nothing, man. I was helping Pops with his new machine, getting it set up. The cops show up, say they got some eyewitness who seen me leaving Gill's place. Pops starts swearing at them, saying that can't take me, but I told him it was fine. I didn't want him getting worked up." He didn't look at them as he spoke.

"Did you leave me another note?"

Tate stared at the glass behind Ryan's head.

Ryan slapped his hand down on the table, startling them. "Answer her. I might not be able to pull strings and get you out of this."

It sounded like if he did, it wouldn't be the first time. Annie wondered how well Tate and Ryan knew each other.

Tate looked at Annie. "I got a note saying if I tried talking to you again, my pops would find out about me sneaking out." His eyes looked damp, and he sniffled loudly. Proudly tilting his chin up as if he could roll the emotion back down his throat.

"Where's the note?"

"I burned it. Listen, I know I made mistakes in the past, but I didn't do anything, Ry. You know I didn't. I've done everything you told me to. And I promised her I wouldn't sneak out no more, and I haven't. I keep my word."

Annie's heart twisted. Was she just a sucker? She totally believed him. She wanted to hug him and tell him everything would be okay. She wanted someone to do the same for her. This was a mess of epic proportions.

"I believe you," Ryan said quietly.

Annie didn't want to label the tone of his voice as defeated, but that's how it felt. "Can they seriously hold him?"

Ryan nodded. "He's eighteen. They have an eyewitness. Until they can discredit whoever it is or until forty-eight hours have passed. At the end of that, they have to charge him or let him go."

Tate cleared his throat. She could see the emotion he fought to hold back. Going to his side, she knelt down. "Listen. We're going to figure this out."

He nodded but didn't look at her, so she gripped his hand.

"Tate. Look at me."

He did. He might be an adult, but he looked so young, her heart broke.

"Ryan and I are going to figure this out." She took a deep breath. Let it out. "I promise."

Chapter Thirty-Three

RYAN DROPPED ANNIE off at her place, saying very little as he watched her walk to the door. He'd be back tomorrow, and they'd share whatever information each of them had been gathering. She wanted to check on Bob or Mira but didn't know if going to either of her neighbors was a good idea.

Taking a glass of wine, she went outside to sit with the sound of the ocean. The stars dotted the sky like miniature beacons. The moon was hidden by a hazy cloud that seemed to fade in and out, making the brightness do the same. Her heart hurt. She didn't know how to help Tate. Something told her that he wouldn't do this, if for no other reason than she truly believed he didn't want to let his pops down.

You promised him. What were you thinking? She stood, leaving her wine on the arm of the chair so she could lean on the porch railing. The rocks below were barely visible as the white foam of the turbulent sea crashed against them. Her brain wouldn't settle any more than her pulse.

Stop. Go back to the beginning. Mystery books and television shows, had a formula. She figured out the culprit in many of the books she read because she logged the clues, looked for subtle nuances in the characters' actions. Gill was dead because…why? That was the billion-dollar question hanging over everyone's head.

She took her wine, downed it quicker than she should, and went back inside. She'd visit the cats. Maybe Shelby could shed some light. Annie smiled at her own ridiculousness. If nothing else, looking at kittens had a way of changing a person's mood.

The air felt more static when she let herself out the front door. She started when she saw a figure outside her house until she saw it was Joseph.

He stopped walking and waved. "Hello, dear. How are you doing?"

"I'm good," she said stiffly, staying on her porch. "What are you up to?"

"My nightly walk. I'm surprised you haven't seen me out here before. I can't sleep without it."

Annie's muscles seized. *Maybe you got it wrong.* "Oh, I thought you walked with Margie in the daytime."

"Good lord. No. I love her, but she has her own nighttime routine. It's one of the reasons she's using to keep us from moving in together."

Okay. Weird. On so many levels. Why would Margie lie? The look on her face when she saw the photo kept flashing through Annie's brain. "You want to move in together?" Was that what they'd been arguing about at the funeral parlor?

How could Gill have gotten in the way of that? He'd said Gill was the one thing holding them back.

He nodded. There were white stripes on his jacket that reflected in the darkness. She noticed he marched in place. "I'm a traditionalist. When you love someone like I love her, you want to end each night together, start the new day beside them. You'll see, one day, when you find the right one."

The words were nice, but her mind buzzed. She was missing the connections. Something needed to snap into place. "I need to check on the cats."

"Right. Gill's cats. I wonder what Mira will do. If she's staying. Even if she does, you've got what, a half dozen of them, I heard?"

She smiled, continued to stick close to the door because at this point, it felt as though she didn't know any of her neighbors. "Four kittens and Shelby." Annie looked over a Gill's house. The lights were all out. "I'll talk to her soon."

"You can ask her bright and early Monday morning. That's the next Homeowners' Association meeting. It should have been in your welcome notes from Margie. On the back of the calendar."

There was a back side? Annie held back her groan. "I remembered all of my pickups and deliveries but didn't see a back side." She felt no guilt for using Raj's suggestion of Costco muffins.

"What time is the meeting?"

"Eight a.m. See you soon, dear. Rest tomorrow. You've hit the ground running since you moved in. Awful things happening, but I can assure you, usually, it's a quiet and lovely place to live." Joseph lifted his hand and power walked away, heading past Margie's house and back to his own.

Annie locked her front door, let herself into the garage, and locked it, too. Shelby looked up from where she slept.

"Hey. How was your night?"

The cat let out a contented sigh. Annie was jealous.

Annie pulled the soft bed the cat never used—Ben had brought it—to use as a cushion. She set it next to the box Shelby continued to use with her babies. When she needed a break from them, she hopped into the bed Annie brought from Gill's. She had her own little kitty apartment right here with the beds and toys, her food dishes, and a litter box. Annie didn't want to admit it, but she'd miss Shelby when Mira was ready for her to come home.

"How am I supposed to know who's telling the truth?"

The cat looked at her like, *I'm a little busy here.*

Annie sighed, her fingers itching with desire to touch the kittens. She could hear Ben's voice, *Not yet.*

"Yeah, yeah." She pet Shelby instead. "You let Ben pet them. Him, you like."

Shelby looked up and purred softly. Annie smiled. At least she and the cat were in agreement on one thing.

When Annie returned to the house, she texted Ben but didn't get a response. Grabbing a stack of sticky notes, she cleared off her parents' coffee table. On one sticky, she wrote Gill's name. On the others, she wrote out here possible suspects with a reason on each. None of her other methods of sorting through her thoughts were working. This way, she could move suspects around.

At the moment, the list was:

GINGER—FOUND CREEPING AROUND; NO ONE SEEMS TO BELIEVE SHE AND GILL WERE AN ITEM

JOSEPH—MARGIE LIED ABOUT HIM; THEY WERE ARGUING AT THE FUNERAL

MARGIE—SHE LIED AND WAS IN THE HOUSE RIGHT AFTER ME; HER RESPONSE TO THE PHOTO

RAJ—ARGUING WITH HIM? HIS CAR? MORE THAN ONE HEATED ARGUMENT ACCORDING TO THE OTHERS, AND WHOSE CAT SCRATCHED HIS HAND?

That one didn't feel right, but she left the sticky.

TATE—AVENGING HIS POPS

CONWAY—SAID HE'D DO ANYTHING FOR MIRA. MIRA THINKS HE'S GUILTY.

The list was too long. She needed to narrow it and didn't know how. Her phone buzzed with a text at the same time someone knocked on the door. She glanced at her phone as she stood up. *Ben.*

Hey. I hope you're okay. I'm going into a surgery. Neighbor's

dog ate something he shouldn't have. I'll call you when I can. Stay safe.

She winced and typed *good luck*.

When she looked through the peephole, she saw Ryan on her doorstep. Pulling the door open, she glanced back at the coffee table.

"Hey." He looked tired.

"Hey. What are you doing back here? Come on in." She shut the door behind him. Maybe he'd learned something else.

He walked to the table. "Good. You've already started." He glanced at her. "I couldn't sleep. Too many things running around my brain, and none of them will settle."

Like they planned to do this very thing, he grabbed the sticky that said RAJ. "He's got an alibi. It's solid. He's on security footage at a casino."

Annie kneeled on the floor next to the table. "You want a drink?"

Ryan looked at her, and beneath the fatigue, she saw the sadness. "I just want to figure this out. Tate shouldn't be at the station. He showed me that photo. I sent it to the detectives, thinking it might make them loop me in."

That answered one question but gave her more. "I'm sorry I didn't show it to you. At first, I told him I wouldn't, and then I kept getting sidetracked." She leaned back on her heels. "You're close to him."

Ryan sighed, leaned back against the couch cushions

while running one hand over his face. "When he first moved here, a few of the people in this complex called in complaints every time the kid breathed. It was hard on him and Bob. He was here trying to start over, but no one would give him a chance. Except Margie. She said her teaching days introduced her to more than her fair share of Tates."

Ryan sat up, letting his hands hang between his knees. "We were having trouble with vandalism up near Rainbow Lodge. Don't know if you're heard about it yet. It's a tourist spot at the far tip of the peninsula. Some kids were goofing around near the boat launch. One of them fell into the water, hit her head. The other kids helped Tate get her out of the water, but they got scared, took off. Tate didn't. He could have done what the others did—called 911, left an anonymous tip. But he stayed. I showed up, and the kid was so scared. He'd grabbed a blanket, wrapped her up; he was holding her, talking to her, telling her everything would be okay."

Annie's throat tightened. "Was she?"

Ryan nodded. "He did the right thing. When everyone around him didn't, he made the hard choice. I check in with him, take him out to the driving range or the batting cages in Trenton. He didn't do this."

Because she trusted Ryan's gut and her own—she didn't think Tate was behind this, either—she took the sticky note with his name and crumpled it.

Ryan gave her a small, tired smile. "We need to talk to

everyone else. I'm going to go talk to Conway. He's been in love with Mira since high school, so I have a hard time seeing him do something that would end things between them for good."

Annie's legs started to tingle so she stood, switched her spot to the chair next to the couch. "Unless he thought this was the way to make her happy. Weren't she and her father estranged?"

Ryan gave a rough laugh. "Gill was estranged from most of the people in his life. I suppose there could be something there, but it doesn't feel right. When they broke up a couple years ago, Conway went to Gill, tried to ask for her hand in marriage. Rumor has it Conway sank a ton of cash into Gill's failing business in exchange for his blessing."

Annie felt her forehead wrinkle. "That sounds pretty antiquated."

Ryan smiled. "Hence the reason Mira didn't get back together with him. She was mad. Stopped talking to both of them. Gill tried to get her to come work for him. He liked to control the people in his sphere."

"Maybe Conway got tired of being controlled."

Ryan tapped his fingers on the table. "I'll talk to him tomorrow. It's too late to do it tonight." He picked up Joseph's sticky, reminding Annie of earlier that evening.

She filled him in. "He's such a sweet old man. We can't forget that whoever did this had to have the strength to actually sink a knife into a man."

Ryan gave her a grim smile. "Fury makes you strong. I can't see Joseph hurting anyone, either, but he has the strength. The guy was on a championship rowing team for years. He went to the Olympics. He's no slouch."

Annie sighed. "How do you do this all the time? It's not nearly as satisfying when it can't be wrapped up in a nice bow."

"I don't have to do this all the time. This town doesn't often see this sort of thing. Even the surrounding towns are fairly low-crime areas. I'd like to think that's why the detectives are botching it so badly, but in truth, I think they're just really bad at their jobs. If they get the chance, they'll pin this on the wrong person just to wrap it up like a good Sandra Brown."

Annie grinned. "You've read Sandra Brown?"

He shrugged. "Among other things. Some of the shifts can be long."

"I have a meeting with the Homeowners' Association first thing Monday morning. I'll see if I can get anything out of anyone."

Ryan stood up. "I wouldn't normally invite a civilian to dig into something like this, but with those two jerks chomping at the bit to blame Tate, I need all the help I can get. Just stay safe. Don't be alone with any of them."

She nodded. "I'm not looking to be a martyr. Everyone needs closure on this. Until Tate is home and Mira knows who killed her father, that can't happen."

She walked him to the door where he paused on the porch. "You're a good person, Annie. I'm glad you came to Rainbow Falls. I'm going to enjoy watching you keep Ben on his toes."

Laughing, she let that go without a comment. She waved him off when he got in his vehicle. The sun had set long ago, and the night was dark with secrets and the scent of the ocean. She inhaled deeply but didn't find the calm that usually came with the smell of the sea. It was hard to find a sense of peace when she was almost positive one of her neighbors was a murderer.

Chapter Thirty-Four

ANNIE WOKE IN the middle of the night, something tugging at all the strings in her brain. She'd fallen back asleep before untangling the knots, and by the time she woke up, her head hurt with the confusion she felt. Crawling to the coffee pot, she remembered something her mother—or maybe it was Margie—had said about the homeowners' manual. Had she seen that?

"Can't see anything before coffee," she muttered, pulling two pieces of bread from the bag and dropping them into the toaster. Once she'd taken several sips of her coffee, eaten one slice of toast, she took it to the living room, leaving her breakfast on the coffee table.

Remembering what Joseph had said about the calendar, she detoured back to the kitchen, grabbed it off the fridge and did a silent prayer to the caffeine deities to kick in soon. She had this intense, uncomfortable feeling that time was running short. She waited until she was settled on the couch to flip it over. Annie groaned out loud.

Margie had handwritten a list of other commitments Annie needed to honor.

-Secretary at all HOA meetings; your mother kept meticulous records

-Liaison with outside agencies: landscaping, snow removal, and the man who takes care of our gate maintenance

-Holiday Decorating Chair; your father suggests a theme each Christmas, researching where we can buy similar decorations for our lawns and homes

"Seriously? Since when are my parents such joiners?" Taking a long drink of her coffee, she set it down so she could check the office for the binder. It wasn't hard to find.

Her mother not only kept meticulous records, her bookshelves and office were pristine. Annie pulled the large book, clearly marked, from the shelf.

"Death by boredom," Annie mumbled as she sank into the overstuffed chair in the corner of the office. The binder weighed at least as much as Shelby. That was a guess since Shelby would probably scratch her eyes out if she tried lifting her.

She flipped through the book. It was divided into years, then months, then meetings. There were special sections for written requests from residents, copies of correspondence with groundskeepers and city officials.

Gill had his own tab. It was filled with complaints he'd lodged against other residents. Everything from *entertaining too loudly on the deck* to *parking crookedly.*

"This requires chocolate." She hefted the binder and brought it into the living room, setting it on the table. Thinking about the double-stuffed Oreos she'd picked up at the store, she started for the kitchen. The knock as she passed the front door startled her.

"I've had more visitors in a couple weeks than all the years I lived with Viv," she said aloud to herself, stepping toward the door.

"Small towns are easily wowed by exciting city girls," Ben's voice came back through the door.

Laughing, she pulled the door open, her mouth watering at the sight of cinnamon buns.

He held them up in their clear covered case. "Grams said to say hello and bring these."

"Come on in. I was just going to get some Oreos, but these are better."

He shut the door behind him. "I don't know. Oreos are pretty delicious, especially the chocolate-covered ones."

When he followed her into the kitchen, she glanced over her shoulder. "How'd late-night surgery go?"

Ben's smile was tired, and she wondered if he'd gotten much sleep. "Good. The dog is resting now. How'd last night go?"

While she plated up the cinnamon buns, which they

took to the table, she told him about the police station, Tate, and then Ryan's visit after.

"He just dropped by and asked for your help?" Ben licked icing from his thumb.

"Yes. I think he's frustrated that the Trenton PD won't let him be part of anything." She stood up, grabbed a couple bottles of water.

"Thanks. He mentioned the other day that he'd tried to offer some help but that Rickers guy just laughed him off. The thing is our police department is tiny. There are only four officers, but they're good at their jobs. You'd think they'd want to work together."

Annie nodded in agreement. "You'd think. Unless they have an ulterior agenda like getting promotions."

"The truth has to come out. It can't stay buried, right?" He winced. "Sorry."

"It's okay. I don't think Mira came back to the house. Do you think she's okay?"

"She's probably staying with Bethany again. I'm not sure what she'll do with the house or who it goes to. Maybe that's the trail Ryan should be following."

"Maybe. It just feels like this was about more than money or an inheritance. Gill had the house and dealership, but from the sounds of it, he also had a lot of debt."

Ben considered that, finishing his cinnamon bun, then taking both of their plates to the sink. He washed his hands, stepping to the side to dry them while Annie washed hers.

He passed her the dish towel, their fingers touching over the cloth. The little spark of awareness was a complication she didn't need to focus on, but it was hard not to when he stood so close. When he looked so good.

His smile was sweet, a little bit shy. "Speaking of Gill's things, how are the kittens?"

Swallowing down desire to step into him and take one of his very comforting hugs, she smiled. "Great. Come say hi. Shelby misses you."

Before they made it to the front door, Ben noticed the Binder of Boredom. "Some light reading?" He pointed.

Annie rolled her gaze, and they detoured. "It's awful. On top of muffin duty and prescription pickups, I have to take notes at the meetings all the residents have. I'm beginning to suspect my parents sailed around the world to get away from Margie's list of chores."

Ben laughed, taking the book from her hand. "Whoa. Heavy."

He sank into the couch, so she sat beside him as they flipped through. She showed him Gill's many complaints. "You just have to take notes?"

She nodded, trying to ignore how good he smelled. Like the sea, but also like Ben. It was hard to cross lines that couldn't be uncrossed.

Ben turned his head, their gazes connecting like a bolt of lightening.

"Have you looked through this for ideas on who might

have had issues with him? If he was complaining about everyone, maybe there's a clue." His voice was low and husky.

Annie shook her head side to side, feeling as if it was weighted down with cloudy thoughts.

"No. I should familiarize myself with the last couple meetings, I guess."

Ben cleared his throat and opened the binder to the last meeting they'd had at the beginning of the previous month.

They both scanned the pages, but she wondered if he was as distracted by her presence as she was by his. She started to say something, to tackle the delicious-smelling elephant in the room. But her gaze caught on her mom's notes.

Ben must have seen it at the same time. "Looks like some of the meetings got pretty heated."

"They really did. My mom wrote everything verbatim. Wow. Looks like these two didn't get along at all." Annie's brows scrunched as she thought about what else she'd learned in the last day or so. With this documented argument and what she'd found out, she was pretty sure there was enough information to pull the spotlight off of Tate.

"We need to call Ryan." Her heart rate accelerated—and not because she was sitting so close to Ben. "I think we know who killed Gill."

Chapter Thirty-Five

T HE THING ABOUT solving a real-life mystery that they never showed in books was how nauseating it was to know the killer was in the same room. What felt worse for Annie, as everyone filed into the Common House, as it was called, was looking directly at the person and still finding it hard to believe.

They'd called Ryan over the night before. It was out of her hands, and yet, she felt consumed by all of the things that could go wrong. Ryan had said to trust him; she did. But that didn't make her feel much better about attending this meeting.

People hovered near the breakfast pastries. Joseph seemed to love baked goods more than the rest of them. Almost as much as he loved Margie. She watched as he handed Margie her coffee, pressing a kiss to her cheek. There was a large farm style table in the center of the room. It might look like a regular, though smaller, house from the outside, but it was actually just a big recreation room with chairs, the table, a kitchen in one corner, and a bathroom off of the main area. It was meant for parties or large gatherings like the Homeowners' Association.

Ginger caught her gaze from across the table. Annie smiled, her nerves spreading impossibly thin. Beside Ginger was Raj and other people that Annie had been introduced to earlier. She couldn't remember all of their names. Looking at the clock, her heart felt like it had taken up residence in her throat. Getting up, she crossed over to the kitchen, helping herself to some water.

Annie startled when Ginger came up beside her, offering a hesitant smile. *Act normal. It'll all be over soon.*

"How are you?" Ginger asked.

Annie glanced at the door, then looked back at her neighbor. "I'm okay. You heard about Tate?"

Ginger nodded, an unreadable look in her gaze. "Yes. I'm just glad they have someone in custody. The funeral was nearly unbearable. I'm not surprised Mira isn't here this morning."

"She hasn't been home since the funeral." Annie watched as Ginger took in the information.

Pain flashed in the woman's gaze. "I hope she and Conway can find a path back to each other. It's a terrible thing not to be with the person you love."

Uncertainty warred with anxiety. "It'll all be over soon."

Ginger's wandering gaze came back to Annie. "What do you mean?"

"The truth is about to come to light. When it does, people will be able to start healing." She hoped this offered the woman some comfort. Whether or not she should have been with Gill—though if he was divorced, he was available—wasn't the issue. People didn't choose who they fell in love with.

"The *truth* is that they arrested Tate," Ginger said, her breath choppy.

Annie tilted her head. "We both know he didn't do it." Soon, any minute now, everyone else would know, too.

Their gazes held. Annie felt every pulse beat in her body and needed these moments to fly faster.

The front door opened, pulling Annie's attention as her breath caught painfully in her chest. Ryan wasn't supposed to be here until the meeting started. They had eight minutes. But it wasn't Ryan who walked through the door.

"Good morning, everyone. We'd like you all to go back to your homes. This meeting has been canceled due to a change in circumstances," Detective Rickers said. He didn't bother to remove his sunglasses. Standing in the doorway, he pushed his suit jacket back to reveal his badge, as if any of them were unsure who he was.

Idiot. What's he doing here? But she knew. She'd trusted Ryan, but he didn't trust himself. He'd called in the cavalry even though the chances of them messing it up were good.

"What's going on?" Margie stood, putting both hands on the table.

"We'd like to not make a scene in front of anyone's neighbors. Everyone back to your homes, now." Rickers stood aside, gesturing to the door.

Ginger gripped Annie's arm, her nails pressing in. "What's happening?"

"It'll be okay," Annie whispered, looking over at Joseph and Margie arguing. Much like they had the day of the funeral. Her heart twisted.

"Let's go!" Detective Black shouted as she stepped in beside Rickers.

Outside, Annie started for her house. She'd done the right thing. Joseph had no alibi; he wanted to rent out his home, but the only person stopping him was Gill. One of the bylaws in the manual stated homes couldn't be rented out unless all eight homeowners were in agreement. Margie had lied more than once for him. She'd even heard Joseph say that there was nothing stopping them anymore. Margie had run off when she saw that photo on the detective's phone. Because she knew it was him. As much as Annie hadn't wanted to believe it, his nighttime walks along with notes of what he'd said to Gill at the last meeting—the venom in the argument the two had—confirmed things. Yet, she felt sick with the thought that it was him.

Annie tried to loosen her fingers which had curled into fists. Breaths rapid, she barely felt the slap of the morning wind. *You did the right thing. You did the right thing.* She was so consumed with guilt and sadness, she didn't even realize, until she was almost at her house, that Ginger was right behind her. Annie glanced behind her to see if Margie and

Joseph and everyone else came out. Everyone but those two shuffled out of the building and back toward their own homes.

"We're supposed to go home," Annie said, distracted.

"I can't be alone right now," Ginger said, her voice shaking.

Annie nodded. "I have to check on Shelby. This will all be over soon."

She let them into the garage, tears prickling. Shelby wasn't with the kittens. Ginger closed the door behind her as Annie walked toward their beds.

"How did you figure it out?" Ginger asked from behind her.

Annie clicked her tongue a couple times, looking around for Shelby before kneeling in front of the cats. "It was a number of things. The meeting minutes about the rental disagreement was the final clue though."

"You're a stupid, stupid girl," Ginger said.

Annie turned, thinking she'd heard her wrong. She jolted out of the way as one of her father's golf clubs swung toward her. Ginger's face was a mask of rage.

"What the hell?" Annie shouted.

"You won't ruin this for me." She swung again but, as Annie attempted to back up, only managed to hit her calf. Pain shot through her leg, making it vibrate like a tuning fork.

"What are you talking about? Are you crazy? Ruin

289

what?" She scanned the garage, seeing several things that could act as weapons, but from her spot on the floor, practically on her back, she had an extreme disadvantage.

Ginger pressed forward, swinging again, hitting Annie in the shoulder. Pain sung through her upper body. She forced herself up, throwing a garbage can in the crazed woman's way. Ginger smashed it with the golf club. Annie moved back, circling around the larger items in the garage to keep some space between them.

"I'm not going to jail," Ginger said, spittle flying out of her mouth. She looked around frantically but, obviously seeing nothing she preferred more, advanced again, holding the golf club up higher, ready to swing.

"*You* killed him?" Annie's shock must have shown because Ginger hesitated. Her relief that it wasn't Joseph was short lived.

Ginger halted. "You just told me you knew the truth."

Annie nodded, her hands moving behind her in an attempt to grab something. Anything she could use to defend herself. Her heartbeat echoed in her ears. What had pushed Ginger over the edge? Gill going back to Bethany? *Keep her talking.* "Yeah. That Gill was killed because he refused to agree with the majority and allow rentals. It was blocking Joseph from moving in with Margie like he wanted."

Ginger's expression went from furious to almost gleefully happy. Annie didn't find any comfort in her drastically changing emotions. "Oh my God. You really are stupid."

She stepped back, lowered the club. "They're here for Joseph?" She started to laugh in an overblown, almost manic fashion.

"I thought you loved him."

Ginger smiled. If she weren't still holding a golf club with a crazed expression in her eyes, she would have looked pretty. "No one could ever love that man. You had the right reason, just the wrong person." She held up the golf club again.

Something wasn't adding up. "I don't understand. I found you in his house grabbing your…" she said, gesturing to Ginger's lower half.

Like this was hilarious, Ginger bent over in laughter. "Good lord. You are such a prude you can't even say *panties*? Did you really fall for that? Give me a break. It was a hand-kerchief, you fool. I used it to avoid leaving prints on the doorknob. You really are pathetic."

Annie's face scrunched with offense. "Hey. You're the one that was trolling around his house. Falling in the back-yard, crying like you'd just lost your best friend." If she'd learned anything from crime shows and mystery books, she knew she needed to keep the woman talking.

Ginger stepped closer, and Annie really wished she could latch on to something to protect herself.

"There's nowhere to go, Annie. But just because you've pleased me so much by being so incredibly gullible, I'll tell you a secret." Her voice quieted at the end of the sentence.

Annie stumbled over a pair of shoes. "Nah. I'm good. I don't need any secrets."

Ginger laughed. "I fell on purpose."

Her heart was hammering so hard, it was a wonder she could hear the woman over it. "Why did you fall on purpose?" Had everyone gone? Where was Ryan?

Ginger inched closer like a snake ready to strike but enjoying the chase. "I dropped my earring when I left that morning. I saw it on the path and had to grab it before you found it." She tucked her hair behind one ear. "Pretty, aren't they?"

The gold and diamonds sparkled. Annie's gaze darted left and right. She needed to get closer to the door.

Ginger smacked the golf club against a box as she was finished playing games. "Here's how this is going to go. You will do exactly what I say, or I will make you wish it was you I killed."

She had to do something. Standing still was going to get her killed. Annie hedged along the wall, slowly trying to get to the garage door. "You're nuts."

"Oh, sweetheart, you haven't seen anything yet. When you get to be my age and live your life a certain way, you'll do anything to protect it."

Annie's thoughts of fleeing or screaming died when Ginger spotted one of her father's fishing knives. She reached for it at the same time Annie lunged. Annie tripped over a can of paint, falling, landing with a thud on the cement floor. She rolled, crawled as far as she could, but Ginger reached the knife first, swung it wildly. Annie got to her feet again, tossing anything she could at the woman. She backed into one of the cabinets, knocking boxes from the top. They tumbled down as Ginger lifted her hand, the steel of the knife glistening like a jagged beacon.

Before she brought her hands down though, she stumbled over a flash of white, cursed as she flailed around, reaching for something to steady herself. Instead, she grabbed on to the golf clubs which tumbled, bringing her down in the midst of clattering irons. Ginger's screech was drowned out by a sound Annie hadn't heard since she moved in—a pissed off cat. Shelby darted behind the boxes as the ringing sound of metal on the cement floor reverberated through Annie's body. She looked over to Ginger, scared the woman would get the knife again.

She was off the floor now but bent in half over the fallen clubs, howling. "Stupid cat broke my nose."

The words registered as Ginger stood all the way up, holding her face. Which was apparently leaking blood.

Little dots blurred her vision along with the rage on Ginger's face. Annie pushed past her, falling against the wall. When she looked back the blood was dripping through the woman's fingers. Annie's hand smacked the garage door opener with muted force as she sank down, as her brain fogged, her words slurred. She thought she heard the whir of the motor, the creak of the door lifting, but she wasn't sure because everything went black.

Chapter Thirty-Six

ANNIE'S BODY THROBBED. Keeping her eyes closed, she tried to decide what hurt the most. Her shoulder felt like it was on fire, her head was fuzzy, and her leg felt as if she'd been kicked by a horse. Warm fingers touched the pulse point at her neck.

"How long until the ambulance, Ryan?" Ben's usually calm voice barked out the question.

Annie opened her eyes. Ben was looking right into them. He shook his head, the relief evident.

"Hey," he whispered.

"Hey." She tried to smile, but it probably looked like a wince.

"She's awake?" Ryan crouched beside her.

"It's Ginger," she said, her voice croaky. How hard had she fallen?

"We know. The detectives have her. The ambulance is one minute out. Can you sit up?"

"No ambulance. I hate hospitals." She tried to lift herself into a sitting position, but both men assisted.

"As much as you hate blood?" Ben's tone held a touch of

amusement.

"Don't make fun."

"If he does, you can tease him about the squeal he let out when he saw you on the ground," Ryan said.

"Shut up, man. I didn't squeal." Ben glared at his friend.

"Ambulance is here," Officer Emily said.

Annie smiled at her, wondering where she'd come from. Confused and tired, she didn't resist when the medics checked her out but did refuse a ride to the hospital.

"I'm fine. I just need to go inside. Where's Shelby?" She looked around, spotting the cat not even a foot away, staring intently at Annie.

"She hasn't moved. She's just staring at you," Ben said quietly.

"She might have saved me."

Ben's face came closer as he pulled her into a hug. His breath fluttered over her skin. "Told you she liked you."

His whisper sent a welcome kind of shiver over her body. "She probably only did it to impress you."

Ben squeezed her tighter, causing her to yelp in pain. The medic gave him a dirty look.

"We need to check her arm. I really think you should get X-rays," the guy said with a heavy note of disapproval.

"I'll drive you. Please?" Ben asked, little flecks of gold sparkled in his green gaze. She figured if she was waxing poetic about Ben's eyes in her head, it might not be a bad idea. She nodded.

BEN TOLD HER to stay where she was before getting out of his truck to come around to the passenger side.

Annie rolled her eyes when he opened the door. "I can open a door."

He took her hand, kept her close as she lowered her feet to the ground. "Indulge me." He put an arm around her waist. "It's going to take me some time to get used to you passing out all the time."

Tipping her head back as they walked up the path, she muttered, "It's not all the time."

When they got to the door, she reached for her keys, but Ben turned the knob. It wasn't locked. Her body froze.

Ben looked down at her with questioning concern. "What's wrong?"

"Did we lock it?" She whispered the words, a chill spreading over her skin.

Turning her to face him, he bent his knees a touch. "Margie and Joseph came over to make sure you had some dinner ready, that the cats were all okay, and the garage was cleaned up."

Tears burned. She stepped closer to Ben, worried they might hear her. "We don't deserve that after suspecting him."

Ben lifted his hand, cupped her cheek. "Don't do that. We had no way of knowing. You figured out most of it.

They aren't upset."

Taking a deep breath, she worked to get her emotions under control. "Okay."

When they went in, Joseph and Margie broke apart as if they'd been in a deep conversation. She started to say hello, to apologize when Ryan came out of the kitchen. He smiled when he saw her, closing the distance between them.

"Are you okay?" He glanced at Ben, then back at her.

"Sore. Bruised. But I'll live." She held his gaze and noticed the hesitation in his. "It's not your fault."

Ryan shook his head, ran a hand over his mouth. "I looped them in. It felt like the right thing to do."

Margie came over, patted Ryan's arm. "It was the right thing to do, Ryan. Don't any of you second-guess yourselves. Now bring that girl in here so she can sit down before she falls."

"Again," Ben whispered.

Annie stuck her tongue out at him then walked toward Margie who pulled her into a hug. When she let her go, Joseph did the same.

"I'm so sorry," she said.

He patted her back, stepping back. "No reason for that, dear. Let's sit you down before Margie scolds all of us."

She sat in the armchair, preferring the straight back so she didn't sink into the cushions and jostle her badly bruised but not dislocated shoulder. Resting her head back, she exhaled. The day had been forty hours long.

Looking around, she saw all of them were on tenter-hooks. Margie and Joseph sat side by side on the couch. Ben sat on the ottoman, while Ryan stayed standing by the fireplace.

"Someone fill in the gaps for me, please," Annie said.

Joseph cleared his throat, scooted forward in his seat. "When those detectives came in, we didn't know what was going on. Margie and I were held back when everyone left. Detained, I'd say."

Margie patted his arm, nodding. "They told Joseph he was under arrest, and I told that Detective Rickers exactly what I thought of him."

"I asked them to wait for me. I was bringing our cops as back up. He and his partner, Detective Black, said they didn't need us. When Emily and I arrived, they had Joseph in cuffs. I don't even think they'd read him his rights. Emily noticed Ginger going into the garage with you. When I asked them what that was about, the detectives said we could figure it out since they'd solved the rest of the mystery."

"Idiots," Ben muttered. His stare was intense when he looked her way.

Annie smiled at him, trying to reassure him without words that she was okay.

"I asked them to wait, but they started leading Joseph to their car. Emily heard something, drew her weapon. They shoved Joseph into the back. I told Margie to stay, but she doesn't listen very well," Ryan said, shooting her a glare.

Margie returned it. "You're not the boss of me, Ryan Porter. I used to change—"

Ben started to laugh, but Ryan cut them both off. "Okay, okay. We heard what was happening in the garage. Margie started hollering, the detectives came over. It happened so fast."

"It didn't feel like it," Annie said, shifting.

"Do you need anything?" Ben asked.

"She'll have some dinner when we're done telling her what happened. I'm glad you're not one of those city girls prone to theatrics," Margie said.

Joseph patted her hand, pulled her close, and it was as though all of them took a cleansing breath.

"Ginger killed Gill." Annie looked at Ryan.

He nodded, came over to the couch, and sat on the other end, closer to Annie. "She's in debt up to her roof with credit cards and loans, but the house is free and clear. Her son and daughter-in-law invited her to move in. She had a plan to do that, rent out her place, pay off her debts, then move home. Gill fought her every step of the way."

"Why wasn't that in the minutes?" Annie looked at Joseph and Margie.

"She went behind our backs. Joseph and Gill had gone more than one round about that, but I guess she approached Gill on her own. First, she tried to sway him on behalf of Joseph. She must have seen some humanity in him because she told him her predicament, and he used it against her."

Margie looked sad as she shared.

"She told us all of this before we got her into the squad car. Because they had Joseph in the back of theirs, we took the collar. Rickers and Black were mad," Ryan said with a smile. "You would have loved it if you weren't passed out."

"Hey," she said, laughing. "Her face was bloody. Shelby tripped her. She went right down into a bag of golf irons, dropped the knife."

"I think she owed you," Ben said, giving her a smile that made Annie feel like they were alone in the room.

"Does Mira know?"

"She and Bethany were both filled in. You were at the hospital a while," Ryan said.

Annie looked at Ben. "Not my choice."

He smiled, looked down at the ground.

"What now?"

Ryan shrugged. "Trenton PD is still trying to take over. They want the case closed in their precinct, but my boss is fighting it. I've got to get back, file my reports. You'll need to come in tomorrow and give your statement."

There was still something she didn't understand. Like she could read her mind, Margie squeezed Joseph's hand and nodded in Annie's direction. "I'll admit, I was worried Joseph and Gill took things too far. When I saw that photo, I had a moment of doubt, thinking Joseph would go to any ends to live with me."

Joseph chuckled. "Even I have limits on my love, Margie."

"Why the lie about the walking?"

"I'm no fool, dear. I watch those big city shows, too. I didn't know where Joseph was at the time of Gill's death. Plus, I don't like admitting how much vanity I have. Skin doesn't stay this smooth without effort you know." She preened a bit, leaning into Joseph. "I had to be sure he hadn't done something rash. But when we talked at *book club*, you didn't bring him up, so I thought you'd ruled him out."

Annie gave a weak laugh. She should have been honest. Margie would have set her straight.

They talked a while longer, but Annie started to drift in and out of the conversation.

"We'll let you eat and get some rest." Joseph stood, held a hand out to Margie.

Annie started to stand, but Ryan stopped her. "Stay there. Rest. I'll see you tomorrow."

"I lived in Portland for six years, never once saw the inside of a police station," Annie remarked.

Ryan chuckled. "Sorry we don't have a frequent customer card like some of the coffee shops."

Ben laughed even while Annie tried not to. The grin broke free. When Ben walked them to the door, he came back, sat on the coffee table across from Annie.

"How are you really doing?" He took her hand, ran his fingers over the bruises on her wrist.

"I'm tired. Really tired. I thought I was good at figuring these things out, but she blindsided me in the garage."

With one hand, he tucked her hair behind her ear, studying the bruise on her chin. He ran a finger along it gently. "It wasn't your job to figure it out. She fooled everyone. You'll feel better after a good sleep."

It was going to take more than a solid twelve hours to erase the memories of today. Ben's fingers grazed Annie's neck. She had bruises everywhere, but when he looked at her the way he was now, she couldn't feel them.

His face inched close enough that she could feel his warm breath when he spoke. "Our town is going to seem pretty boring after all of this."

Annie lifted her chin, just a bit, putting them in the perfect position for seeing if this chemistry was real. "Somehow, I doubt it. It's over now, and I'm definitely not bored."

They must have moved at the same time because with the next breath, there was no more space between them. His hand cupped her head, fingers tangling softly in her hair as they kissed. He pulled back before she would have, pressing a kiss to the center of her forehead.

His soft smile spread warmth through her entire body. "Let's get you something to eat." He stood, still holding her hand.

"I'm not sure I'll eat much, but something smells good."

They walked to the kitchen where Annie stopped, stared at the table. When she glanced at Ben, she saw it was, once again, his turn to blush.

He dropped her hand so he could run it through his hair. "I didn't know she set the table."

Annie stepped forward to where Margie had set two places, wine glasses and candles creating an obvious ambiance. The candles flickered softly, reflecting off the glass and the darkness settling outside.

She looked at Ben, then stepped closer to him. Putting her arms around him, she rested her head on his chest. His arms closed around her like they belonged there. Like they fit.

"I'm glad you're okay," he whispered against her hair.

"Me, too."

She wasn't sure how long they stood there, but when they stepped apart, Annie felt calmer. She sat while Ben served them, then they talked over candlelight about anything and everything except neighbors or murder.

As the evening wore on, Annie knew there were still a lot of loose ends that would need to be tied up but for now, she was safe. She was home.

Chapter Thirty-Seven

THOUGH HER BREATH caught as she entered the Common House, her nerves fled as soon as she saw the way it was decorated. Ben's hand touched her back, nudging her forward but also reminding her that he was there. Most of the others had already arrived. Margie and Joseph were talking with Tate, the guest of honor. Mira, still dressed all in black, chatted with Ryan. Tate's pops ambled over to him without oxygen and put a hand on the boy's—young man's—back. He said something that made the others laugh.

Raj and a woman Annie didn't recognize were seated at the table, looking at a photo album. A banner was hung up over the kitchen area that read: HAPPY BELATED BIRTHDAY, TATE.

It was Annie's idea to celebrate the occasion. After he was released from police custody, Tate had given her a long hug and a promise to come clean with his pops about his transgressions. Ryan had gone with him to remind his grandfather what a good kid he actually was and to explain everything that happened.

There were a few residents of the complex she didn't really know yet. Annie was more than fine taking her time to get to know them. She could strike up conversations on her delivery days. She was pleased when Ben's grandmother; grandfather; Ashley; Stephanie; and their brother, Levi, showed up.

There were hugs all around, presents put on a table off to the side, and a selection of appetizers and snacks that called to Annie.

She excused herself from Ben and his family to go grab something to eat. Mira joined her, picking up a plastic plate.

"How are you doing?" Annie held an empty plate but turned to look at the woman.

"I'm good. Better than I was. Thank you for your part in helping to find the truth."

She hadn't seen Mira in the week and a half since Ginger had been formally charged.

"I didn't do anything. Honestly, I'm lucky I didn't get more people hurt."

Mira reached out, squeezed Annie's arm. "You pushed for the truth. That's more than those two detectives did. Ryan told me they're under investigation." She shook her head before continuing. "I'm glad you made it out okay. I'm so glad Tate didn't take the fall for this. I still can't believe Dad is gone." Her tone shifted, her gaze looking past Annie. She blinked a few times as though ridding herself of memories or tears before meeting her eyes again.

"I'm sorry. What will you do now?" Annie realized she

didn't know much about the woman.

Mira's smile bloomed, changing her face, making her look younger. "I'm going to stay. Part of me feels like it'll help me be closer to him. That's probably dumb, but it feels right to stay."

Annie smiled. "If it feels right, then you definitely should. We'll be neighbors."

Mira nodded. "Yes. I keep to myself a lot. One of the things my father and I fought so much about was me coming to work for him, but I'm not a people person. I like burying myself in research and archives. I work at the museum in Trenton."

"It surprised me that your dad owned a dealership. He…" Annie's voice trailed off. Her cheeks heated.

"Didn't seem like a people person?" Mira laughed. "You're right. He wasn't. It was why he let Conway buy in. He liked the cars, the paperwork, and the money. Conway did the rest."

Annie didn't want to pry. Well, she did, but she didn't want to cross a line. Turning to start adding food to her plate, she asked as casually as she could, "Do you think you'll patch things up with him? He seems to really care about you."

Mira's expression grew solemn. She set the plate down. "He told me he'd crossed a line he couldn't uncross. I blamed him for my father's death, but that wasn't what he was talking about. He reported my dad for tax fraud. He thought I wouldn't forgive him. But I think if he can get over me accusing him of killing my dad, it's worth being open to the idea of trying again. We've been through a lot."

Ben came up to her side. "Having a hard time choosing what to eat?"

Mira smiled shyly at him. "Hi, Ben."

"Hey, Mira. How are you?"

"I'm okay." She glanced at Annie, started to walk away, but Annie put a hand on her shoulder.

When Mira met her gaze, Annie leaned in. "Take a risk. When someone cares that much, they don't just stop feeling it."

Mira nodded. Annie turned back to her plate, noted that Ben had eaten the cheese she'd put on it. Laughing, she added more. He ate that, too.

"Get your own, mister."

He looked at her, and her stomach did that whirly thing only he inspired. "You look really pretty today." His voice was low. Her heartbeat kicked like a bass drum.

"You, too." She closed her eyes, groaned. When she opened them again, humor flashed in Ben's gaze. "You know what I meant."

He shook his head, his smile growing. "Is it my hair? Or my shirt? Does the color match my eyes? Or bring them out? Is that how you say it? What do you think is prettiest thing about me?"

She glanced around. People were laughing and talking

and healing. It was…really nice. These were good people. Annie was lucky to have them for neighbors. She looked back at Ben, who was still smiling at her.

"I think you're prettiest when you stop talking," she teased.

Ben leaned in so close, his nose was nearly touching Annie's. "Hmm. What could I do with a pretty girl that wouldn't require talking?"

She'd never had someone make her want to burst into laughter while simultaneously stirring up all her feelings. She put one hand on his chest, calling his bluff. "If you don't know the answer to that, I'll be *pretty* disappointed."

His gaze widened. Annie wanted to give a triumphant *ha* when desire flashed in those green eyes.

"Annie," Ben's grandmother said, joining them. Ben stepped back, cleared his throat, and gave his grandmother a tight smile.

She embraced Annie. "I'm so happy you're okay. What a whirlwind adventure for you."

Annie nodded, adding to her plate. "I'm just glad it's all over."

Desiree leaned in closer, putting a hand on Annie's arm. "I hope you'll join us on Thursday. We'll be just a regular book club again, I guess."

That was fine by Annie. "I'm looking forward to it."

Desiree smiled, leaned in. "This month's selection is erotica."

Annie's face heated. "Okay. Maybe a little less now."

Ben snorted with laughter. "I'll meet you guys over there. Please never fill me in on book club."

Shaking her head, Annie shoved a large cracker into her mouth so she wouldn't have to respond.

It would only work for so long so Annie was grateful when Margie stood at the front of the room and tapped a fork to her wineglass.

Everyone turned her way. Joseph sat in a chair, his adoring gaze on the woman he loved. Ben's gaze caught Annie's; his smile settled down the galloping horses in her chest. Funny because looking at him sped them up as well.

"I just want to wish Tate a happy birthday. I'm sorry we didn't do it sooner. We're also sorry for all the trouble that came your way." Margie paused, looking at Tate, who smiled awkwardly and shifted in his spot. Then she looked around the room at everyone else. "We're neighbors. I know that can mean many things. We don't have to be close or best friends, but it's natural, at times, for our lives to intersect. When bad things happen, we want to do what we can to assure ourselves we're safe. With everything that's we've been through, I feel lucky to know that you're a group who will watch out for each other, lean on each other for more than muffins."

The group laughed. Annie glanced at Mira.

"There are changes coming. Mira is moving into Gill's. Ginger's family is selling her home." Margie looked at Joseph. "And Joseph is selling his to move in with me."

People clapped. "About time," Tate's pops called out with a raspy voice.

Margie looked at Joseph, her smile shining right from her eyes. "I know not everyone is lucky enough to call their neighbors friends, but I feel honored I can do that with so many of you." She raised her glass.

Others followed suit before breaking off again to chat in smaller. Annie watched, listening from her seat. She wondered how her parents were doing on the open seas. Their waters had probably been less choppy than her own, but she was still glad she came. Margie was right; not everyone got to call neighbors their friends, but Annie had a feeling, no matter how long she stayed in this little town, the people in this room were going to leave a lasting mark on her heart.

BEN WALKED HER home about an hour later. By silent, mutual agreement, they went into the garage. Ben opened two canvas chairs, set them next to the cat beds. When Annie sat down beside him so they could stare at the little balls of fur, it felt natural, excitingly so, to reach for his hand.

"Mira said she was okay with you keeping one?" Ben looked over at her.

"She's going to come visit Shelby every day so they can get familiar again. She said she knows people who want kittens, so if I want one or two or all of them, fine, but she

HOME IS WHERE THE BODY IS

can home them if not."

Ben chuckled. "Four cats. That's a lot all at once."

"Tell me about it. I was worried about one. But then I was worried about only one, you know?" Annie looked away from the cats, met Ben's gaze.

"Yeah. Two is always better than one. Especially since they're so perfectly named in pairs."

"Exactly. But two is a lot for someone who has never had a pet."

Ben leaned forward in his seat, pulling Annie closer. "Not if that someone has a vet on speed dial."

Annie arched her brows even as she leaned in. "You think you're on speed dial?"

Trailing one finger down her cheek, he nodded. "I should be. With how often you pass out, it would be smart."

The distance between them was starting to disappear with each breath she took. Still, Annie held back. "I only pass out at other people's blood."

"Two is a solid choice. Sherlock and Watson." His lashes lowered slightly. They were enviably long enough to notice.

"A good team."

Ben's thumb traced over Annie's lower lip, making her breath catch. "A very good team."

When she felt Ben's breath on her lips, her eyes fluttered closed. A loud protest in the form of a cat howl stopped them both. Her eyes popped open when Ben made a slight "oof" sound. Shelby sat on his lap.

Annie scowled at the cat. "Really?"

Ben's laughter made it impossible to hold the frown. He stroked the cat's back. She purred. Loudly.

Annie leaned in close to the cat, nearly nose to nose. "I'll allow it because you saved my life and I appreciate it."

Shelby responded by cleaning her paw. Ben reached out with the hand not petting the cat to take Annie's hand again.

When he squeezed it, she felt all of the things neither of them needed to say. There was plenty of time for whatever came next. But for now, like Ben, she was content to just sit. To enjoy the moment. And the company.

The End

Don't miss the next book in The Wannabe Sleuth series, *Homecoming and Homicide*!

Join Tule Publishing's newsletter for more great reads and weekly deals!

If you enjoyed *Home Is Where the Body Is,*
you'll love the next book in…

The Wannabe Sleuth series

Book 1: *Home Is Where the Body Is*

Book 2: *Homecoming and Homicide*
Coming in January 2023

Available now at your favorite online retailer!

About the Author

Jody Holford writes sweet romance and cozy mysteries with sweet romance in them. She's published several books including the cozies in The Britton Bay Series. She's unintentionally funny and rarely on time for anything. If she's not writing, she's reading, hanging out with her family, or doodling. She also writes romcoms under the pen name, Sophie Sullivan.

Thank you for reading

Home Is Where the Body Is

If you enjoyed this book, you can find more from all our great authors at TulePublishing.com, or from your favorite online retailer.

TULE
PUBLISHING

Printed in Great Britain
by Amazon

85172964R00187